Death Wish

Fortress Security, Volume 18

Rebecca Deel

Published by Rebecca Deel, 2024.

This is a work of fiction. Similarities to real people, places, or events are entirely coincidental.

DEATH WISH

First edition. January 23, 2024.

Copyright © 2024 Rebecca Deel.

ISBN: 979-8224920174

Written by Rebecca Deel.

To my amazing husband. You are always the hero in my story. I love you.

Chapter One

Jesse Phelps walked into Brent Maddox's outer office and stopped in front of Gloria, the CEO of Fortress Security's gate keeper. "Good afternoon, Gloria."

She smiled. "Good to see you again, Jesse. Go right in. Brent is waiting for you."

"You know all things. Mind giving me a hint about what this meeting is over?" He had to admit to some trepidation. Brent had never called him in alone, always with his team. His team, however, had scattered to the four winds and wouldn't return to the area for another week.

"Sorry, my friend. I know nothing. Even if I did, I wouldn't tell you. My boss is a hard taskmaster." Her eyes twinkled, belying her words.

"Stop pumping my administrative assistant for information," Brent said from the doorway of his office. "Get in here and find out for yourself."

"Yes, sir." Jesse winked at Gloria and entered Brent's office.

"Take a seat."

He sat in a comfortable visitor's chair in front of Brent's massive oak desk. "What's this about, sir?"

"First, sorry to interrupt your time off. I need a favor."

"Name it." Brent rarely asked for favors from anyone. That he felt the need to do so increased Jesse's unease. No matter the favor, Jesse felt obligated to say yes. After all, the boss had put his reputation and his life on the line to protect his people more than once.

"An undercover assignment."

His blood ran cold. "Sir?" He didn't take undercover assignments, not since he left law enforcement. He hated those assignments as a Texas cop and swore never to take another one.

However, Jesse and his teammates owed Brent. And for ask him this favor while his team was out of the area was even more unusual.

"We accepted the assignment this morning, and you're the best person to handle part of this job."

Alarm bells rang in Jesse's head. "Part of the job?"

A slight smile curved Brent's mouth. "Caught that, huh?"

"And you're delaying. I won't like this, so spill it already, sir."

"I'm sending you in with a partner."

He stared. A partner? Many scenarios raced through his mind as he waited for the blow he knew lurked in the offing. He wasn't wrong. "Who's my partner?"

"A computer hacker."

No. Way. The only hacker he knew willing to take on any challenge was Simone Kent. But she wasn't an operative. "Simone?"

Brent inclined his head.

"Sir, she's not a trained operative."

"She doesn't need to be. You are."

"No."

His boss's intense gaze bored into Jesse. "You're refusing the assignment?"

"I'm asking you to assign another hacker."

"None of the other hackers we employ are operatives, either." He remained silent for a moment. "I could send you in with Zane, I suppose."

"He has a family," Jesse said flatly. "Although no one is better at hacking than Z, he has responsibilities. His wife and son need him." Jesse knew well the dangers of going undercover. Anything could go wrong and usually did. You made plans? Good for you. They wouldn't work without big changes on the fly. Such was the nature of undercover assignments.

"For this kind of specialized work, I have two hackers in my arsenal. Zane and Simone."

He scowled. "What about Jon Smith? He's in the same league as Z and Simone."

"He's tied up with something else at the moment."

So, Jon was out, too. "What kind of work are we talking about?"

"Tracking down the creator of a computer virus being developed to steal information and blackmail governments and companies around the globe."

Jesse frowned. "The program isn't finished?"

"No, and your job is to stop the development before the program is completed."

"If we stop the program development, what's preventing some other hacker from coming up with another program capable of the same destruction?"

"Cybersecurity is part of our service, Jesse, and we're being offered a lucrative contract to find the creator of this virus and stop him before he succeeds."

To risk bringing in a rookie to take on an undercover assignment meant something bigger was at stake than a nasty computer virus. "What aren't you telling me?"

"The program targets the military and private companies who provide services and products to the military and governments."

Jesse whistled. "Who's the client?"

"Our government." Brent smiled. "For a pretty penny, of course."

The medic rolled his eyes. "Of course. Brent, I don't want to make you angry."

"But...."

"Simone has only been working at Fortress for a few weeks."

"Remember the discussion earlier? You'll go in with either Simone or Zane. Frankly, I can't afford to have Z gone that long. He's vital to our operation. Simone is our only other option. No one else is in their class. I need her to do this."

He still didn't like it. "So many things could go wrong."

"And will. That's where you come in. Your job is to make sure she's safe, no matter what happens."

"Can't she do this from the comfort of her couch or here in the office?" Hacking was hacking, right? Simone could do the work anywhere.

Brent shook his head. "We have rumors. No computer footprints to follow back to the source. Zane thinks the programmer is creating the virus on a computer disconnected from a network. Simone won't be able to locate and destroy the program if the computer isn't online. She has to have a target. Right now, she doesn't have one."

Jesse stood and paced. "She's too green. Do you have any idea where she should start looking?"

"Again, we have rumors that pinpoint a specific company but not the designer. Simone will have a starting place. The problem is she'll have to be on site to accept a job offer and work for the company."

"Which company?"

"Dragon Alley."

He stopped pacing, his head whipping toward his boss. "You're kidding."

"Nope."

"Dragon Alley is a huge outfit of computer programmers."

"Exactly. Their services are in high demand, especially in Europe, Mexico, and Central and South America. Their presence here is already established, but they have a lot of competition."

"If we agree to do this, where would we go?"

A chilly smile curved Brent's mouth. "Guess."

Jesse's heart sank. "Mexico?"

A nod. "The Chihuahua province."

He groaned and dragged a hand down his face. "Great. Just great. Will I have backup?"

"The Shadow Unit is down there for three more days, unless they finish their mission early. Artemis will replace them. Look, Jesse, I know how much you hate going undercover. If you refuse to go, the mission will still go forward."

He didn't like the setup, but what choice did he have? If he didn't agree to go with Simone, Brent would send her undercover with someone else. He hated that idea even more than the prospect of going to Mexico with the feisty computer hacker he'd met a few weeks earlier. "Before I commit, what's my role in this?"

"Security for Simone and Dragon Alley." Brent paused. "You're also going in as Simone's boyfriend."

Jesse stared. Boyfriend?

"Problem?"

None except he'd wanted to take his time romancing Simone Kent, and he'd been stepping lightly around her from the moment he met her. Now, he'd have to play the role of Simone's boyfriend when he wanted the role to be real.

"If there is, tell me now and I'll send someone else. Just thought you might want the job yourself."

"I do." No way would he step back and allow someone else to spend that much time with a woman he was interested in dating. "Our covers are ready?"

"Zane is completing the finishing touches as we speak."

"Accommodations?"

"Already taken care of. I called in a favor from a friend. You and Simone will stay in a house outside Sayulita, Mexico."

Sayulita, the hometown of Dragon Alley's Mexico headquarters. "Any terrorist organizations in the area?"

A snort. "What do you think?"

"Wonderful. So, when will this fun assignment begin?"

"Tonight. Jet leaves in six hours."

And the fun just continued. "Does Simone know?"

A knock sounded on the door, and Gloria said, "Simone Kent is here."

"Send her in."

Seconds later, Simone Kent, hacker extraordinaire, strode into the room, confidence practically oozing from every pore.

Brent stood. "Take a seat, Simone," Brent said, motioning toward the chair near Jesse's.

Jesse joined her.

"Am I in trouble already?" Simone asked, mischief in her eyes.

Brent's eyebrows rose. "Should I be concerned about that statement?"

"Might be best not to ask."

He chuckled. "Why am I not surprised? Hackers are all alike. You can't resist the bright and shiny things behind closed doors, can you?"

"Guilty."

"I have a special assignment for you that will involve a trip out of the country."

"That's why Jesse is here, too?"

He nodded. "The mission is dangerous. Jesse will go with you to keep you safe."

"Dangerous missions and computer hacker don't go together, sir."

"Under normal circumstances, that's true," Brent agreed. "The job is in your area of expertise. The location and circumstances are not."

"I'm listening."

"You don't have to do this, Simone," Jesse said. "Brent can find another hacker."

"He's right," Brent said. "I could. But I'm hoping you'll take on the task."

Simone looked from Brent to Jesse and back. "Must be important."

"It's critical, and time sensitive."

"Tell me more."

"What I tell you may not go beyond the office door. National security could be at stake and the security of other nations. Do I make myself clear?"

"Crystal."

"Good. You've heard of Dragon Alley?"

She straightened. "Who hasn't? They're one of the best programming companies in the world. Their hackers are world class and sought after by other companies and governments across the globe. What does this mission have to do with Dragon Alley?"

"Credible rumors are circulating that someone inside the company is creating a program to steal classified information from military installations, defense contractors, and governments around the world, then infect the computers with a virus. If this program is completed, our soldiers and sailors will be at risk of exposure and our military operations will be for sale to the highest bidder, putting thousands of people in harm's way."

The longer he spoke, the grimmer Simone's expression grew. "Who would do such a thing?"

"Someone who wants a truckload of money to restore the information and keep what he learned off the market," Jesse said.

"We can't let them get by with this."

Brent smiled. "I hoped that's what you'd say. I only have two programmers or hackers in the same class as those employed by Dragon Alley. You and Zane."

She shook her head. "You need Zane here, and he has a sweet little boy and beautiful wife to care for. I should go."

Yep, Jesse had known that would be Simone's exact response. The beautiful hacker was as eager as anyone he'd seen to right a wrong. Funny, considering what she did for a living and also on the side for fun. She hacked into websites and databases without authorization. Some of the hacking was sanctioned by Fortress. Some was not.

"Excellent. You'll be going undercover as a new hire at Dragon Alley starting tomorrow. You and Jesse will leave for Sayulita, Mexico in six hours."

Simone's eyes widened. "Six hours? That's a little fast, isn't it?"

"The clock's ticking. We can't afford to lose an extra day. Every day, this programmer is moving closer to finishing the program that will endanger our troops."

"Do I have a cover story?" She looked uneasy. "If I go in as Simone Kent, I'll have to invent another identity for myself. People at Dragon Alley have long memories."

"We have that covered. Zane has created alternate identities for you and Jesse. When you leave my office, go to the communication center. He'll give you what you need."

"Are you sure you want to do this?" Jesse asked Simone. He wanted her to say no, to back down. This mission would be dangerous.

"We don't have a choice." She looked at Brent. "So, what's our cover story for Jesse going along on this adventure?"

"He's your over-protective boyfriend who is also starting a new job in security at Dragon Alley tomorrow."

She smiled. "Gives him access to every part of the building complex. Brilliant. Are you sure no one in the company will figure out we're not who we pretend to be?"

"As long as you stick to your stories, you'll be fine." Brent paused. "Under no circumstances should you mention who you work for in real life. Fortress Security isn't looked upon with favor in the Chihuahua province."

"When will you tell her the rest?" Jesse said.

"The rest?" Simone's eyes narrowed. "What does he mean, sir?"

"Our client is the US government."

She groaned. "I should have known there'd be a catch. I'm not a fan of the government."

Brent chuckled. "Neither are we. We appreciate their prompt payment of the bill, however."

"That's not all," Jesse said wryly.

"More good news?" Simone asked. "I'm not sure I can stand anything more earth shattering than knowing I'm working for the government, my arch nemesis and frequent target."

Brent pointed at her. "I did not hear that statement from you. While you work for Fortress to complete this government contract, if you and Jesse are caught and turned over to the Mexican authorities, our government won't lift a finger to get you out of Mexico."

Simone stared. "You're saying I could go to a Mexican prison if I'm caught?"

He inclined his head. "You'll either die in prison or disappear when they're tired of feeding you."

#

Chapter Two

The door closed behind them as Simone stumbled from the office, stunned beyond belief. Holy cow. An undercover assignment after a few weeks on the job, and she could end up in a prison or buried six feet under if she blew her cover.

She shook her head. She hadn't signed up for this when she joined Fortress Security. This was insane. Who would take this on?

Simone sighed. Apparently, she would because she couldn't stand the thought of their military personnel and contractors being targeted by enterprising blackmailers who were using a computer program. In her personal hacking code, the action was dead wrong. Who would put American patriots' lives in harm's way by selling information to the highest bidders, all of whom hated Americans and would love nothing better than to see masses dead in one strike?

Once they were in the elevator, Jesse said, "You okay?"

"Ask me again in a few hours. Talk about a hit and run." She looked at the medic. "Does Brent do that kind of thing often?"

"If you mean blindside you, yeah, he does. I'm paid to deal with this kind of situation all the time. You aren't. You're a hacker, not an operative. Simone, you don't have to do this. If you're uncomfortable with this assignment, we can go back upstairs and tell Brent you've changed your mind about the job. He'll find someone else to handle it."

She'd love to do just that if not for her strict personal code. "You heard him, Jesse. We can't turn him down. He doesn't have another hacker who can do this at the speed required to stop the programmer. If the program is finished and sold, all we'll be able to do is sell a patch for the computer systems affected by the virus. We won't be able to stop them from selling the information without the target company paying millions for ransom to get their information."

"And even then, there's no guarantee they'll honor the bargain." Jesse's expression was grim. "They could double dip."

"Sell the information back to the company they stole it from and to the highest-paying interested party on the market? That's a given, and it would be a disaster. We have to stop them, Jesse."

They exited the elevator and turned toward the comm center. Jesse tapped on the door frame, and a dark-haired man in a wheelchair spun around to motion them inside the room.

"Just in time," Zane Murphy said. "I finished your identification packets five minutes ago." He zoomed across the office to one of several drawers. He opened the drawer and pulled out three packets. One he tossed to Jesse. The other two he handed to Simone.

She opened the first packet and peered inside. Multiple forms of identification, including credit cards with the name Simone Kenyon emblazoned on the front.

Nice. She'd always wished for a more exotic name than Kent. Simone ripped open the second packet and frowned. Jewelry? "What's this?"

"Jewelry with GPS trackers embedded in them. You need every piece," Zane said, giving her a hard stare. "No arguments, Kent. The trackers ensure we'll know where you are at any time."

"Just in case?"

"Exactly. Put them on right now and don't take them off until you're back on US soil. Hear me?"

"Yes, sir." She emptied the contents of the packet onto a table and put on the jewelry.

"One more thing left to do, then you should prepare to leave town. Jesse, take your new girlfriend down to the medic on duty."

"Why?"

"She needs one more tracker in case her jewelry is stripped from her."

Simone narrowed her eyes. "What does that mean?"

"You'll find out soon. Suck it up, Buttercup. You wanted in on this mission. Time to help ensure your safety. Do what you're told, Kent. I want you back in one piece at the end of the mission."

"Yes, sir."

"If I find out you didn't obey orders, you and I will have a long discussion when you return, and you'll have a written reprimand in your personnel file." He shooed them out of the comm center as another call came in.

"He's not kidding, is he?" Simone whispered to Jesse in the hall.

"Not about your safety. Trust me when I say you don't want to tick off Zane. He'll set you down hard and make you wish you could turn back time and undo the damage. After he finishes with you, Brent will lay into you. You never want to be reprimanded by a Navy SEAL."

She stopped walking to stare up at the medic. "Both of them were SEALs?"

"Yes, ma'am, and both were Tier One operators. No one is tougher than those men. They won't tolerate deliberate disobedience from anyone."

Oh, boy. Simone swallowed hard. She should have realized. Seemed like almost everyone Fortress employed was military or law enforcement trained.

Jesse walked Simone to the infirmary and opened the door. "Hey, Jake. Long time since I've seen you," he said.

A tall, dark-haired man smiled and held out a hand to Jesse. "Great to see you, Jesse. Who's your friend?"

"This is Simone Kent, ace computer hacker, new to Fortress."

The medic shook Simone's hand. "Pleased to meet you, Ms. Kent."

"Simone, please. Zane sent me down here for another GPS tracker."

"Got it right here." Jake picked up a small packet. Inside was a tiny chip, about the size of a grain of rice. "I'll need to slip this under the skin on your back. The best place is near your shoulder blade or your lower back. What's your preference?"

"Um, nowhere?"

Jake chuckled. "Not an option. Choose the site, or I'll choose for you." He sobered. "The tracker is for your safety. Jesse has two of them implanted beneath the skin of his back."

Her head whipped toward Jesse. "Seriously?"

"It's true."

"But why?"

"Our missions can be dangerous, Simone. While we do our best to stay out of enemy hands, sometimes it's inevitable. If we're taken captive, Fortress can activate the trackers to locate us and hopefully send a team before time runs out."

Oh, man. She hadn't considered that Jesse's job was so dangerous. Stupid of her. She knew he worked in black ops. He was a medic, though. Somehow, she viewed him as working on the sidelines, patching up the wounds of the other members of his team. But Jesse was as well trained and deadly as his teammates, along with that store of medical knowledge in his brain.

Simone turned to Jake. "Let's do this. I need to pack my gear for this mission."

Minutes later, the deed was done.

"You shouldn't have a problem with the cut. However, since you're traveling to a tropical climate where any cut could become infected quickly, I'm going to give you an antibiotic." He handed her two packets. "The blue-and-white capsules are to prevent infection. Two a day. Take them all. No arguments. The white caplets are mild pain killers if you need them. You probably won't. The incision is like a paper cut. You shouldn't have a problem with sleepiness or sluggishness if you need to take the pain meds. Jesse will check the incision every day until it's healed. Let him. You can't afford to take a chance with your health."

"Yes, sir."

"Anything else I can do for you?"

"I need to restock my supplies," Jesse said.

Jake waved him toward the drug cabinets. "Take what you need. I'll replenish from the storeroom anyway." He handed Jesse a bag.

"Thanks."

The other medic motioned for Simone to follow him to the other side of the infirmary. "Have a seat," he said, indicating a chair near one bed. He sat on the bed. "So, Simone, you're an ace computer hacker, huh?"

She shrugged. "I'm good, and I enjoy the challenge. What about you? How long have you worked for Fortress?"

"Several years now. I'm actually filling in for a medic out sick today. Normally, I'm assigned to the Wolf Pack as their medic."

"You're trained like Jesse."

"That's right."

"Any words of advice before we fly to Mexico?"

"Yeah. Stay close to Jesse. Don't tell anyone what you're really doing in town. Never mention the name Fortress. We don't have many friends down in that neck of the woods." He thought a minute. "If you're in a restaurant, don't leave your drink unattended. If you do have to leave it, order another one. Assume your drink is drugged."

And the fun just continued. She blew out a breath. "So noted. Anything else?"

"Know how to use a weapon?"

Simone flinched. "No. My weapon of choice is a computer. I leave the gun wielding to Jesse and his pals."

"Consider carrying a knife or a stun gun."

"Are you serious?"

"Yes, ma'am."

"Would you give your wife or girlfriend the same advice?"

"I have. My wife carries a small stun gun. She's in medical school, training to be a doctor. Her schedule is weird and if I'm deployed, another operative might not be available late at night to pick her up or walk Lacey to her car."

"Has she ever had to use it?"

"Once. Dropped the guy instantly, giving Lacey time to run to safety and call the police."

Jesse rested his hand on Simone's shoulder. "Ready?"

She nodded.

He held out a hand and tugged Simone to her feet.

"Stop by the weapons vault," Jake said. "For Simone."

After a curt nod, Jesse escorted Simone from the infirmary and into the elevator. They rode the car to a subterranean level where the medic guided her to one of the many rooms along a long corridor. The doors were steel.

"What is this place?"

"We have two floors of vaults filled with weapons and medical supplies. They're kept well stocked." He unlocked the door by using his key card, inputting a long string of numbers on the keypad, and having a retinal scan.

"Overkill?"

"Nope." He opened the door and motioned Simone inside. "We have enough weapons and ammunition stored on these two levels to win a war."

Simone stared in awe at the rows and rows of guns, ammunition, knives, throwing stars, and many other things she couldn't name because she didn't recognize them. Jesse hadn't been exaggerating.

He walked to the far wall to a set of cabinets and opened one door. After scanning the contents, Jesse grabbed a small pink gadget and showed it to her. "How about this? The female operatives and spouses of operatives all carry one of these. It's easy to use and efficient."

"Is that a stun gun?"

He nodded and flicked a switch with his thumb. Instantly, she heard the snap of an electrical spark. "All you have to do is touch this to your attacker's skin, and he'll go down. As soon as he drops, get away from him. Don't stop until you're with me or you're locked in where no one can get to you."

"Is all this necessary?"

"I hope it's overkill. If it isn't, you'll be ready to protect yourself until I can get to you."

"Sounds like I should have opted to take a truckload of self-defense courses instead of computer classes," she muttered.

Jesse chuckled as he ushered Simone from the weapons vault and into the elevator. "We've worked together on a few self-defense moves since you moved here."

"You don't seem worried about this mission."

He glanced at her. "I'm not happy about taking you into the lion's den. I'm trained to do this. You aren't."

"So you're in less danger than I am?"

"Just as much, but I'm better prepared to handle the danger."

She considered that. Made sense. He should be confident about his training. Jesse had certainly had plenty of it. "You realize I'm not athletic at all, right?"

His eyebrows shot up. "What does that have to do with handling danger?"

"I'm not prime material for self-defense lessons, despite your best efforts. Besides, you can't teach me everything I need to know to toss bad guys over my shoulder while we're on the plane."

"You might be surprised what you can do. Your center of gravity is lower to the ground, and that gives you an advantage over a taller opponent."

"Yeah, if I know what to do. I don't."

"By the time we land in Mexico, you'll have more training that will hopefully give you a chance to escape." He paused. "Provided you have time to use the training."

That didn't sound good. "What if I don't?"

"That's where the stun gun comes in handy. Keep the weapon on you or it will be of no use."

"Jake said the same thing."

"Good. Pay attention to his advice. I'll get you through this, Simone. Concentrate on finding the programmer who's selling out our people. I'll handle the rest."

"You should have more help."

"I'd prefer my team, but they're not available until next week unless Zane or the boss calls them back sooner. I hope not. We can handle this by ourselves. If we need help, backup will be close. We'll be fine."

"Famous last words." She hoped they didn't regret it.

Chapter Three

Jesse opened the jet's hatch and stepped onto the top of the stairs. He surveyed the area, looking for anything that pinged a warning on his internal radar. Even at midnight, the air was hot and muggy, typical for the climate in this area.

The private airstrip was quiet, only necessary lighting illuminating the company jet. Although he saw nothing out of the ordinary, Jesse's skin crawled. Someone was watching them.

Seconds later, a vehicle's engine cranked, and two sets of headlights approached.

Jesse glanced over his shoulder. "Jordan, we have company."

The pilot stepped to the hatch, weapon in hand and held by his thigh. "The boss said we'd be met with a vehicle."

"I hope that's what we're seeing. Simone, stay inside until I tell you it's clear."

"Be careful, Jesse. I don't want my boyfriend to have bullet holes."

He chuckled. The little minx was enjoying herself. She was calmer than when they left Nashville.

The two vehicles parked near the bottom of the stairs, and four men climbed out. One man came to the bottom of the stairs. "My boss sent an SUV for you as a favor to Maddox."

Jesse glanced at Jordan, who nodded. The pilot would monitor Simone. Jesse descended the stairs. "Thanks for the delivery this late at night."

"It's no problem. My boss says he owes Maddox and is glad to repay the debt." He handed over two key fobs. "Steel plates run underneath and surround the vehicle. The glass is also bullet resistant. My boss transports his family in this SUV, so it's safe. When you no longer need the vehicle, bring it back here. This airstrip is on the Reyes property. No one would dare come onto our land to bother the vehicle."

Jesse gave a brief nod. "Tell your boss we appreciate the help."

The four men climbed into the second SUV and drove away.

"Keep watch," Jesse said to the pilot. He stepped onto the tarmac, grabbed a small plastic device from his pocket, and slowly circled the vehicle while watching the green chaser lights. So far, so good. The electronic sniffer didn't detect any devices to track their movements or listen to their conversations.

Once he finished the circuit, Jesse slid the device away and crawled under the vehicle to check visually for a bomb. He trusted his boss's judgment. Trusting the unknown Reyes with Simone's life was another matter.

When satisfied that Simone would be safe, Jesse climbed to his feet and returned to the jet. "We're clear."

"I'll help load your gear," Jordan said.

Between them, Jordan and Jesse grabbed the bags and Jesse's mike bag and carried them to the SUV. Once they loaded everything, Jesse returned to the cabin. "Ready to leave?" he asked Simone.

She rose and came to him, her gaze locked with his. "What about Jordan? Isn't he going with us?"

He shook his head. "He'll refuel the jet and take off to pick up Artemis."

Simone scowled. "Who is that?"

"I'll tell you about them on the drive to the safe house." Was that a little jealousy he heard in her voice? A positive step forward if he was right. Then again, he was probably imaging things.

Once he helped Simone into the shotgun seat, Jesse turned and shook Jordan's hand. "Appreciate the lift. See you soon, my friend."

"Yep. Be safe, Jesse. People who sell out their country won't think twice about turning on you and Simone."

"We'll be careful." Jesse climbed behind the wheel and cranked the engine. He plugged in the GPS coordinates of the safe house into his phone and drove away from the airstrip.

"Tell me about this Artemis person," Simone demanded. "What's she like?"

"Artemis is a team of female operatives. Each member of the team is skilled in hand-to-hand combat, has sniper training, and can gut you like a fish in two seconds flat if you're a threat to her or one of her principals. I think you'll enjoy meeting them."

"Why?"

He glanced at her. "They're as tough as nails and feisty to boot. You have a lot in common with them, Simone. That's an enormous compliment. They're more than capable of protecting you and watching our six."

"How many women are on the team?"

"Five, although I've heard rumors that Brent is considering adding a second all-female team. That way, members of the two teams will work together on assignments where many female operatives are needed."

"Were these women military as well?"

"Some were. Some were law enforcement. Sometimes they go into an undercover assignment alone. Most of the time, their teammates are close or they take temporary jobs right along with the chief operative."

"Are they good?"

"They're one of the best teams I've ever worked with."

Her head whipped in his direction. "You worked a mission with them before?"

"More than one. We've been backup for them twice, too. They didn't need us to intervene. We got paid to work on our tans on those missions."

"What do you know about them?"

"Not much," he admitted. "Brent kept them under wraps until the last year. They still keep to themselves a lot. Most of the other teams have heard about them but wouldn't know the faces of Artemis if they passed the women on the street, a deliberate move on the boss's part. Some teams believe the rumors of an all-female team are a myth."

"Did you like working with them?"

He thought about that. "I appreciate their skills and their ability to blend into any environment. Their skills are lethal. I wouldn't want to go up against them if they decided to go rogue."

"You have that much respect for these women?"

"Definitely. You will too once you meet them."

"Where will they stay while they're watching over us?"

"Another safe house close by. Two of them will watch the house at night so we can sleep."

"Wouldn't it make more sense for them to stay with us?"

"We can't afford for them to stay in the same house. If we're followed to our safe house one night and our tail spots Artemis, that would compromise their identities. Their presence would also compromise our story. No one will believe I'd tolerate a house full of women when I'm supposed to be persuading my girlfriend to marry me."

"Marry you?" Simone's voice rose. "Brent and Zane didn't mention that part of our cover story."

Jesse chuckled. "We have to make it believable. Besides, you can sell a refusal to be rushed to the altar."

"I don't have a ring," she protested. "Who's going to believe we're engaged without you shoving a ring on my finger to warn off other men who might be interested?"

"It's in my Go bag."

"You can't be serious. We were never apart at Fortress headquarters. When did you get a ring?"

"Zane slipped it into my identification packet. The ring also has a GPS tracker embedded in it."

"Of course it does. Good grief, Jesse. How much money does Fortress spend on trackers every year?"

"A lot," he admitted. "They're worth every penny."

He steered the SUV around a large curve. "Let's go over our cover story again."

"I'm tired. Can't this wait?"

"It's the perfect time to see if you remember what we've been memorizing on the flight." He quizzed Simone on her story first, then had her do the same to him. They both passed their tests. Now if they could do the same under pressure and in everyday conversation with their coworkers, they'd have a better shot at getting out of this with their skin intact.

"Well, Jesse, did I pass muster?" Simone teased.

"You were great. Just remember to stick to the story unless we're inside the house, and only after I've confirmed no bugs or cameras were planted in our absence. To survive in undercover assignments, you live and breathe your persona every minute. Less chance of slipping up that way."

"You don't trust anyone much, do you?"

"Never. Only my teammates and their wives." Jesse glanced at her. "And now you."

Minutes later, he parked at the back of a small house outside of Sayulita. "Home sweet home, Simone."

She said nothing for a moment. "It's kind of small, isn't it?"

"Small is good. We'll have an easier time spotting things out of place if we see the same spaces all the time."

"Can't argue with that logic. Does it have more than one bedroom?"

He turned off the engine. "Don't know. We'll deal with the accommodations, whatever they are. If there's only one bedroom, I'll sleep on the floor."

"You can't do that," Simone protested. "We're in a tropical climate. You might share the floor with scorpions and snakes."

Jesse laughed. "I'll search the room before I lay down. Stay here while I check things out. You'll be safe inside the vehicle." He handed her a key fob. "If anything happens, get out of here and drive to the American consulate. They'll keep you safe until a Fortress team arrives to help."

"I'm not leaving you alone to face off with thugs. We're a team. We stick together."

"Do you remember Zane's orders?"

She scowled. "Yeah, yeah. Do what I'm told."

"It's for your safety and mine. I'm well trained, Simone. I'll be fine, especially if I know you're safe."

"I don't feel right about leaving you, so let's not put those orders to the test."

Stubborn lady. "Stay here. I'll be back soon." He exited the SUV and locked the doors before doing a circuit around the house. Everything appeared to be in good order. No obvious signs of tampering around the doors or windows. He located the safe house key hidden behind the back porch light.

Jesse unlocked the door, palmed his weapon, and turned the knob. He slipped inside the door and waited. No sign of anyone lying in wait, a sense of disturbed air, or alarming scents. Nothing.

Room by room, he searched the home, including checking for cameras and listening devices. All was as it should be, including a refrigerator and pantry filled with food. Very nice. He and Simone shouldn't have to eat out much. He was also pleased to see four cases of bottled water. No chance of dealing with a virus or parasite from drinking tap water.

Once he was satisfied Simone would be safe inside the house, he returned to the SUV. "Clear."

"I'll help you carry in our gear, then we can sleep. We have to be at work in a few hours."

"We'll be fine."

"Ha. Speak for yourself. I like my sleep, thank you very much."

"I'll keep that in mind." So, the lady was cranky if she didn't get enough sleep. He already knew she was a coffee addict. He'd have to keep her well supplied.

Jesse carried his bags into the small guest bedroom and dropped them on the bed, then returned to the kitchen where Simone was peering into the refrigerator. "Hungry?"

"A little."

"So am I. How does an omelet sound?"

"Like heaven."

"I'll whip up a couple after I set your bags in your room."

She turned. "There are two rooms?"

"Yes, ma'am. You'll be staying in the main bedroom." He carried her bags to her room, then returned to find Simone whipping eggs together in a bowl. "You cook?"

"Since I like to eat, cooking is one of my favorite pastimes."

"Same here. What do you like in your omelet?"

"Anything. I'm not picky."

He got to work washing and chopping a bell pepper, onion, and tomato and returned to the refrigerator for a block of cheese. After locating a grater, he shredded enough cheddar cheese for two omelets.

Jesse found a saucepan and cooked the pepper and onions until they were soft.

"Ready for the vegetables?"

"Yep. Dump half of them in this omelet."

Soon, Jesse plated the omelets, hung up the dishtowel he'd used to dry the dishes and utensils, then joined Simone at the small table.

She set a small glass of juice in front of him and poured another for herself. "Hope apple juice is okay. I'm not a fan of orange juice."

"I'm not picky." Couldn't afford to be on missions. You never knew what you'd have to eat or drink when the rations ran out.

When they finished their meal, Jesse and Simone washed the last of the dishes and utensils and set them on the drainer to air dry.

"This way," he said, leading Simone along the short hall to the main bedroom. He turned on the light and stepped aside so she could enter the room. "What do you think?"

"I'll let you know in a minute." She went straight to the bathroom, turned on the light, and walked inside. Seconds later, she returned to the room. "This works."

"Good. Get some rest, Simone. No one will bother us tonight. We're safe."

She frowned. "How do you know? You've been with me since we arrived."

Jesse smiled. "Two members of Shadow unit are outside, keeping watch. They'll let us know if we have a problem. I'll also be setting up more security inside the house before I sleep."

"Want help?"

He shook his head. "I've got it. Won't take me long. If anything makes you feel uneasy, I'll be in the room across the hall, and my door will be open. See you in the morning." Jesse would give anything to kiss her goodnight. He couldn't, though, so he turned and left, closing the door behind him.

In his room, Jesse unzipped his Go bag and pulled out the portable security devices he'd brought to Mexico with him. Small but mighty, these little gadgets would do the job of warning him if anyone tried to enter the premises without his knowledge. Didn't see how a person could slip by their Fortress backup, but things happened you didn't expect all the time. Better to be safe.

Minutes later, he finished the work and got ready for bed in the hall bathroom. Jesse climbed into bed and dropped into a light sleep. In a few hours, their job would begin. He hoped Simone could maintain her cover without a slipup.

No matter the cost to himself, Jesse would keep her safe. No question, he was the muscle on this operation. Simone was the key partner. Everything hinged on her.

Chapter Four

Simone could barely contain her excitement as they drove up to the guarded gate of the Dragon Alley campus. Hard to believe she was really here, the place where she'd dreamed of working for years. And here she was. Undercover, perhaps, but an official employee of DA.

Too bad she'd never be able to tell anyone about this opportunity. What a boost to her reputation that would be. Ah, well, if she needed to find another job in the future, dropping the name of Fortress Security would also add some weight to her work history.

Jesse lowered the driver's side window. "Porterfield and Kenyon reporting for work." He handed over their identification.

The well-armed guard retraced his steps to the guard shack and entered something into the computer. He returned and handed back their identification. "Employees park at the back of the main building straight ahead. The spaces are numbered. You and Ms. Kenyon are assigned to number 242. Report to the front desk. The receptionist will tell you where to go. Have a good day." He opened the gate for them.

"Why does this feel like a prison camp?" Simone said as she looked at the campus. "Razor wire on top of the fence? Who does that?"

"You'd be surprised," Jesse murmured.

"I know their programs are sought after worldwide, but this is ridiculous."

"Consider where they're located. Sayulita has two terrorist groups working in tandem to control the drug and weapons trade in the area. The Federales enforce laws the terrorist groups want enforced. This isn't a safe place to live or work."

"You wouldn't live here?"

"No way. I'd never try to raise a family in this area."

That said something, didn't it? Simone eyed the razor wire with more appreciation. "I should look at the over-the-top security as a protection measure to keep the terrorists out rather than keep the workers inside the facility."

"Maybe. We'll see once we're inside."

Yeah, see, that didn't help her feel better about the situation. Simone hated feeling penned in. She'd had enough of that with her former boyfriend who had now turned to her current stalker. The Jerk. One good thing about being in Mexico. Trevor White wouldn't know where to find her.

Jesse parked in their assigned space and came around the hood to open the door for Simone. "Remember, we're on the stage as of right now."

"I got it."

"Good. Don't act surprised when I kiss you."

She stared, heart racing. "Why would you do that?"

He snorted. "Come on, Simone. Have you looked in the mirror lately? You're drop-dead gorgeous. A man who didn't want to kiss you would have to be dead. I'm very much alive."

Her face heated.

He winked at her and held out his hand. "A boyfriend always holds his girlfriend's hand."

"He does, huh?"

"It's a rule in the boyfriend handbook."

Simone laughed. Couldn't help it. Jesse Phelps had a keen sense of humor, and she loved it. "Is there a girlfriend handbook? If so, I need a copy because apparently I wasn't a good girlfriend."

Jesse stopped and turned to her. "What does that mean?"

She waved that aside. "Long story. I'll tell you about it later. We need to get going or we'll be late for our first day."

He gave a slight nod. "All right. I'll let it go for now but we will go back to that topic tonight because I think you're wrong."

"Wasn't me who said it, but I appreciate the vote of confidence."

The medic escorted her to the front of the building where a chirpy woman greeted at the front desk. "Welcome to Dragon Alley. How may I assist you?" she asked with a bright smile.

"We're new employees. Jesse Porterfield and Simone Kenyon."

She glanced at her screen. "If you'll take a seat, someone will be here shortly to escort you to your stations."

Seriously? They had to have an escort to their desks? Simone took a seat beside Jesse on the cushioned sofa. "Will we have to have an escort to the bathroom, too?" she whispered.

His eyes twinkled. "To work here, you'll deal."

"Yeah, but I'll fuss and fume every time if it's true."

He squeezed her hand and went back to casually looking at everything in the lobby.

Except it wasn't so casual. Simone could almost see him cataloging everything in that massive brain of his, mapping out escape routes and every potential weapon in the large room.

One of the elevator doors slid open, and two people walked toward Jesse and Simone. She'd bet the burly guy was security, while the woman with the quirky clothes in bright colors worked in the programming division.

Jesse stood and held out his hand to Burly guy. "Jesse Porterfield."

"Bastien Boudreaux. I'm your supervisor. This is Trina Kirk, programming development supervisor."

Jesse held out his hand to help Simone to her feet. "This is Simone Kenyon."

Trina held out her hand to Simone. "Nice to meet you, Simone. Come with me, and we'll start your orientation."

Yay. Not. Orientation would be boring as dirt. "I'm looking forward to working with you and the rest of the team. Working for Dragon Alley is a dream come true for me."

"We love to hear that. DA is a great employer. Everyone here is so nice, and we look out for each other."

Jesse squeezed Simone's hand before he turned her face up to his and brushed his mouth over hers. "Have a good day, sweetheart," he murmured and released her.

"You, too." Wow. A little peck on the mouth shouldn't cause fireworks to go off inside her. It did anyway.

Simone followed Trina from the lobby into the elevator. Soon, they stepped out on the sixth floor. She glanced around, curious about her new working area. Nothing much to write home about yet. Office after office, all with doors closed. A conference room in use. More offices.

And there at the end of the long hallway, a large room with multiple cubicles. This was what she'd expected. Programming could be a lonely business. Being part of a cubicle farm meant she'd have people walking by and looking into her space to see the new girl and look at what she was working on.

If she'd been a legitimate employee, she would have enjoyed the camaraderie. Under the circumstances, though, she'd have to be clever and fast to snoop around online with no one catching her. Good thing she enjoyed a challenge.

"I'll introduce you to your mentor, then leave you to your work." Trina led the way to the back of the room to the space next to the corner cubicle. "Joy, this is Simone Kenyon."

Joy spun around in her chair and stood. She held out her hand. "Welcome to the Farm, Simone. I'm Joy Walters."

"Nice to meet you, Joy."

"Let's get you set up in the corner cubicle, and you can work through your orientation packet online. When you finish, I'll help you begin your first assignments."

"I'm ready."

Joy grinned. "That's what we like to hear. Enthusiasm is welcome and appreciated."

"Who wouldn't be enthusiastic working for Dragon Alley?"

"Let's get started." Joy took Simone to the cubicle and motioned for her to sit at the desk, then she handed Simone a piece of paper with her login information. She'd just given Simone instructions when her desk phone rang. "I need to take the call. I'm working under a deadline and expecting information for the next stage of programming."

"Go. I'll set up my password."

"You'll find your online orientation in your email. Work on that, and I'll check in with you soon." She hurried off.

Perfect. The sooner she finished her orientation, the faster she'd be able to poke around in personnel files and coworker emails. When she and Jesse returned to the safe house, Simone's actual work would begin.

She logged in and created a complicated password. Working with a horde of computer programmers and hackers made an excellent password necessary.

Simone checked her DA work email and found three welcome letters, one each from the CEO, the head of the programming division, and the head of the special projects division, a man named Griffin Daley. She needed an introduction to Daley. If Dragon Alley had instructed one programmer to create the program Fortress was targeting, Daley had assigned the work to someone in his division.

After scanning the emails, Simone logged into the orientation program and worked through the reading and testing portions of the program. More than once, her mind drifted, and she had to corral her brain into the rookie training. She'd been right in her guess about the orientation program. Necessary but boring as dirt.

Although she'd expected intense training from a company with Dragon Alley's reputation, the basic information surprised Simone.

A list of the top people in each division was the only interesting thing to come out of the four-hour orientation.

Joy rolled her chair around the edge of the dividing wall between their cubicles. "How's it going?"

"Just finished orientation. What's next?"

The other woman stared at her. "You're finished?"

Simone tilted her head. "Yeah, why?"

"Orientation took me two days to get through, and I had one of the fastest times. Holy cow, Simone. I can't believe it."

She shrugged. "You can check if you like. The program is like one I had at my previous job."

"Where did you work?"

"Game Theory," she said, naming one company Zane had created in his off time, a company which had a stellar reputation in the gaming community. Since Z owned the company, he had loaded her fake personnel file and work history into the company's system in case anyone at DA checked more closely into her background.

"Whoa," Joy whispered. "I didn't know you worked for them. It's super hard to get on with them. How did you do it?"

"A recommendation from a friend got me an interview with the owner. Since he liked my work portfolio, he gave me a programming job as a skills test. I finished the job faster than he expected. The owner offered me a job on the spot."

"No wonder you finished orientation so fast." Her mentor sounded awed. "You're going to be a big hit around here, Simone. The higher ups at DA are always looking for new talent with exceptional skills. I think they'll discover you quickly and put you to work in a different division."

She frowned as though she hadn't poked around enough to notice the special division. "There's another division other than programming?"

"Oh, yeah." Joy scooted closer and lowered her voice. "It's called Special Projects. That group is an elite bunch of programmers. Their projects are hush-hush, and they're not allowed to talk about them even after the work is finished."

"No one knows anything about their projects?" Simone sounded skeptical. "Come on. This is like a small town. Rumors must fly around the company."

"All I know is the projects are top secret, and anyone who talks is handed a pink slip without a severance package."

"How do I get noticed by the upper ranks? I'd love to work in a division like that."

"Who wouldn't? Don't worry, Simone. From what I can see, you'll be out of this programming area soon. All you have to do is complete the assignments you're given in record time. Trust me, they'll pay attention since you're new, especially coming from Game Theory. Someone will monitor your work for the next few weeks. Getting noticed doesn't take long around here."

She'd figured on having to create a program to prevent anyone from keeping tabs on her computer searches while she was working at DA. Waiting for weeks to be noticed wasn't in the cards. They had days to stop the target programmer from finishing the work. "Who's in Special Projects? Can you tell me that much?"

"Griffin Daley is head of the division. Patrick Meyers, Allison Norbert, Beckett Francen, and Wyatt Hatcher all work for Griffin." Joy sighed, a dreamy expression on her face. "Griffin is drop-dead gorgeous, Simone. I would give anything to be noticed by that man." She laughed. "Who am I kidding? I'd love to go on a date with Griffin but he hasn't noticed me that way either."

"That handsome, huh?"

"Wait until you see him. You'll melt into a puddle at his feet."

Simone shook her head. "I don't think so. I'm involved with someone."

"He can't hold a candle to Griffin."

"You haven't seen Jesse yet but you will."

"How?"

"He just started working in the security division of DA."

Joy's eyes widened. "Really? That's great for you, right?"

"Can't beat living and working together."

"I'm looking forward to meeting this guy. Is he a good man?"

Simone smiled. "The best. He's wonderful."

"Introduce me when he comes around."

"Sure. Now, what's next?"

"Lunch. Log out, and I'll take you to the company cafeteria. We have the best food here. The CEO hired two professional chefs to make meals for the employees."

She logged out and rose. "Let me text my boyfriend to let him know I'm going to lunch."

"Is he a control freak?" Joy asked.

"Well, yeah, he is, but not in a bad way." She'd had that with Trevor. Jesse was nothing like The Jerk. "Jesse is very protective. Frankly, I'm glad he is, especially down here in Sayulita. I wouldn't want to live here without him."

The other woman led Simone from the cubicle farm. "What do you mean? I've had no problems here. My neighbors are all really nice, especially when they find out where I work."

Simone slid her phone from her pocket and shot off a quick message to Jesse. "Jesse checked the crime stats and researched areas where cartels and terrorists were active. Sayulita is home to two terrorist organizations."

Joy stopped and turned to face Simone. "Are you serious?"

She nodded. "He wouldn't let me come to Sayulita without him. I'm lucky Dragon Alley had an opening in their security division. Jesse is perfect for the job."

Her phone vibrated with a reply to her message. She smiled when she read the text. "Jesse will meet us in the cafeteria."

"That's great." Joy led Simone from the cubicle farm and down a long corridor to a bank of elevators. They rode to the second floor and stepped out into a large room with many circular tables and employees eating their lunches. "This way."

The two women walked to the front of the room where several tables of food were set up with food service workers manning the stations and refilling serving dishes as needed.

Simone's eyes widened at the assortment of food. "They have this kind of spread going all the time?"

Joy nodded. "I've had to work late into the night before when my project was on a deadline. When I took a break to investigate the food offerings, I scored apple pie and vanilla ice cream and coffee for my snack."

"Excellent choice."

"Can't beat sugar, caffeine, and ice cream for energy."

Jesse walked up to Simone. "Hi, babe." He bent his head and brushed his lips over hers.

Good grief. She'd never get used to that simple gesture of affection, fake or not. Fire sizzled in her veins every time he kissed her.

She glanced at his uniform. "You look sharp."

"You're biased."

"Maybe." Definitely. Jesse Phelps was smoking hot. A nudge from Joy reminded Simone she'd promised to introduce her new friend to Jesse. "This is my mentor, Joy. Joy, this is Jesse Porterfield, my boyfriend."

"Hopefully, soon to be her husband," Jesse said, smiling as he shook Joy's hand. "My woman has a stubborn streak."

Simone laughed. "Told you."

"I'm glad to meet you, Joy."

"Same here."

They selected their meals and carried loaded trays to a nearby table. Jesse pulled out Simone's chair for her and did the same for Joy. Once Jesse seated them, he took their glasses and filled them with iced tea.

"You weren't kidding about him being protective," Joy whispered. "You're a lucky woman, Simone."

"I know."

"So, why aren't you jumping into marriage with him? If you don't, some other woman will take him up on the offer. He's too good to pass up."

"I'm skittish," she said, opting for the truth. This question hadn't been in the arsenal of background information Zane had created for her. "I was in a terrible relationship before I met Jesse. I don't want to make a mistake like that again."

Joy's hand wrapped around Simone's, and she squeezed. "I'm sorry. Looks like you got a good one this time, though."

"I did." She wrinkled her nose. "However, I don't want to be too accommodating. Jesse will appreciate the challenge of having to win my heart." Simone laughed. "Truthfully, he's already got my heart. I just want him to work at catching me."

"Smart woman."

Jesse set two glasses of tea in front of the ladies and placed the final filled glass in front of his plate. "What did I miss?"

"I was telling Joy why I'm leading you on a merry chase instead of giving in and marrying you."

"Yeah? Enlighten me, too. That way I'll be able to come up with better arguments why you should do what we both want, anyway."

"Bad breakup before I met you."

He froze, his gaze locking with hers. "How bad?" In the depths of his eyes was the real question he wanted to ask and couldn't in front of Joy. Was this real or made up for Joy's benefit?

"I ended up in a hospital for a week when The Jerk lost his temper. I filed charges and had him arrested for assault and battery. The cops delivered the message that I was finished with him when they arrested The Jerk, and that he was never to set foot on my property again."

"How did he take it?"

"Not well. He doesn't want to take no for an answer."

"You should have told me." Jesse trailed the back of his fingers along Simone's cheek. "If he contacts you again, I want to know. I'll take care of it."

"Jesse, that's unnecessary."

"Yeah, it is. No woman should feel threatened. No real man would threaten a woman, especially one he claimed to care about."

"We're in Mexico. He's not. The Jerk isn't a problem."

Jesse watched her a moment. "He'll find you. That's how stalkers work. Promise you'll tell me when he pops up again."

"What can you do about him?"

His eyebrow rose.

Yeah, okay. Her question couldn't be answered truthfully. Otherwise, Joy would be even more curious about Jesse than she already was. "Never mind. I don't think I want to know."

"I want your promise, sweetheart."

This was pretend, right? It didn't matter what she answered. Except Simone knew her answer mattered to Jesse. Somehow, he had figured out she told Joy the truth and planned to take care of the problem for her if The Jerk showed up again. *When* he showed up again. He was like a bad penny, turning up when you least expected or wanted. "I promise."

Joy sighed, her chin resting on her palm. "Do you have brothers, Jesse?"

He chuckled. "I do. They're married with two kids a piece."

"Isn't that how things always work?" she said. "All the good ones are taken."

"Except for Griffin?" Simone teased.

Her friend's face flushed. "As if he'd ever notice me. I've been here for two years, and he hasn't so much as looked in my direction yet. So, Jesse, how has your first day on the job been?"

"Uneventful, just how I like them when I work security."

"What work were in you before this?"

"Army," he answered with his cover story. "Military police."

"Did you like it?"

"Sometimes. A lot of boring stretches with no action interspersed with heavy firefights to ramp up your adrenaline." He grimaced. "Most of the time I drank too much terrible coffee and dealt with sand everywhere."

Joy laughed. "You should feel right at home in Sayulita."

"What about you?" Simone asked to get attention off of her and Jesse. "Where did you work before you came to Dragon Alley?"

"A computer programming job in San Francisco."

Seriously? Some coincidence that Joy was from Simone's home town. "Why did you apply for a job here? San Francisco is home to many good tech companies who could use your skill."

"Bored with my job. I wanted a challenge, and working in a foreign country sounded exciting." She smiled slightly. "I had a nasty breakup, too, and needed a change of scenery. I applied here on a whim and was thrilled when I landed an interview. As soon as DA offered me a job, I jumped at it and moved, telling no one where I was going. My mother thought I moved to Georgia to get away from Todd, my ex-boyfriend. I finally told her where I was a few months ago but only after Todd had married my former best friend. They have a kid now." Joy shivered. "I'm glad I escaped. I feel sorry for Beth and her little girl."

"I'm happy you're safe." Simone sipped her tea. "So, we just got into town last night. What places do you recommend Jesse and I visit and the best restaurants?"

"I hope you like Mexican food because that's all there is in Sayulita except for a Mediterranean restaurant and a Chinese place." She told Simone and Jesse the names of the restaurants and her recommendations for the best ones to try. "We have an excellent theater company and good ballet if you're into that kind of thing. We also have two movie theaters and more bars than you can shake a stick at. Oh, and coffee shops on every street corner."

"Sold on the coffee shops." Simone finished the last bite of her lunch. "What self-respecting computer programmer doesn't live on caffeine?"

Joy laughed. "That's what I say. If you want, I can take you to my favorite coffee shop after work tonight. They have an excellent selection of baked goods, too."

"That's a winner," Jesse said. "We won't have to cook breakfast in the morning before we head here."

"Well, you wouldn't have to do that, anyway. You can always eat breakfast here. The cafeteria is open 24/7 for all employees."

"Good to know. We might take advantage of that perk if we run late one morning." Jesse captured Simone's hand and kissed her palm. "Simone can be a distraction."

Her face flushed at that innuendo. Oh, man. Jesse was lethal. He was also excellent at this undercover role. He was playing the role, right? The line between reality and role playing was blurring.

"Oh, Simone." Joy laughed. "I can't believe you've held out against this man. If you decide you don't want him, point Jesse my way. I'll take him off your hands in a heartbeat."

"He's mine," she said. "I don't share."

Jesse winked at her. "I don't share, either." He turned to Joy. "Sorry, Joy. I think you're out of luck."

"You never know. Surprising things happen all the time around Dragon Alley."

#

Chapter Five

Jesse drove Simone back to the safe house, taking a circular route. When he was satisfied that he'd lost the tail they'd picked up from the campus of Dragon Alley, he headed toward the house.

"Why did we take the scenic route?" Simone asked.

"We had a tail."

"What?" She twisted in her seat to look out the back window for herself.

"Don't worry. I lost him. Otherwise, we wouldn't be this close to the house. I don't want to invite further trouble by leading our enemy straight to the place where we sleep."

"Did I mess up today?"

Jesse glanced at her. "Don't worry, Simone. I'm sure you did fine. This is probably a precaution by Dragon Alley. If they've commissioned the program we're here to find and destroy, the power behind the decision to create the program will be skittish about new hires, especially one with your programming skills."

"Unless you put a mouse in my pocket with a listening device on his collar, you can't know I didn't screw up today."

"I have faith in you. You can't be afraid to talk to people, sweetheart. Clamming up will draw the wrong attention. Be yourself and stick to the cover story. You'll be fine. Remember, you're the brains of this outfit. I'm the brawn. It's my job to make sure you're safe."

That comment reminded him of their lunch conversation. "How much of the story of your ex-boyfriend is true?"

"All of it. You'll notice I didn't give Joy a name, and I won't. The name would give her too much information about me if she tracked down The Jerk, including my real name. My ex would follow her computer tracks back to Sayulita to find me again. By the way, Joy is from my hometown."

Jesse scowled. He didn't like the sound of this. Too much coincidence with the women being from the same hometown. Although he wanted to gripe over Simone not telling him about her ex-boyfriend, he didn't have the right. Yet. He wanted it, though. Badly. "Your ex sounds like more than a jerk, Simone. He sounds like a stalker."

She remained silent.

Guess that answered his question. "I meant what I said in the cafeteria. If he shows his face or contacts you in any way, I want to know about it."

"Jesse...."

He shook his head. "No arguments. I take care of those in my inner circle." Especially the woman who was coming to mean so much to him in a short amount of time. "That includes you."

"Trevor can be dangerous."

"What's his last name? I'll run his name through our system to see what we have on him." He smiled. "I have to keep busy while you're working tonight."

Her head whipped toward Jesse. "His name last name is White. How did you know I was planning to work after supper?"

"Easy. I watched you recharge after midnight a few weeks ago when we were helping Poppy and Logan. You're a night owl, like me." The other couple had needed Simone's hacking skills to ferret out the culprit who was targeting Poppy.

"I suppose we'll both be working late, then."

"Good thing we have a large supply of coffee, hot chocolate, and herbal tea to keep us fueled and ready."

Jesse drove another circuit around the block, turning squares to be sure he hadn't missed a tail. When the mirrors showed no one following them, he turned into their driveway and parked. "Wait here while I check the house."

"Be careful."

"Always." He slipped from the vehicle and locked the doors. Walking around the side of the house to the backyard, Jesse studied the lock. No scratches to announce someone had broken into the place. Same with the locks on the windows.

He unlocked the back door and slipped inside the darkened kitchen. Only the light over the kitchen sink burned.

When all remained quiet, Jesse walked through the house, checking every room for signs of an intruder and using his electronic signal scanner to see if any unwanted electronics had been placed in the house. At the end of his search, he'd found that all was as he and Simone had left it this morning, and his security measures were working perfectly.

He returned to the SUV. "Clear." Jesse helped Simone to the asphalt driveway and escorted her to the house. "Do you have a preference for supper?"

"Anything as long as it's edible."

Jesse chuckled. "That's easy enough. I'll change clothes and work on our meal."

"What can I do?"

"You can be my sous chef or you can start on your night work. Your choice."

"You won't mind if I leave it all to you?"

"Of course not. I'm decent in the kitchen as long as you don't expect gourmet meals. My job is to take care of you and that includes feeding you. I can't hack into databases and emails but I can handle the rest of this assignment."

"I'll help you in the kitchen. If I work before supper, I won't want to stop."

"I understand." He took a chance and curved his hand around her nape. "Get into comfortable clothes, and I'll meet you in the kitchen." His thumb caressed her throat. When her eyes widened, Jesse released her and went to his room to change.

Had he gone too far? The last thing he wanted to do was scare her off. He didn't want to be locked into the friend zone, either.

Jesse changed clothes, washed his hands and face, and returned to the kitchen to find Simone had beaten him back. "That was fast."

She shrugged. "What can I say? I'm hungry."

He chuckled as he opened the refrigerator and scanned the food choices. "How do you feel about steaks and nuked potatoes?"

"No vegetables?"

Jesse narrowed his eyes. "Live large."

She laughed. "I'm in. I'll handle the potatoes if you want to man the steaks since I'm no good with grilling."

"I've got you covered."

They worked together to prepare the meal. In less than an hour, they sat at the table to eat. "How was your day?" she asked. "Anything interesting happen?"

"Nope. Just the way I like it. Dragon Alley has a lot of security measures in place, and Bastien is a stickler for following policies and rules."

"So, you're not best buds, huh?"

He snorted. "Not hardly. He liked the background Zane created for me but that's about all he had to say unless he was spouting off orders like a drill sergeant."

"Any holes in security?"

"They're lax about checking employees as they leave the facility."

She frowned. "I noticed that. I'm surprised since the employees are working with highly classified and competitive programs. Anyone can download something to a flash drive or upload things to the cloud and make out like a bandit by selling the programs to the highest bidder."

"That causes me to suspect there are more security measures in place that I haven't seen yet. Be careful when you're poking your nose where it doesn't belong, okay? Chances are excellent the higher-ups are tracking every keystroke, download, and upload."

"I will. I'd feel better if I knew whether DA installed cameras to spy on workers in the cubicle farm."

"We'll go in early tomorrow morning. I'll check the farm for you."

"That would be great, Jesse. Thanks."

When they finished their meal, Simone helped him clean the kitchen and wash the dishes and utensils.

Jesse took the dishtowel from her and hung it up to dry. "Get started on your work, Simone. Do you need anything while you're working? Coffee? Water?"

"Coffee. I'll switch to water after midnight."

"You got it. Where do you want to work?"

She nodded at the table. "This is as good a place as any. If I work in the bedroom, I'll fall asleep."

"Same here. I'll prep the coffeemaker, grab my computer, and join you."

Simone left the room and returned a minute later with her Fortress-issued laptop. She sat down, logged in, and dove into the work.

Jesse smiled as he prepared the coffeemaker. Although Simone wouldn't appreciate him saying so, she was adorable in work mode. If he had the talent to draw, he'd fill sketch books with her funny expressions and terrible posture while she worked.

He retrieved his laptop and carried it into the kitchen where he set up across the table from Simone. That way he'd be able to keep tabs on her energy and fatigue level through the next few hours. She might prefer to work at night but she also had a day job for the moment. Simone needed to be sharp for both sides of her work on this mission.

When the coffeemaker finished the brewing cycle, Jesse poured two mugs of coffee and carried one to Simone.

"Thanks," she murmured without taking her gaze from the screen.

After taking a sip of coffee, Jesse booted up his laptop and clicked on the icon for one of the Fortress databases. He entered Trevor White's name and narrowed his eyes at the results. So, good old Trevor had a record. This guy had been in and out of jail since he was a teenager. What was Simone doing with this guy?

He read screen after screen, growing more angry as he went deeper into Trevor's record. Simone's ex-boyfriend was a real creep.

Jesse saw a link to a hospital report and clicked on it. He froze as pictures of Simone appeared on the screen. Didn't take a genius to know what had happened to her. Trevor had beaten Simone so severely that she'd landed in the hospital for over a week. She'd filed charges against him from her hospital bed and the SFPD had taken care of the rest. They'd convinced Trevor that pleading guilty to assault and battery was a better deal than going to court and risking being found guilty of attempted murder.

At least Simone was given enough breathing room to pack up her belongings and move out of state while White was incarcerated. He'd meant what he said earlier. If Trevor showed up, Jesse would make sure he didn't bother Simone again. He wouldn't touch her.

Wonder if anyone would care if the abusive jerk disappeared permanently? Jesse sighed. Most likely, someone would miss him. Nothing could blow back on Simone.

"You okay, Jesse?"

"No."

"What's wrong?"

"Trevor White."

She rolled her eyes. "He's out of my life."

Jesse's eyebrow rose. "Really? Did I misunderstand you earlier?"

"No," Simone muttered. "You didn't. Look, he's a jerk and a creep, all right? I know that. I learned from my mistakes and will never go down that road again with any man."

"How did you meet him?"

"We grew up in the same neighborhood. Everyone assumed we'd be a couple since we dated off and on through high school. I just went along with it."

"How long did you date him?"

"Three years." She held up her hand. "I know what you're going to say. Don't bother. He wasn't a bully in high school. Yeah, he was in trouble a lot but most of the guys around the neighborhood were exactly the same. No one thought anything of it."

"White was more than a bully, sweetheart. He was abusive."

She stared. "You saw the pictures?"

"I plugged his name into the Fortress database. What do you think?"

Simone flinched. "I didn't want you to see me like that."

"If he comes after you again, I'll stop him by any means necessary. You know that, right?"

She nodded. "All I ask if that you do nothing to get you into trouble with the cops."

"No guarantees," he countered. "He hurt you. That's unacceptable. If he comes around again, I'll stop him from touching you. Period. He'll have to go through me first, and I'm difficult to get around. Not only that, you have my teammates plus Brent and Zane who will also go after Trevor with everything they have. Take my word for it, Simone. If he bothers you again, he's toast."

"Hopefully, he'll find someone else to pester."

"Don't bet on it. He's not just a pest. White is obsessed. Men like that don't quit until they're behind bars or dead."

She shoved her fingers through her hair. "I can't think about this right now. I need to focus on work. If I don't, I won't sleep at all tonight." After another quick glance at Jesse, she went back to her task.

Jesse seethed inside, a volcano ready to blow at the first sighting of one Trevor White. He'd seen several pictures of the creep and knew what he looked like. He'd be looking for him. If he showed up, White would regret showing his face.

He shoved back from the table. "I'm checking the perimeter," he said and left the house without another word.

What he needed was a good hard run of ten miles but that wouldn't happen. It would leave Simone alone and vulnerable. A circuit around the property would have to do.

He returned minutes later, grimaced at the taste of the cold coffee in his mug, and poured out the drink in favor of the steaming brew still in the pot.

Jesse resumed his exploration of White's life, growing more disgusted with the information he learned as each minute passed. Simone's ex-boyfriend had been arrested on multiple charges over the years. Attempted rape, assault, battery, illegal drugs and weapons. You name it and the authorities arrested White for the crime. Unfortunately, he'd been released more often than not except for the charges Simone had filed against him. As soon as the police told her she could leave, she moved out of state and attended college where she met Poppy Reynolds Fletcher. They graduated together, then Poppy moved to Tennessee to be closer to her sister Sage. Simone stayed near Washington, D.C.

Simone had to know what White was like. Jesse hated she had felt as though the creep was her only option for a dating relationship. She deserved better, and Jesse intended to show her as much if she gave him the chance.

The woman at the forefront of his mind pushed back from the table and stretched, looked at him, and froze. "Jesse, what's wrong?"

He couldn't help it. Everything protective inside Jesse demanded he act. He rose, circled the table, and pulled her gently into his arms. "I wish I had known you before last month."

"Why?"

"I feel like I'm too late to make a difference in your life."

She was silent a moment. "You're talking about Trevor."

"I'm sorry, Simone. No woman deserved the treatment you received at his hands."

"So you said at lunch today."

"I meant every word. If I'd been in your life sooner, I would have stopped him from abusing you."

"Lucky for me you don't have to intervene."

"But he keeps popping up, doesn't he?"

"Sometimes."

Right. He resolved to dig deeper and figure out how this guy was tracking Simone. She was too good with computers to leave electronic footprints for White to track back to her. Was someone at the think tank where she'd worked before joining Fortress to blame? Perhaps she kept in contact with someone in her old neighborhood.

In his pocket, Jesse's phone vibrated. Leaving one arm around Simone since she seemed content to remain in his embrace, he checked the screen. "We have a visitor."

She leaned back to look at him. "Who?"

"Iona Byrne, leader of Artemis."

"Do we have a problem?"

"If we did, Iona would have said as much." Pushing just a little more, Jesse kissed Simone's cheek and released her.

A knock sounded on the back door.

Jesse unlocked it and motioned Iona inside. "How's it going out there?"

"Quiet." The woman smiled at Simone and held out her hand. "I'm Iona, a member of Artemis. Brent sent me and my teammates to watch over you and Jesse."

"I'm Simone. Thanks for keeping us safe."

Iona shook her head. "That's Jesse's job. We're here for backup and to make sure your bodyguard/boyfriend sleeps at night."

Simone's eyes widened as she swung around to face Jesse. "Why wouldn't you sleep?"

"Your safety is my priority."

"I could have helped you keep watch. You already know I sleep little myself."

"You can't afford to have brain fog, sweetheart. The success of this operation depends on your brain working at top speed."

Her cheeks flushed. "It's still not right for you to do all the heavy lifting on this mission when I can watch to see if someone approaches the house."

"That's our job," Iona said. "We each have a role to play, Simone." She turned to Jesse. "Anything we should know?"

"Picked up and lost a tail from Dragon Alley today."

"Making someone nervous on your first day?"

He shrugged. "I don't think it's me. The program is attracting a lot of interest. The people involved will suspect anyone new, especially someone with Simone's skills."

"Biased much?"

"Nope. Honest. Simone is in Zane's league."

"High praise. I'll be on watch tonight with Tegan. Sleep, Jesse. We have your six. You and your lady are safe with us."

"Appreciate it. Need any food or coffee?"

She shook her head. "We're set. Thanks for the offer, though." Iona glanced at Simone. "If anything happens overnight, follow Jesse's orders to the letter. Between us, we'll get you out. Description of the vehicle that tailed you, Jesse?"

He rattled off the description as well as what he'd been able to see of the occupants. "Whoever followed us is not hugging the poverty line. The vehicle looked retrofitted."

"A lot of money is at stake. They don't want to lose control of the situation and the money that comes with selling out American patriots."

"You think the people following us work at DA?" Simone asked.

"Makes the most sense. They work there or were hired by someone who does."

She sighed. "Must be someone higher up the food chain. Employees are paid well but not enough to pay for hired muscle like that. How am I supposed to figure out who that person is and who the programmer is?"

"Focus on the programmer," Iona advised. "If Jesse can't persuade him or her to give up the name of the boss, one of us will." She smiled. "We enjoy playing hardball." A minute later, Iona was gone.

Simone shook her head. "That woman is intimidating. I believe she can handle anything thrown her way."

Jesse chuckled. "You'd be right. You stopped working to take a break. Do you need a snack, water, more coffee?"

"A snack would be great." She wrinkled her nose. "I shouldn't be hungry after our supper. I am, though."

"Walk around for a couple of minutes while I put a snack together."

"You're going to spoil me, Jesse."

He sobered. "That's my intention, sweetheart."

"I shouldn't get used to it. We're playing a role here. Losing you will hurt like crazy as it is."

"Not going to happen." He nudged her toward the archway between the kitchen and the rest of the house. "Walk. Your snack will be ready in a couple of minutes."

After Simone left, Jesse blew out a breath. He was moving too fast and knew it but couldn't stop. He was crazy about the feisty little programmer. Losing her would gut him, too, so he had to convince Simone to give him a real chance.

Pushing his concern aside for now, he headed for the refrigerator. He saw a couple of excellent possibilities. However, remembering her earlier comment at lunch about her favored late-night snack, Jesse poked around in the freezer. Score!

He grinned as he removed a frozen apple pie. This would be perfect with the vanilla ice cream he'd spotted earlier.

Jesse turned on the oven to the correct temperature and prepped a new pot of coffee. Simone wouldn't mind the wait with this feast as the reward. He'd just placed the pie in the oven when she returned to the kitchen.

Gaze fixed on the oven, she asked, "What are you baking?"

"A surprise. You don't mind a brief wait, do you?"

"If sweets are involved, nope." Simone returned to the table and sat down to resume work.

He watched as the coffeemaker began the brewing cycle, considering what he'd learned about White so far. Not enough. The first step was to find out where he was. If he was still in California, then Jesse would leave him to his own devices until this mission was over.

However, if another operative was in the San Francisco area and didn't mind making a point to White, Jesse would be glad to owe the coworker a huge favor.

He thought about that a minute and decided sending a friend to confront White didn't feel right. This was something Jesse needed to handle personally.

When the coffee finished brewing, he filled their mugs and returned to his computer to search for White's whereabouts while he waited for the apple pie to finish baking.

Less than an hour later, Jesse cut the pie and placed a steaming slice in a bowl, topped it with ice cream, and carried the bowl and spoon to the table for Simone.

Her eyes lit and she breathed deep. "Oh, man. That smells fabulous. Thanks, Jesse."

"Need more coffee?"

Simone shook her head. "I'm ready to switch to water now."

After handing her a bottle of water, he dished his own dessert into a bowl and joined her at the table. "How's it going?"

"Slow. Joy told me the names of the people in the special projects division, so I've been looking into their backgrounds. Nothing has stood out yet, but it's just a preliminary run. They're just computer geeks like I am."

"They must have some impressive qualifications to land a job at Dragon Alley."

She spooned up a bite of pie with the ice cream and chewed, an expression of bliss on her face. "This is so good. A perfect chaser to dinner. Anyway, to answer your question, the four of them have impressive skills and programming wins to their names. They're also good enough to bury their backgrounds online."

"Did you run them through the Fortress databases?"

"Not yet. I wanted to see what was out there on the Web first. Everything in cyberspace is carefully crafted. I need to see behind the mask."

"Zane has probably already done a preliminary run on them, especially since you're one of his employees. He leaves nothing to chance with his people."

She swallowed another bite. "I imagine you're right. I'll check the databases and a couple of other sites before I call it quits for the night. What about you? How are you making out with your research?"

"Not making as much progress as I wanted either."

"Maybe I can help."

"You could but you don't want to get involved in this one."

Simone stared. "You're looking for Trevor, aren't you?"

"Yes, ma'am."

"Why? He's a jerk and will always be one."

"White's not going away. We'll have to deal with him, eventually."

"We?"

"I'm not tossing you to the mercy of the wolf. He's already shown what he's capable of doing. If I can head him off and keep him away from you, I'll do it."

"He's not your problem, Jesse."

"He's your problem, and I care about you."

"You can't do this. He hurts people."

"I've seen his record. He's at least as bad as the perps I arrested when I was a cop. He's the type of man who enjoys lording over others and hurting them. If you want to be part of stopping him, we'll do it together. Otherwise, I'll deal with him on my own."

"I want to let someone else handle the problem but it's not right."

"Then we'll devise a plan where you can help."

She gave a wry laugh. "Like I was so successful when I tried to deal with him alone."

"You're not alone now." Hopefully, she'd accept that truth before they had to put it to the test.

Chapter Six

Simone peered at the bedside clock and groaned. She'd awakened an hour before she needed to rise.

She swung her feet over the side of the bed and walked to the bathroom. After a quick shower, she pulled on jeans and a blouse and slipped into her running shoes. She glanced in the mirror. Her appearance was good enough for work. Good enough to impress Jesse? That was another matter.

Simone frowned at her reflection. Since when did she care about her appearance? She needed to fit in with her DA coworkers. Jesse's opinion shouldn't matter.

But it did. The question was, why? They were friends, coworkers on this undercover assignment. The dating gig was a ploy for the Dragon Alley people so they wouldn't question why Jesse had moved to Mexico with her and landed a job at her new place of work. The relationship wasn't real.

She repeated that to herself but didn't believe what she was selling. This was madness. Of all women, Simone shouldn't be interested in dating. Trevor had caused her years of trouble and popped up to annoy her and press his case once in a while.

Simone rolled her eyes. Okay, more like every couple of months. However, he'd lost the trail after her house was destroyed. She should be safe for a couple of months.

Maybe. Lately, Trevor had become more persistent and faster at finding her. How? He wasn't a computer geek. How was he finding her every time she chose a new location for her base of operations?

Something to ponder in quiet moments. Right now, she had other priorities. It was her turn to cook breakfast, and she craved pancakes. While poking into the pantry yesterday, she saw a bottle of unopened maple syrup that would be perfect on those pancakes.

Hurrying into the kitchen, Simone got to work preparing batter in a large bowl. Maybe their guardian angels would like pancakes for breakfast as well. She'd ask Jesse to invite them inside when the food was ready.

Soon, the kitchen was redolent with the scent of chocolate chip pancakes, her favorite variation. Hopefully, the handsome medic wouldn't mind chocolate in his breakfast. She shrugged. If he did, she and the Artemis ladies would enjoy breakfast without him. He could make something different.

Twenty minutes later, she lifted the last pancake from the skillet and laid it on the pile of pancakes resting on a large platter.

Jesse walked in, hair still wet from his recent shower. "Good morning, beautiful. The pancakes smell great. Need help?"

"Yeah. Invite Iona and Tegan inside for breakfast while I make coffee."

"You got it. They'll appreciate the food. Standing watch all night is boring as dirt."

"Unless something exciting happens."

"There's that. I'm glad the night was quiet for all of us." He grabbed his phone and shot off a text. Seconds later, he received a response. "On their way."

She glanced at Jesse. "I hope you don't mind chocolate chips in the pancakes because that's my favorite kind."

"Who doesn't love chocolate?"

Oh, man. Definite brownie points for Jesse.

A knock announced their guests.

Jesse unlocked the door. "Come in, ladies."

"Smells amazing," Iona said. She motioned to the other woman. "Simone, this is Tegan, my teammate."

"Thanks for watching over us last night," Simone said. "Take a seat. Jesse, carry the platter to the table while I get the plates and forks."

Jesse did as she asked. "Do you want coffee or something else?" he asked their guests.

"Coffee for me," Iona said. "Hot tea or chocolate for Tegan. She's the only one of us who doesn't live, eat, and breathe coffee."

Tegan laughed. "What can I say? I have excellent taste."

Simone handed out plates and forks, then returned to the refrigerator for maple syrup. While the coffee finished brewing, she hunted through the pantry until she found a variety box of herbal tea.

Mint tea sounded like a winner to her. Hopefully, Tegan would like that one. She grabbed the packet, filled a mug with bottled water, dumped the tea bag in the water, and nuked it. A minute later, she set the tea in front of Tegan. "Do you want sugar or something else for the tea?"

Tegan shook her head. "This is perfect. Thanks, Simone."

She joined the others at the table. "Jesse said the night was boring."

The two women exchanged glances. "We saw the same SUV twice." Iona shrugged. "Could be a neighbor coming and going to various places."

"Or not," Jesse said.

"We sent the license plate number to Riley. She hasn't gotten back to us yet. We'll let you know when she does."

"If she can't track it down by tonight, let me know," Simone said. "I can check into it."

"No worries." Iona sipped her coffee. "Riley's not in your league but she's pretty good with computers."

"Offer's always open."

They finished breakfast minutes later, and Iona and Tegan shooed Simone out of the kitchen. "You cooked. We'll clean," Tegan said.

"What about the rest of your teammates? Will they want pancakes, too?"

Iona shook her head. "They're already working on breakfast for themselves. Thanks, though."

"Sure." Simone glanced at Jesse. "I'll be ready to leave in fifteen minutes."

"Good. I'll walk you to the cubicle farm and look around before anyone else arrives."

While she was freshening up, Iona and Tegan returned to their watch until they were relieved by two of their teammates. Simone found Jesse waiting for her in the kitchen. "Who's watching the house while we're working today?"

"Riley and Rayne. You ready?"

She nodded. "Let's do this." The sooner they found the programmer and destroyed the program, the better. Maybe all the talk about Trevor last night had spooked Simone, but she felt as though her skin was crawling. "I feel like we're being watched." Her face flushed. "Aside from Artemis, I mean. Am I being paranoid?"

"I hope so." He sent off a text and received a reply within seconds. "No sign of anyone watching the house. Doesn't mean you're wrong. Always pay attention to your gut, Simone. If you feel like something is wrong, it probably is."

He opened the door and stepped out on the patio to scan the area. The sun was just beginning to turn the sky a dark gray. "Clear." Jesse clasped her hand in his and tugged her outside. Once he locked the door, Jesse escorted her to the SUV and helped her inside. After she put on her seatbelt, he circled the vehicle while watching a gadget in his hand.

Satisfied with what he saw, the medic slid the plastic device into his pocket, climbed behind the wheel, and headed toward Dragon Alley.

"Why did you circle the SUV?" Simone asked. "What were you looking for?"

"Unwanted electronic signatures."

Her heart lurched. "A bomb? But no one followed us here, and the women didn't see anyone."

"Someone tried. I lost them. As much as I trust Artemis, your safety is at risk."

"I hate this, Jesse. I don't want to be looking over my shoulder constantly, and I don't want you in danger because of me."

"I'm exactly where I want to be."

"In the line of fire?"

"By your side. Anywhere, anytime with you is worth every risk."

Tears pricked Simone's eyes. "Are you real?"

He chuckled. "Yeah, sweetheart. I'm real. Why?"

"You're everything I dreamed a man in my life would be. No one else has come close."

"Lucky for me, you've been dating the wrong guys." For the rest of the short drive, Jesse asked her questions about the work she'd been doing.

"Grunt work." She scowled. "In order for me to have an inroad into the special projects group, I need to be noticed. Grunt work won't do it."

"Things will turn around soon. Don't worry. DA won't allow outstanding talent to go to waste."

"I hope you're right. Otherwise, I might have to see about doing some night work at DA so I can poke around."

"Not without me to watch over you. Non-negotiable, Simone."

They arrived at Dragon Alley's campus a few minutes later, checked in with the gate guard, and drove to their assigned spot.

Once again, Jesse circled the hood to open Simone's door and help her from the vehicle. "Remember yesterday's performance?"

Boy, did she. A smoking-hot kiss that wasn't an actual kiss. She nodded.

"Same song, second verse, okay?"

"You think someone is watching us?"

"I know they are. I saw a curtain move in a window on the fourth floor. The watcher hasn't moved."

"Go for it, Jesse." She smiled. "Let's give him or her a genuine show."

He cupped her nape. "Are you sure?"

"Chicken?"

"Oh, no, baby. Just not sure you know what you're asking for."

"I have a pretty good idea, considering the fireworks going off like the fourth of July inside me the last time you barely kissed me."

Jesse watched her a moment, then nodded. "Come here. I'll do it right this time." He slowly urged her toward him until Simone was in his embrace. A bit at a time, he lowered his head until he captured her mouth with his.

The world stopped turning while fireworks exploded in her veins. Heat roared through her body as she inched closer to Jesse and wrapped her arms around his neck.

This was what she'd been missing every time she dated. Fireworks. Heat. Care for her as a person. How Jesse conveyed those things with his hold and his mouth moving over hers baffled Simone.

And how could this tough medic have a touch as gentle as anything she'd felt in her life? Was this the real Jesse Phelps? Or was this only for show?

Simone broke the kiss and stared up at the handsome operative. "Real or show?" she whispered.

"Both."

She dragged in a shuddering breath. "We need to do that again." Over and over a million times.

He chuckled. "Agreed. Not right now, though. We have a job to do, and you're a distraction. I shouldn't have kissed you like that." Jesse quartered the area as he escorted her inside the building to sign in, then to the bank of elevators.

She glanced at him as the silver doors slid shut. Gone was the dreamy kisser and in his place was the operative alert for a threat. They were on stage, she reminded herself. Someone in security who would report their movements and discussions to someone higher up the food chain monitored everything they said and did in this building.

They stepped out on Simone's floor, and she led Jesse to the cubicle farm where she worked. Suspecting they were being observed here, too, she threaded her fingers through Jesse's and tugged him to the back corner of the room where her cubicle was located.

As soon as she rounded the wall dividing her space from Joy's, Simone knew someone had been snooping around her desk and computer. Good or bad? Perhaps someone was being extra cautious or Simone might have aroused suspicion yesterday.

She waved toward her workstation with a big smile on her face. "Here's my station, baby. It's kind of dull at the moment. I need pictures of you to decorate my space. I missed seeing your handsome face and gorgeous eyes yesterday."

"We'll do something about that soon," he murmured, and trailed a finger down her cheek and neck. When she shivered, Jesse smiled and bent his head as though nibbling on her ear. "What's wrong?" he whispered.

"Someone has been poking around my space."

"Can you check things out while you chatter about nothing important?"

"Please. Multitasking is my strong suit."

He captured her mouth in a quick kiss. "So, you still want to go out to dinner tonight?"

"Absolutely," Simone said as she dropped into her seat and logged in to the system. As the computer booted up and loaded the programs, including the one she'd added to mask her work on the keyboard, she scanned everything on her desktop.

Someone had moved the pen holder and desk phone. How did she tell Jesse without blowing their cover? "Joy mentioned a couple of restaurants in Sayulita that have good food. Plus, we got in so late from work last night we didn't have time to explore the town. I'd love to see the shops and get a feel for the town itself."

"Sounds good to me. Ask Joy to join us."

"Great idea. I'll ask her when she arrives." She reached for a pen and deliberately knocked the container over. Pens spilled onto the desk and rolled to the floor. "Oops." Simone smiled wickedly at Jesse. "You kept me up too late last night, Mr. Porterfield. I'm afraid I'll be a klutz today."

"Want me to keep my hands to myself, babe?"

"No way. I'll deal with the fatigue. Well worth the sacrifice of sleep." She wrapped her arms around his neck and kissed his neck. "Phone, too."

He gave a slight nod, kissed Simone's temple, and released her. "I'll take care of the pens while you start work." He grabbed the empty pen holder, knelt and gathered the pens. As he picked up pens, Jesse used the desk to hide his examination of the holder.

A moment later, he removed a small black disk from the interior and slid the object into his pocket. Jesse stood, dropped the pens into the container, and handed it to Simone. "I have to leave in a minute to report in for work. Want to see if any of the restaurants Joy suggested require reservations? If so, I'll call and set it up when I'm on a break."

She remembered three restaurants Joy had mentioned but pretended that she couldn't recall the names by searching for restaurants in Sayulita. As she did, Simone moved her cubicle phone closer to the keyboard as though simply repositioning it for her own convenience.

Jesse hovered behind her. When she pulled up one restaurant, he leaned closer to the screen. He pointed. "Can you pull up the menu? I'd like to see what my options are before we walk into the place. Joy said it was one of the most popular restaurants in town."

Using his body as a shield, he moved the phone to Simone's lap and turned it over. No weird black disks on the bottom.

He leaned down as though to see the screen better and opened the housing of the handset. Inside was a twin to the disk in her pen holder.

Great. Looked like she tripped somebody's alarm bell yesterday. Why? She'd been careful not to say too much. Was this overkill in caution or had she messed up yesterday?

Jesse removed the disk and slid it into his pocket with the other one while he talked about different menu options that sounded good. "Talk to Joy. Choose the place she likes the most, and we'll go there. Let me know if I need to make reservations, and I'll make the arrangements."

He stood. "I need to go. You'll be okay here?" he murmured.

"I'll be fine."

"No cameras yet."

She relaxed. Excellent. "Watch your back."

"Always. Call or text if you need me." After another quick kiss, he left.

How would he dispose of the bugs? Flush them, she decided. That was the easiest and quickest way to get rid of them. That's how she'd do it.

Simone checked her computer meticulously to see if anyone had tampered with her computer or the program she'd uploaded. Both seemed untouched. Wouldn't last, though. When the person who bugged her station realized the bugs were gone or had stopped working, they'd take other measures to spy on her.

Checking her company email, Simone found a document giving her instructions and assignments for the day. Her eyebrows rose at the long list of things to finish before her work shift ended.

Huh. A challenge or a deliberate move to cause her failure. Either way, the division head was in for a disappointment.

Simone dove into the first task. She lost track of time as she sped through the assignments. Some were easy, some difficult. None of the assignments were the stumbling block her division head had assumed they would be.

By the time Joy arrived an hour later, Simone had completed all the easier tasks and was halfway through the difficult ones.

"Good morning, Simone." Joy peered over the cubicle wall. "You look like you've been here a while."

"More than an hour." She shrugged. "Couldn't sleep so Jesse and I thought it best to get started here."

Joy smiled. "Good way to be noticed, my friend."

"Maybe. Jesse and I are going out for dinner tonight. We want you to join us. Our treat for being so kind to me yesterday."

"I'd love to go if I wouldn't be intruding on your date."

"I told you yesterday. I want Jesse to work at getting me to agree to marriage. Nothing that comes easy is appreciated, and I want him to appreciate me. Please, say you'll come with us."

Joy laughed. "I'd love to. It sounds like fun. I just wish Jesse had an unmarried brother. He's a great guy."

"He's the best," she said simply. It was the truth, and she was finally coming to believe what her friend Poppy had been telling her about the medic. Although Trevor had soured her on men, Jesse had slipped underneath her protective walls and was fast arrowing toward her heart.

"You're so lucky, Simone."

The day passed much as the day before. Lots of work. Her division head swung around to see her after lunch.

"Simone, you've been blazing through your assignments today. How do you like the work?"

She shrugged. "Nothing to write home about yet. Frankly, I was hoping for a little more challenge."

Trina Kirk's eyebrows rose. "The work's not challenging enough?"

"Not yet. I had to work harder to finish tasks at Game Theory than I am at Dragon Alley. I finished all my assignments yesterday and pestered Joy for more so I wouldn't be sitting here twiddling my thumbs. I've already finished everything assigned today as well. I need more."

A slow smile curved Trina's mouth. "I wondered if that would be the case. I told my boss you wouldn't be satisfied with the jobs we were assigning you. Don't worry, Simone. I'll pass the word to my boss. Something more up your alley will turn up soon."

"While I'm waiting for interesting assignments, how about sending something else so I can keep busy?"

Trina laughed. "I'll see what I can do. Be looking for the next batch of assignments in your email in the next ten minutes."

"Perfect. Thanks."

A head shake. "I've never had an employee beg for work. You're an anomaly, Simone."

Good or bad? Had she overemphasized her skill? Overplayed her hand? In truth, she had finished everything for the day unless Trina gave her something else. She needed to catch the attention of the person who commissioned the computer program she and Jesse were targeting. The only way she knew to do that without putting herself or the medic at risk was to work at her natural fast pace.

Once Trina was gone, Joy peered around the edge of the cubicle wall, her eyes wide. "Holy smoke, Simone," she murmured. "You're bored?"

"Come on, Joy. I must have driven you crazy yesterday, asking for more work."

"I thought you were just trying to impress me with how fast you were churning out the assignments but that's your natural pace, isn't it?"

"Actually, I was holding back yesterday. I decided this morning before I arrived I needed to work at my normal speed. Otherwise, I'll be bored most of the time I'm employed here. I came to DA to stretch myself. I know it's early days in my career here, but so far, I'm not stretching myself at all."

Joy shook her head. "Girl, you'll be lucky to stay in this division with me if you keep up this pace. The supervisors in the special projects division are always looking for more talent. They push their workers pretty hard, so they burn out fast."

"Oh, yeah?" Simone scooted her rolling chair closer to her friend. "What kind of work do they do?"

"Very hush hush programs. Programmers in the cubicle farm dream of working in that division. I don't think I'll ever reach that level."

"I don't know. You're pretty good."

"I'm not at your level. I'm so far back in the pack, I doubt the special divisions supervisor even knows my name."

"That would be his loss."

"Are we still on for supper tonight?" Joy asked, changing the subject.

"Absolutely. Jesse and I are looking forward to spending time with you."

Her friend beamed. "I really wish he had a single brother. He's a special man."

"I agree."

"You should put the man out of his misery and say yes, Simone. You don't want to lose him to some other woman. Guys will only wait so long before they move on."

"Believe me, I'm aware of that. I'm thinking hard about his proposal. He'll have my answer soon."

Simone's computer dinged with an email alert. She glanced at her screen. "Oh, yeah. More work." She rubbed her hands together and scooted back to her station. "Time to shine, Joy."

Her friend laughed. "Let's do it, then have some fun after work."

"Deal."

Simone dove back into her work, relishing the extra assignments. The first few were a continuation of the simple things she'd worked on for the past two days. The last four assignments were more of a challenge. Better. Again, she breezed through the work and asked for more.

Trina was as good as her word and assigned even more challenging assignments.

By the end of the day, Simone had cleared the assignments in her email and still had thirty minutes to burn before she could clock out.

This time it was her turn to peer around the edge of the cubicle wall. "Hey, you have anything pending?"

Joy swung around to stare at her. "You're finished?"

She nodded. "Can I help you with anything?"

"I have a couple of issues with two programs that I haven't been able to find. I finally had to give up and move on to something else. I planned to come back to them but I'm stuck on the Tidewater program."

"Send the programs to me. I'll look at them while you finish with Tidewater."

"Thanks, Simone. I really appreciate the help."

"No problem." She rolled back to her station and clicked on the email Joy sent her. She pulled up the first program and read through multiple lines of code, searching for a problem.

Simone found the first mistake halfway through the program, fixed it, then continued on through the rest of the lines of code. Finding no more issues, she downloaded the program and ran it. Perfect.

She sent that program back to Joy, then started working through the second program. Multiple problems with the code slowed her down, but she untangled the codes, ran the program to be sure her corrections worked, then saved it and sent the program back to Joy.

Her friend whooped with happiness. "Yes! You're a miracle worker, Simone."

"Not even close. You overlooked the issues because you've been staring at them for a good while. I was a pair of fresh eyes."

"Ha. Don't lie. You're incredible. I say we clock out, eat great food, and have some fun."

"I'll text Jesse to let him know we're coming down." Simone clocked out, sent the text, and stood.

Hopefully, she wouldn't have the same problem with bugs tomorrow. Not holding her breath, though. Simone had deliberately made a splash today, hoping to draw attention. With that attention would come more measures to spy on her.

She smiled. Let them. She had an ace in the hole. One drop-dead gorgeous medic who was well versed in security protocol. He wouldn't let anything slip past him or her.

Simone stood and circled the cubicle wall to see Joy logging off her computer and grabbing her purse. "Ready?"

"Yes." She grinned "I can't believe it. I finished everything today with your help. I can't thank you enough, Simone."

"Glad to help. Come on. I'm starving, and we deserve a reward for all the hard work."

They rode the elevator to the first floor where Jesse met them at the bank of elevators. He gathered Simone into his arms and kissed her lightly. "How was your day, baby?"

"Busy."

"Better than yesterday, then."

"Much better. Joy and I are starving."

"I made reservations at La Hacienda. Our table will be ready by the time we arrive."

Twenty minutes later, Jesse gave his name at the reservation desk, and the hostess led them to a table at the back of the restaurant and in the corner. Typical of Jesse and his teammates. Wouldn't surprise Simone if Artemis had the same tendency.

Already knowing where Jesse would sit, she took a seat next to the one he'd choose and motioned for Joy to sit in the chair beside hers. "What's good here, Joy?"

"Everything."

"Well, I could order one of everything on the menu but I doubt we'd be able to eat it all. What's your favorite food here?"

"Can't beat their quesadillas and burritos."

"Sold." Simone scanned those sections of the menu and selected one of each. If she couldn't finish them, she'd ask for a box to take the leftovers to the house. Might be breakfast or a middle of the night snack.

When the server arrived to take their orders, Jesse chose the same items plus a large order of nachos for the three of them to share.

Their food was delivered fast, and the meal was as excellent as Joy said it would be. "You were right, Joy." Simone sat back in her chair. "I don't think I've tasted better food anywhere."

"High compliments from a native of California."

She shrugged. "We have a lot of Tex-Mex food but this is authentic. Where are you from?" Simone waited to see if her friend would tell her the truth.

"San Francisco."

"What brought you here?" Jesse asked.

"The usual. A yearning for adventure and to get away from a boyfriend who was possessive and mean."

"Is he still bothering you?"

"Not since I left California. The last I heard, he'd hooked up with my former best friend. Good luck to her, is all I have to say. I wouldn't wish Chip on anybody."

"Was he involved with her while he was still with you?"

Her smile was wistful. "How did you guess?"

"Familiar story. You're better off without him."

"Oh, I know. Believe me. Doesn't make me any less lonely, though."

"I can't believe one man at DA isn't interested in you," Simone said.

Her friend crumpled her napkin. "I've had a few offers but I'm afraid to accept, though. I don't really know the men who asked me out. What if they're creeps, too?"

"If you'll give me a list of their names, I'll do a background check on them," Jesse said.

Joy's eyes widened. "Really? You'd do that for me?"

"Women can't be too careful these days. I'll be glad to help."

"Thanks, Jesse. Are you sure you don't have a single brother somewhere?"

He laughed. "I'm sorry."

"Too bad." Joy took a pen from her purse, grabbed a clean paper napkin, jotted down a list of four names, and slid them across the table to Jesse. "I appreciate this. Are you sure you won't get into trouble?"

"I'll be fine. Are you ladies ready to go?" When they nodded, he stood and helped both of them to their feet.

After paying the bill, he escorted them outside. "We'll follow you home, Joy."

"You don't have to do that. I don't live too far from here."

"We want to be sure you get home safely."

She looked surprised. "Thanks."

Jesse wrapped his arm around Simone's waist and walked with the women toward their vehicles in the parking lot.

They stepped into an aisle of vehicles. Somewhere close, an engine revved and tires squealed.

A vehicle's headlights were flipped to the bright setting. The vehicle raced directly toward them.

Chapter Seven

Jesse shoved Joy into the space between two vehicles, grabbed Simone, and rushed toward safety.

Joy screamed.

Simone didn't make a sound as they hurtled to safety but her grip was tight around him as though making sure he didn't stay behind.

Once they were safe, Jesse turned with his weapon drawn and aimed at the vehicle barreling past.

No shot.

He kept his weapon aimed at the vehicle as the large SUV raced from the parking lot into the main street and disappeared.

"Are you okay, Joy?" Simone asked.

"I'm fine, thanks to your boyfriend. Who were those crazy people? Who drives that fast through a parking lot? They could have killed someone." She wrapped her arms around her middle. "The driver must be drunk. No one would be that reckless on purpose."

Jesse disagreed, but he didn't think the information would help Joy sleep tonight. "Come on. Let's get you home."

"Shouldn't we call the police?"

"What do we tell them? Someone almost ran us over and disappeared before we could get the license plate?" He shook his head. "We wouldn't get anywhere with the report."

"We can't let them get by with this," Joy insisted. "If they're that drunk, they could kill someone while driving."

Jesse urged Simone's coworker toward her car. "I don't think the driver was drunk."

Joy stopped. "What do you mean? Of course he was. What other explanation could there be?"

"Someone tried to run us down," Simone said, her tone grim.

"That's ridiculous. Who would do that? We're worker bees at Dragon Alley, no one special."

"I don't know yet," Jesse said. "But I will find out."

"How?"

He smiled. "I'm in security. I have access to things that aid in identifying vehicles and drivers. Leave this to me. I'll take care of it. In the meantime, let's get you home."

"Are you sure you don't mind, Jesse?" Joy looked uncertain. "I'll be fine."

"I know you will because I'm going to make sure you are." He waited while she unlocked her car, climbed inside, and strapped in.

Once she was inside her vehicle, Jesse escorted Simone to their SUV. "Wait here," he murmured as he slid his electronic signal detector from his pocket.

After turning on the device, he circled their vehicle while watching the chaser lights. They stayed green until he reached the passenger side wheel well.

He grabbed his penlight and crouched beside the tire. Jesse searched but spotted nothing. Running his fingers along the outer lip of the well, he found the small black GPS tracker and removed it.

He attached the tracker to a pickup truck three slots down and returned to check the vehicle again in case he'd missed another signal. This time, the search came up clean.

Unlocking the vehicle, Jesse helped Simone into the passenger seat. "I'm going to check Joy's car for tracking devices. Be right back."

"We had a GPS tracker?"

He nodded. "Someone wants to keep track of our movements."

"Or desperately wants to know where we're living. I don't like this, Jesse. What if Joy's in danger?"

And not a bit of concern for her own safety. He couldn't help himself. Jesse brushed his mouth over hers. "We'll do what we can to protect her, all right? But we have a mission to complete before more of our military members and contractors are targeted. We have to stay focused."

"Not at the expense of Joy's safety."

"Agreed. If she needs protection, I'll contact Maddox and have him assign someone to shadow her."

"Thanks, Jesse."

He gave a curt nod and shut the door before searching Joy's vehicle as well. Her wheels came up clean.

So, he and Simone had aroused suspicion. Why? Had they slipped up somewhere or was it suspicion of two new people who now worked at Dragon Alley? They'd have to find out soon.

He climbed behind the wheel of their SUV. "Her car was clean. Let's follow her home and see if there's been any activity at her house."

"I hope not. I don't want our actions to affect her."

Five minutes later, Joy turned into the driveway of a small bungalow. Jesse parked the SUV behind her car and circled the hood to the passenger side. He helped Simone to the concrete, and they followed Joy to her front door. He held out his hand. "Do you mind if I check your house before you walk inside?"

"Why do you want to do that?"

"Your safety is important to us. While I don't think there's anything to worry about, I'd feel better if I did a cursory check first."

Without a word, Joy handed Jesse her key.

"Thanks. Do you have a pet?"

She shook her head. "I've been thinking about getting a dog but haven't taken the time to go get one."

"You should. Dogs are better than security alarms for letting you know if something isn't right."

"I'll try to go to the animal shelter tomorrow after work."

Jesse unlocked her door, slipped inside the house, and shut the door behind him. He waited a moment, listening for signs of someone else being in the house.

Nothing.

He searched the small home room by room until he was satisfied that no one waited for Joy. However, unless their DA coworker was the messiest housekeeper on the planet, someone had searched her home in her absence. If so, what was he looking for?

Gut knotting, Jesse returned to the front porch where the two women waited for him. He looked at Joy. "Come see the house. Looks like someone broke in while you were gone."

She gasped and rushed past Jesse. Joy came to a sudden stop just inside the doorway. "Oh, no. Who would do this?"

"Touch nothing," Jesse said. "Just walk through the house. See if anything is missing. Once you finish, pack a bag."

"Why?"

"Your home is a crime scene. The police might not want you to stay here tonight."

"I don't care what they want. I'm going to a hotel." Joy shuddered. "I don't feel safe here. In fact, I might move to another part of town. I feel violated."

"I'm sorry," Simone said. "Do you want me to walk through the rooms with you?"

Joy shook her head. "I can handle it as long as I know you two are in the house with me."

"We're not going anywhere. Promise."

"While you do a walkthrough, I'll call the police," Jesse said.

He waited until their friend left the room before turning to Simone. "I would have offered to let her stay with us."

Simone shook her head. "It's not safe," she whispered. "You know we're the reason she was targeted."

"Perhaps. We don't know that for sure."

"No coincidences in your business."

"Accurate statement." Jesse wrapped his arm around her waist and eased Simone against his side. She leaned against him. Man, he could so get used to having this woman in his arms. The feel of her against him was addictive.

Jesse dialed the police and reported the break-in. Although he didn't hold out much home that the Sayulita police were good at their jobs, he planned to wrap this case up as soon as possible so Joy was no longer under suspicion because of her association with him and Simone.

When he ended the call, Jesse wrapped his other arm around Simone and held her close. "Are you okay?"

She shook her head.

"Let me rephrase. Were you hurt when the car tried to run us down in the parking lot?"

"No, thanks to you." She looked at Jesse. "You saved my life."

He squeezed her gently. "I would do anything for you."

Simone blinked. "Jesse."

He heard Joy heading their way. "Later."

Joy entered the room with an overnight bag in her hand. "I'm ready. When will the police arrive?"

"Any minute. We should wait for them on the porch. They won't be happy to learn that we walked around a crime scene."

"Tough. I needed to pack a few things."

"Did they take anything?" Simone asked.

"Not that I can tell." Joy frowned. "I don't understand why they would go to the trouble of searching my house but not take a thing. Although I don't have all the latest and greatest gadgets, I have several game systems and video games." She shrugged. "It's part of what I do, you know? Those items alone would have brought a lot of money in the right circles. I also have my grandmother's jewelry in a case in the bedroom. Jewelry is scattered across my dresser but nothing is missing, not even the cash I keep under the mattress."

Jesse's eyebrows rose as he shepherded the two women outside to sit on the porch bench. "You shouldn't keep cash in the house, Joy. You're begging for someone to break in and rob you."

Her face flushed. "I know. My ex-boyfriend said the same thing. I've always kept ready cash at home."

"If you insist on keeping cash, at least store it in a safe so it's not easily confiscated."

"I'll do that. I promise." She sighed. "Another thing to add to the to-do list. Top of that list is getting a dog."

"Smart move as long as the dog isn't an ankle biter. You need a medium or large-size dog, one that barks loud and intimidates anyone who might decide to break in to the house."

"I wish I had an alarm system. I planned to get one but never got around to it."

"If you want me to, I can evaluate the security companies in the area and give you a recommendation."

"I would appreciate that, Jesse. You're the best." She smiled as the police car screeched to a stop in front of the house. "If Simone ever dumps you, ask me for a date first."

He chuckled. "I'll keep that in mind."

Two officers climbed from the cruiser and approached the porch with their hands on their weapons. "One of you the homeowner?"

"That would be me," Joy said. "I'm Joy Walters. Someone broke into my house while I was at work today."

"Quiet neighborhood. We rarely have reports of any crimes in this area."

"That's good to know." She crossed her arms over her stomach. "Whoever broke in left an enormous mess inside."

"Did they take anything?"

"Not that I can tell. I was afraid to touch anything."

The shorter officer nodded. "That's good. Hopefully, we'll lift some fingerprints but I wouldn't hold my breath."

"What about an alarm system?" the taller officer asked. "Do you have one?"

"No, I don't." She glanced at Jesse. "It's one of the first things I'm going to take care of tomorrow."

The officers looked at Jesse and Simone. "Who are you?"

"We're friends of Joy's," Simone said. "We work together."

"Where?"

"Dragon Alley."

The officers exchanged glances, then the shorter officer entered the house, leaving his partner behind to ask them all questions. Once he'd gleaned as much information as possible from Joy, the officer questioned Jesse and Simone.

By the time he finished, the shorter officer returned to the porch. "Ms. Walters, come with me. I'd like you to look through everything to see if anything is missing." The two disappeared inside the house.

"How long have you worked at Dragon Alley?" Tall Cop asked.

Simone smiled. "Two days. We're new in town and to the company."

"I'm sorry you had to see the bad side of Sayulita." The radio attached to his shoulder crackled as the dispatcher called a unit number. "Excuse me." The officer moved toward the patrol car, activating the radio.

"This isn't good," Simone whispered. "We shouldn't be attracting this much attention. Did I do something wrong?"

"Might have been me since I removed the bugs in your cubicle. Would you rather I had left them in place?"

She shuddered. "No, thanks. I hate the idea of someone spying on me."

"We'll have to be careful going home to make sure we lose any tails."

"How do you know we'll have one?"

"They knew where we were going tonight and did their best to hurt us in the parking lot. Now Joy's house is broken into? Definitely not a coincidence. Someone wants to know what we're up to or wants to warn us to keep our noses out of places where they don't belong."

"They scared Joy."

"I know. They won't be able to scare her once they're behind bars or dead."

Simone's head whipped his direction. "You'll kill them?"

"If they give me a reason to do it."

The shorter officer returned with Joy who looked remarkably flushed considering the trauma she'd suffered tonight.

"Are you sure you're all right?" Shorty asked Joy. "I can have an ambulance come check you out or transport you to the hospital."

"No, thanks. I'm fine, especially after you walked through the house with me so I could see that nothing was taken. I feel better having you nearby."

He gave her a slow, sultry smile. "You have my card, and I have your phone number. Do you mind if I call you later to check on you?"

Joy smiled. "I'd like that."

"Good. I'm looking forward to talking with you." His gaze swung toward Jesse and Simone. "My partner finished interviewing you?"

"He did," Jesse said. "The dispatcher contacted your partner right after he finished with us."

"I'll check with him. If he hasn't thought of anything else to ask, you'll be free to go."

"We planned to follow Joy to a hotel to make sure she arrives safely."

Shorty glanced at Joy. "Is that what you want to do? I can escort you to your hotel if your friends need to go."

"Do you mind? I don't want to interfere with your duties."

"Of course not." He edged closer. "It would be my pleasure, Joy."

"Thank you, Mateo. I'd feel safer if you went with me."

He beamed at her. "I'll inform my partner and be right with you." He glanced at Jesse and Simone. "Stay here until I return. I'll make sure Joy is safe tonight."

Although Jesse wanted to escort Joy to the hotel himself, her reaction to the police officer showed a deep interest in the other man. He inclined his head in silent agreement and watched the other man as he strode away to talk to his partner. After a brief conversation, he returned. "You're free to leave. Joy, if you're ready to go, I'll follow you to the Hacienda Hotel. Do you know where that is?"

"I do." She looked hesitant. "I'm not sure I can afford to stay there, though."

"The manager is my cousin. He'll see to it you are safe and can afford the stay. All right?"

She nodded and turned to hug Simone. "Thanks for a splendid dinner. It was fun. Maybe we'll be able to go on a double date soon."

"We'd love that. Be safe, Joy. See you tomorrow."

Jesse said, "Joy, once you're settled in the hotel room, stay inside. Only open the door for one of us or Mateo. All right?"

She stared. "Do you think the burglars will follow me to the hotel?"

Mateo frowned. "Why would they do that?"

"Just taking precautions," Jesse said. "We work in a very competitive business, and Joy might be a prime target for retaliation."

He didn't think that would be the case but it wouldn't hurt to have the young police officer looking out for Simone's friend.

Mateo straightened, his expression grim. "Don't worry. I'll escort Joy to her room and check the accommodations myself. No one will harm her under my watch."

"Good enough." Jesse held out his hand. "We appreciate you watching over Joy tonight."

"My pleasure. Truly."

"See you tomorrow, Joy. Do you want us to swing by the hotel and follow you to work in the morning?" Simone asked.

"I'll be fine. Really. You go on home and get some rest. If tomorrow is anything like today, you'll have your hands full with assignments."

Simone laughed. "I hope so. That was fun."

Jesse escorted her to the SUV and helped Simone inside. After climbing behind the wheel, he backed into the street and drove away from the house.

As soon as they turned the corner, he activated the Bluetooth and made a call.

"Yeah, Murphy."

"It's Jesse. We might have a problem."

Chapter Eight

Might have a problem. Boy, what an understatement. Simone frowned as she reviewed her interactions with her colleagues at DA. She couldn't think of anything she'd said that would have triggered this level of hostility and worry. Was she being paranoid? Was this a coincidence?

She considered that a moment. No, not paranoid. This was too much to be a coincidence. Jesse was right. No way would this be totally unrelated to their investigation. Did she make a mistake or were these people so suspicious of everyone that they automatically assumed the worst?

"Talk to me," Zane said to Jesse.

"You're on speaker with Simone." He explained the incident at the restaurant and the break-in at Joy's place.

"What do you need?"

"Find video feed near the restaurant around eight o'clock. The vehicle was a large black pickup truck. Late model. Black or blue. Extended cab. Chrome wheels and trim. Tricked up ride. The truck moved too fast through the parking lot for me to see the plates. I'd like to know who owns the truck and get a look at the driver."

"I'll see what I can do. No guarantees, though."

"I understand. Anything will help."

"Simone, how are you?"

"I'm fine. Jesse made sure of it."

"That's what he's being paid to do. How's the work?"

"Boring as dirt. I finished everything they gave me yesterday and today, and asked for more. They obliged. I think this is the only way to get the attention of the special projects supervisor. I'm pretty sure a person who works in that division will have the skills to create the program. No one in the cubicle farm has the skills necessary."

"You do."

"Maybe." Probably. She'd see if they offered her a job in that division. If not, she'd have to convince Jesse to come in to work overnight when things were quiet so she could poke around in the computers in that division.

But would the programmer they wanted work on the specialized program on his work computer? If so, he figured out a way to keep the program from being detected by Zane which was quite a feat. She needed to get into the special projects area. Perhaps each worker had a dedicated computer without Internet access for programs such as the one they were hunting for.

"Anything I can help you with, Simone?"

"Not yet. I may have to ask for an assist later, though."

"Anytime. Watch yourself at DA. They're well known for having a back door to their employee computers."

"I've already installed a program to prevent them from tracking my keyboard work."

"Not enough. Find the back door and close it, Simone. Installing the program will only pique their curiosity."

"Yes, sir. I'll take care of it first thing tomorrow morning."

"Jesse, anything else I can do to help?"

He glanced at Simone, then said, "A background check on Mateo Ortega, a Sayulita police officer. He's showing interest in our friend, Joy Walters."

"You got it. I'll get back to you as soon as I can. Later." Zane ended the call.

"You're checking out Ortega." Simone smiled. "Worried about the cute cop?"

Jesse's head whipped toward her. "Cute? You think Ortega is cute?"

"Well, sure. He's not in your class, but he's attractive enough. I think he'll be perfect for Joy. He seems to be a good man."

"Maybe. We'll see."

She squeezed his forearm. "Thanks for asking Z to check Mateo's background. I'll feel better about his interest in Joy if you clear him."

"Pretty fast work on the cop's part," he said.

Jesse drove them toward the safe house along a circuitous route, frequently checking mirrors, and making sudden turns to see if someone was tailing them.

Although Simone was no expert in the art of following a suspect, she didn't see anyone tailing them all over the countryside.

Finally, they arrived in the neighborhood of the safe house. Instead of pulling into the driveway, though, Jesse circled the area twice. "I think we're clear." On the next pass, he parked at the back of the house. "Stay here while I check inside." He exited the vehicle and disappeared inside the house.

Simone scanned the area, looking for anything that didn't fit or pinged on her trouble radar. Everything looked the same as it did when they left for work this morning. Hopefully, no one had invaded the house in their absence. Someone from the Artemis team should have noticed if someone was nosing around their place and either intervened or notified Jesse of the breach in security. As far as she knew, the women hadn't been in contact with Jesse.

The medic returned and opened her door to help her to the ground. "We're clear. No bugs or cameras added in our absence."

They entered the house together, and Jesse locked the door behind him. "Since Zane is checking out the cop, what do you want to work on tonight?"

"Deeper background search of the people in the special projects division. What about you? What are you going to work on?"

"Finding your ex-boyfriend."

She swung around to face him. "Why? He's out of the picture."

"Is he? You told me he keeps popping up, and that's why you didn't stay in one place for long. He's exhibiting stalker behavior, Simone. Based on what you've said, he won't give up."

Maybe. Okay, that was definitely true although Simone didn't want to hear it. "He doesn't know where we are."

"You're a computer whiz, sweetheart. Looks like Trevor has a connection with someone who is at least as good as you are at uncovering hidden tracks. If I can't find him, I'll put Zane on this. Your focus has to be locating the programmer and the program itself."

She gave a curt nod and went to her room to grab her laptop. Let him look for Trevor. She couldn't worry about her ex. Maybe he'd given up now. After all, he was dating her former best friend. Why come after her now?

Simone ignored the internal warnings going off in favor of starting a pot of coffee and setting up her computer for the hours of work still ahead of her. Time to dig deep into the backgrounds of those in the special projects division.

Once the coffee finished brewing, she poured herself a mug and one for Jesse. After setting Jesse's by him, she rounded to her side of the table and dropped into the chair.

She logged into the Fortress system, plugged the first name on her list into the database, and settled back to read. Griffin Daley, head of the special projects division, was the boy wonder at Dragon Alley. A computer genius, his list of credentials was impressive going back to when he was in high school. More interesting than that, Daley had worked for the Department of Defense for five years before Dragon Alley lured him away from government work with the promise of a seven-figure salary.

On and on his list of accomplishments went, giving Simone a pretty good idea of his intellect and his special skills. No wonder DA went to a lot of trouble and expense to woo him away from the feds. Too bad he worked for DA. Zane would have loved to add him to the stable of programmers at Fortress Security.

Was he the programmer they were searching for? She frowned. Although he was brilliant, Simone had never heard of any significant program that he'd created. Why not? Was it possible he'd risen above his level of skill and experience? If so, he wouldn't be the only division head to be promoted beyond his ability to handle the work he assigned to others.

Simone saved what she'd found in a file and went on to the next name on her list. Patrick Meyers. Married with three kids, all of whom were attending very expensive Ivy league universities. What a tuition bill he must have to pay for those boys. One in law school and two in medical school. From all appearances, though, Patrick was the equivalent of a boy scout and always stayed on the right side of the law. No hint of impropriety. Well, she'd see if his reputation held up when she ran his name through the dark web.

Her next background run was on Allison Norbert, new to the special projects division. She was single with a mother in a special facility that handled dementia patients. Simone's heart squeezed as she read more about the rapid progression of the mother's illness. The facility wasn't cheap, either. Three siblings, all brothers, but none of them contributed to the mother's care. From what she could find, the brothers hadn't visited their mother since she moved into the facility.

Out of curiosity, Simone checked out the facility and discovered the place was outside of Sayulita. That might have been one reason the brothers didn't visit. All of them lived in Texas. The more she dug, though, the more Simone believed the men wouldn't have visited the mother if her facility had been located down the block from their own homes. They cut off communication with her once they turned eighteen years old. Talk about cold.

Next, she turned her attention to Beckett Francen. A serious gamer, other gaming companies all over the world recruited him. This guy had written several very popular games that had made

Dragon Alley a boatload of money. Not married. No family to speak of. Parents were dead. No siblings. A loner unless he was involved with someone.

She considered Beckett for several minutes, then decided he would probably stay on her suspect list. Gaming was a different type of work than the program she was hunting but Beckett had skills for the program and the ability to adopt a different mindset.

The last name on her list was Wyatt Hatcher. She read through the pages of information from the Fortress database. Hmm. Wyatt definitely had the skills required. He'd also worked for the Department of Defense and written computer programs for them for ten years before Dragon Alley lured him away. He also earned a seven-figure salary. No ties or family, debt free, and living conservatively. His only indulgence was a couple of Russian terriers that he treated like his children.

Since she did not know what a Russian terrier looked like, Simone entered the name in her search engine and goggled at the size of the dogs. "Holy smoke! They're huge."

Jesse looked up from his computer. "What's huge?"

"Wyatt Hatcher's Russian terriers. They're big, black, and look like I could ride them to work every day."

"They're stubborn and hard to train, but absolutely loyal to their owners if they're treated right."

"Well, Wyatt treats them like his children so I'd say they're living a cushy life."

"Does he have a family to protect?"

"He's single. No family, no ties. Just Wyatt."

"Huh. Interesting. Flag him for a deeper run."

"Maybe he just loves these dogs."

"Maybe he has a reason for keeping guard dogs in and around his house."

"Right. He's flagged. How's your search going?"

"Nowhere." He rose and went to the coffeepot to refill his mug. "I can't find him."

Simone scowled as her heart skipped a beat, then settled into a faster rhythm. "That's impossible. He has to be somewhere."

"Oh, he is, but he's gone off the grid."

She swallowed hard. That wasn't what she wanted to hear. "I'll set up my bots to scan the dark web for mentions of the special projects division members, then look for Trevor."

"Be my guest. In the meantime, I'll run your special projects team through the DA database and see what they have in the system."

"Wait a minute. Won't they know you're the one running the names?"

"Of course. I have to log in under my identification code. I've been systematically going through every employee's file in my downtime at work, and I already told my supervisor I was running the names so I could get to know each employee and their backgrounds. He won't be surprised to see my ID code in the system attached to the runs."

"Make sure you run other people's names, too, Jesse. I don't want them looking too closely at the list of names. If you only run the special division names tonight, they might become suspicious." Perhaps she could go into the system and fix it so Jesse's search wouldn't show up. No, she decided. That wouldn't work. The computer geeks would know someone had hacked into the system. Better to let Jesse's story about getting to know each employee better stand.

"I will. Need more coffee?" When she nodded, Jesse refilled her mug, then prepped another pot.

Smart man. Their after-hours work would probably last long into the night. Caffeine was a priority.

Simone set her bots to search the dark web and turned her attention to locating Trevor.

An hour later, she sat back, stunned. How could this be? Was she mistaken?

"What's wrong, Simone?" Jesse asked.

"I found Trevor."

"Where?"

She drew a deep breath, dread swamping her. "He's in Sayulita."

#

Chapter Nine

Simone stared at her computer screen, hoping she was mistaken. She wasn't. The information was right in front of her. Her ex-boyfriend was renting a house outside of Sayulita. Oddly enough, he was staying a couple of blocks from Joy. Was that a coincidence?

"Are you sure?" Jesse asked.

"Positive. He's renting a house near Joy's place."

He frowned. "Find a traffic or security camera near his home. Let's see if he was anywhere near Joy's place today."

As Simone turned her attention back to her computer, she shuddered at the thought of Trevor being in the same town. Why was he here? Might he have legitimate business in Sayulita?

She conceded the chances of that being true were little to none. He always needed money. How would he afford to come to Mexico?

If he didn't have a legitimate business interest in town, that left only one reason he'd come to a foreign country and rent a place in the same town.

Simone.

Another shudder wracked her body. Simone placed her fingers on her keyboard, shocked to see her fingers trembling.

Jesse walked around the table to crouch by her side. "Look at me, sweetheart." When she did, he reached for her hands and sandwiched them between his own. "Everything will be all right. I promise."

"You can't guarantee it."

"He won't touch you again, baby."

She blinked. Baby? Sweetheart? Why did those sweet names turn her insides to mush? She'd never allowed Trevor to call her anything except Simone. Jesse doing it didn't bother her in the least. "You don't know him, Jesse. He's tenacious and downright mean. He'll find a way to get to me."

Would she have to run again? She didn't want to leave. Didn't she deserve a life away from her past?

"Simone."

She focused on the medic. "Sorry. I zoned out for a minute."

He stood, tugging Simone to her feet, and wrapped his arms around her.

She snuggled in and sighed as his warmth seeped into her bones. Comfort and safety. That's what his arms meant to her. That, and the sweet, honorable man holding her was in a class of his own. Trevor was nothing like Jesse. How she had been stupid enough to settle for Trevor was beyond her.

"He won't touch you again," Jesse murmured. "He'll have to go through me first, then the Artemis team. Trust me, Simone. He doesn't stand a chance of getting through all of us. You're safe."

"For the first time in my life, I believe that." She tightened her hold around his waist. "Thank you for giving me security."

He tilted her head up toward his and captured her mouth in a sizzling passionate kiss that burned Simone to the bone. On and on the kiss went, sending her into the stratosphere.

When he finally lifted his head minutes or hours later, Simone stared at him. "What was that?"

"A sample of what we're capable of together."

"We don't have an audience."

"I don't want one. This is about you and me, not an audience. So, what do you say? Are you willing to take a chance on me?"

"What about Trevor?"

"What about him?"

"He's not going away. If he thinks I betrayed him with another man, he'll go ballistic. I don't want you hurt because of me."

"I'm exactly where I want to be, by your side. We'll handle Trevor together. Regardless of whether we're dating for real, I will keep you safe from him."

Did she dare take a chance? She knew what Trevor was like. His obsessive personality was the reason she'd fled from San Francisco. If she agreed to date Jesse, she would be dragging him into the line of fire. As things stood, Trevor didn't know for sure if she was involved with the medic.

Stupid. Of course he would suspect she and Jesse were involved. They were living in the same house. Trevor would jump to the obvious conclusion that she and Jesse were more than roommates.

"What's your answer, Simone?"

She grabbed onto her courage with both hands and leaped into the unknown, praying she'd have a soft landing. "Yes."

A slow, heated smile curved his mouth. "You won't regret it. I swear I'll treat you like a princess."

She snorted. "I'm no princess but I appreciate the sentiment. I'm just a cranky, obsessed computer hacker who spends most of her time behind a computer screen."

"We'll have to change some of your ways. A date now and then to break up the monotony."

"I hope I don't disappoint you."

"Be yourself, and I'll be the happiest man on the planet." After another slow kiss, Jesse said, "Think you can focus enough to search for the cameras around Trevor's house now?"

She nodded. "If you change your mind about dating me, just say so, okay? I don't want to find out from someone else that you're unhappy."

"I don't play games in relationships, babe. If I have a problem, you'll know about it. I expect the same from you. We're exclusive unless we decide we aren't. Deal?"

"Deal." It wasn't like she had a line of men begging for dates. The last time she'd been on a date was with Trevor. Definitely not anything good to remember on that one. That was the last time

Trevor had laid a hand on her, and she'd filed charges against him because of her injuries.

"Need a snack before we go back to work?"

She shook her head. The thought of eating anything made her stomach lurch.

"If you change your mind, let me know."

Simone returned to her seat and searched for security and traffic cameras near Trevor's rented house. Three hours later, she pushed back from the table and stretched. Time to call it quits for the night. Her head hurt and her vision was blurry. "I just sent you the camera footage I found around Trevor's house."

"Perfect timing. I just sent you information I gathered from DA's database on the special projects members. Planning to stay up and review the information tonight?"

She shook her head. "I'm wiped out. I'll review everything tomorrow."

"Go get ready for bed, then."

Simone studied him. "You're not coming?"

"Not for a while."

"Why not? Do you need help with anything?"

"What I need to do isn't for you to complete."

That didn't sound good. "Jesse, what are you planning to do?"

"Visit Trevor."

"You can't. He's dangerous."

"We can't let him run around Sayulita, Simone. He knows who you really are, and as vindictive as he's shown himself to be in the past, he won't think twice about blowing our cover."

"What are you going to do with him?" Jesse couldn't just kill him, could he?

"Not what you're thinking." His lips curved. "I'm going to have a chat with him, then ship him off to a black site until we're out of Mexico."

"I should go with you. I know how he thinks."

"No, baby. You shouldn't see him at all or you'll fuel whatever fantasies he's created for himself. Trust me, Simone. I promised I would take care of you. This is my time to find out what he wants and get him out of your hair for now. We'll come up with a more permanent way to keep him away from you once we've finished this mission. While I'm gone, I'll ask the members of Artemis who are on watch to come into the house. You won't be alone at any time."

Seeing that he was determined to follow this course of action, Simone said, "All right. You'd better come back to me unharmed, Mr. Phelps. I won't be happy if you return with new holes or scars."

"Is your ex typically armed?"

"Always. He likes to carry around a Sig and three knives. He always said that was the magic ticket to protection."

"Thanks for the information. I'll be careful."

"I wish you weren't going alone."

"My only other option would be to take a member of Artemis with me."

She grimaced. "Whoever goes better be as tough as nails. Trevor doesn't respect women at all."

"I know just who to ask to go with me."

"Who?"

"Rayne Weatherly. She used to be a cop in Chicago and won't put up with anything, especially disrespect. I wouldn't want to meet her in a dark alley if she had a grudge against me."

That said something about Rayne. Tough, indeed. "She's part of Artemis?"

He nodded as he slid his phone from his pocket. "Let me find out if she's available to help. If not, I'll ask one of the other women to go with me."

"I wish your teammates were here." Not that she didn't trust Jesse. She did. Simone also knew Trevor. He'd be easier to handle with two men, not a man and a woman.

"We'll be fine. Don't worry."

Easy for him to say. He wasn't the one left behind to wait and wonder. Her breath caught in her lungs. This was what she was in for when Jesse deployed with his team. No wonder her friends Poppy and Sage mentioned supporting each other when their husbands were gone. Simone finally got it. The problem was the silence, waiting for word on when they were coming home. *If* they were coming home. The black ops teams at Fortress routinely went into dangerous situations and returned home with injuries. Some were minor. Some weren't.

No wonder Poppy and Sage stayed busy while their husbands deployed. Their work kept them from dwelling too long on the what ifs. Since worry accomplished nothing, the women worked. Simone would adopt a similar coping tactic.

Jesse sent a text and received a response seconds later. "We're set. Rayne will be here in five minutes. Iona and Tegan will stay with you while I'm gone."

He studied her a moment and frowned. "Are you all right?"

"I will be." She had to be, or she'd lose the best thing that had ever happened to her. Jesse.

"What's wrong?"

Time to drag up more courage and speak the truth. "I realized the worry and anxiety I'm feeling is a taste of what's coming when you're deployed."

Jesse's expression went blank. "Are you backing out?"

"No way. I'm making plans to work overtime while you're gone. Will I be able to communicate with you while you're deployed?"

"Of course. You already have a satellite phone. We can communicate by text unless I call you. If I can call, I will."

"But sending a text will be safer."

"In some situations, yes. If you need help and I'm not answering a text, call Zane or Brent. They'll take care of you. Our families are everything. Brent is the first one to tell new recruits that their families are part of Fortress. You're an employee, Simone. That means you're already considered part of the Fortress family. If you need help, you'll get it within minutes."

"Zane told me as much. I still find it hard to believe."

"They mean it."

A soft knock sounded on the back door. When Jesse opened the door, a tall woman walked inside. She held out her hand to Simone. "I'm Rayne."

"Simone. Thanks for going with Jesse."

"Glad to help. I'll watch his back, Simone. We'll return before you know it. Your boyfriend is very good at what he does."

Simone kissed Jesse. "Be careful. Promise me."

"You have my word. I won't take chances. That's why I have Rayne."

Iona and Tegan entered the kitchen. Tegan smiled. "Party time, Simone. I hope you have popcorn and soft drinks."

She laughed. "What's a party without those? We'll see what's in the pantry."

Jesse kissed her and stepped back. He glanced at Rayne. "I'll grab my gear, then we can go." When he returned, Jesse carried two bags. "Ready." He looked at Iona, who gave a slight nod, then shifted his gaze to Simone. "If anything happens, do exactly what Iona and Tegan tell you to do. They'll take care of you until I return."

"We'll be fine. We're having a party, remember? Don't underestimate Trevor. He's a snake who likes to bite when your back is turned."

"Yes, ma'am." He winked. "Save some popcorn for me."

Then he was gone.

Simone stared at the closed door for a beat, then shifted her attention to the two women. "Popcorn and soft drinks is all you want?"

Tegan brightened. "You have something else in mind?"

"Maybe. Let me see what's in the freezer." She and Jesse had polished off the apple pie last night. Hopefully, the people who stocked the kitchen had bought more than one.

She peered into the freezer and hit pay dirt. Not apple, but cherry which was even better in her opinion. "Score."

Simone removed the box from the freezer and turned on the oven to preheat. "Cherry pie for the win. We also have vanilla ice cream. Sound good?"

Iona laughed. "It's perfect. Who doesn't love a good cherry pie?"

"My thoughts exactly."

"How about a movie to go along with the pie and ice cream?"

She thought about the work still yet to be done and knew she wouldn't be able to concentrate on anything except Jesse. "Great idea. Any preferences?"

"No sap," Tegan said. "Just came off a nasty breakup. I don't want any reminders."

"Got it." When a signal showed the oven was at the desired temperature, Simone slid the pie inside and headed for the living room. "Let's see what the owners of this place have in the DVD cabinet."

After a little debate over the offerings, the women settled on National Treasure. A little romance but not too sappy. Adventure because who didn't love a good treasure hunt story. A happy ending. A perfect movie.

The only hitch was her two companions took turns checking the perimeter and watching out the windows. No way for her to forget that Jesse was heading into trouble. No doubt in her mind that Trevor wouldn't cooperate. Worse, if pushed too hard, he would resort to violence.

Chapter Ten

Jesse parked a few houses away from Trevor White's rental bungalow and turned to his companion. "You know your role in this?"

"Of course. Silent bad guy." Rayne laughed. "My favorite role to play. Thanks for giving me the chance to do this, Jesse."

"Listen, White thinks he's a tough guy. He doesn't respect women and thinks nothing about laying his hands on them." Jesse scowled. "He put his hands on Simone and sent her to the hospital."

Rayne's hands fisted. "I hope she had the good sense to file charges against him."

"She did. He spent time in the gray bar hotel for it. My guess is he has a grudge against her for that plus he doesn't like the fact that she escaped his clutches."

"Well, then, this little interrogation should be a lot of fun. Ready?"

After a nod, Jesse opened the door and met Rayne on the sidewalk. Together, they approached White's residence.

No lights burned in any room. Was White out or sleeping? Jesse signaled Rayne to activate the comm device in her ear and to check the front of the house. He rounded the side of the house to inspect the backyard and the locks on the door and windows.

Simone's ex wasn't a trusting sort. Everything was locked up tight.

"No entry." Rayne's voice came across as a whisper in Jesse's ear.

"Copy. Come to the back."

She walked around the corner of the bungalow and joined Jesse. "Locked?" she whispered.

"Yeah."

"Allow me." She slipped past him and crouched in front of the door with her lock picks in hand. Seconds later, the tumblers dropped. "Done."

"How did you do that so fast?"

"Leftovers from misspent teenage years. Sometimes it comes in handy."

His lips curved. Nice. Following a last glance around to be sure he hadn't missed a security system or a camera, Jesse signaled Rayne to stand to the side of the frame in case White or someone else was waiting for them.

Twisting the knob, he eased open the door and waited for a reaction inside the house.

Nothing.

Breathing a little easier, he slipped into the bungalow and motioned for Rayne to join him. They waited in silence for two minutes.

Nothing stirred in the darkness.

Excellent. They conducted a room by room search until they came to the last room with a closed door. Must be the main bedroom.

Jesse grasped the knob and twisted. He pushed the door open a crack and peered inside the darkened room.

White lay on the bed, a large lump under the covers, snoring peacefully.

Not for long. Grateful he hadn't picked up a companion to warm his bed for the night, Jesse slipped into the room and walked to the side of the bed. On the nightstand, White had laid a pistol. Tsk, tsk. Wonder where he'd scored a weapon so fast.

Didn't matter. He wouldn't be able to use it against Jesse or Rayne. Jesse confiscated the Glock 19 and slid it into one of his cargo pockets.

When Rayne was in place on the other side, Jesse shook White hard with his gloved hand. "Wake up, White. We need to talk."

"Huh? What?" He blinked a few times, then squinted up at Jesse. "Who are you? How did you get in here? I'm going to sue the owner of this dump. He promised me this was a safe neighborhood."

Jesse snorted. "Didn't you know? Nowhere in Sayulita is safe." He yanked the covers off. "Out. Now."

"Who are you? What do you want?"

"Only to talk if you cooperate."

"And if I don't?"

"You don't want to do that."

"Get out. I'm calling the cops. If you're smart, you'll disappear before they arrive."

Jesse grabbed his arm in a painful grip and jerked him out of bed. "Let's go."

"Ow! Hey, that hurts. Let go of me."

"Hey." Rayne motioned toward the wall across from the foot of the bed.

He glanced over his shoulder, and his blood ran cold. Photographs of Simone covered the wall. Furious, he turned his glare on Simone's slimy ex-boyfriend. What had she seen in this guy? She was worth a thousand of this man, easily.

"We're going to chat, White." He propelled the stumbling man into the kitchen where Rayne set up a chair. Jesse shoved Simone's ex onto the seat, and Rayne secured his hands behind his back with a zip tie.

"Hey, what's going on here? What do you want?"

"That's not how we play this game. I'm the one who asks the questions. All you have to do is answer them and we'll be out of your life." Not one hundred percent accurate but close enough for Jesse.

"What do you want?" White yelled.

"Answers."

"To what? I ain't no encyclopedia, man. I don't live here, you know. I'm just visiting. Whatever you want, I can't help you."

"Why are you in Sayulita?"

A scowl. "None of your business, dude, but it ain't got nothing to do with you. So, chill, all right? Cut me loose, and we'll forget this ever happened."

"Told you he'd want to do this the hard way," Rayne murmured.

White glared over his shoulder at her but there was no way he could see her face clearly. Her back was to the window, and no light shined in the room. "I ain't talking to you."

"Too bad. I'm sure your conversation would be quite stimulating."

"Shut up."

Rayne looked at Jesse, eyebrow raised in a silent question.

He gave a slight nod.

The other operative gave an exaggerated sigh. "You shouldn't show disrespect to the people who hold your life in their hands." She reached down and squeezed the pressure point between White's trapezius muscle and his collarbone, digging in hard with her thumb.

White screamed as pain ripped through his body.

Jesse clamped a hand over his mouth to stifle the noise. Wouldn't pay to have a nosy neighbor call the cops.

A minute later, he flicked a glance at Rayne who released her grip. White moaned, beads of sweat trickling down his face. "Let's try that again, White. Why are you in Sayulita?"

He cursed at Jesse and Rayne. Another round of pain had him sobbing.

"Answer the question and the pain stops. Why are you here, White?"

"I'm looking for someone, all right? That's all. Nothing to do with you, like I said. Now get out and leave me alone."

"Who? I want a name."

For a few seconds, White debated telling Jesse what he wanted to know but gave in quickly enough when Rayne rested her hand on his shoulder. "My girlfriend. Nobody you know. She ran off on me. Got to teach her a lesson and drag her back home where she won't ever get away from me again."

"Your girlfriend have a name?"

"Simone."

"Why did she run from you?"

"Because she's stupid, that's why. She got angry because I knocked her around a little and she turned me in to the cops."

Knocked her around a little? Simone had landed in the hospital for several days because of this creep. Jesse wrestled with his temper and finally beat it down enough to think clearly. "How did you know she was in Sayulita?"

"Got a friend. I'm glad I found her again. I've got plans for that woman."

"You've been tracking her. How?"

"Told you. A friend." He laughed. "Somebody really has it in for my woman. Everywhere she goes, someone narcs on her."

"Who?"

"What's all the interest in my personal life? It ain't got nothing to do with you."

"That's where you're wrong. You have any other business in Sayulita, White?"

A sly look came into the other man's eyes. "Maybe. What's it to ya?"

"We know your background. We know you're into drugs and guns. Looking to make a connection in Mexico?"

"Oh, I get it. You're the competition, aren't you? Well, you won't get nothing from me."

Rayne sighed again. "Wrong answer, Trevor." Another two minutes of pain and pressure, and White begged for her to stop. "Answer the man's question or I'll increase the pain."

"You don't want that," Jesse said. "Too much of that pressure will damage the nerve and cause permanent paralysis." Definitely not true but good old Trevor didn't know the truth. "Are you looking to make a connection in Mexico?"

White glowered at him. "Why do you care? It's my business."

"I'll take that as a yes."

"I got to make a living, don't I? It's easy money."

"It's illegal."

A snort. "So? Lots of people deal. Just providing a service to the customers, ya know?"

"You're selling poison to kids and adults."

"Hey, it's their choice, all right? I don't make them buy nothing."

Disgusted, Jesse shook his head. "You're a real prince, White."

"Team's here," Rayne murmured.

"They can have him."

"What are you talking about?" White's eyes widened. "You said if I answered your questions that you would let me go and you'd walk away."

Jesse unzipped his mike bag and pulled out a syringe he'd prepared before leaving the safe house. "I lied."

"What's that?" His voice rose. "What are you going to do? Don't kill me, man. I'm begging here."

"Why shouldn't I kill you?" Jesse snapped. "You put Simone into the hospital more than once. Why she put up with you for as long as she did, I'll never know but it stops now."

"You know her?"

"Oh, yeah. I know her." He leaned down and jabbed the needle into White's neck and depressed the plunger.

The slimy man screamed. "No, don't kill me."

"You shouldn't have touched what's mine," Jesse said. "Simone is off limits to you. If I ever see your ugly mug again, you'll leave our encounter in a body bag. Am I making myself clear, White?"

The other man's eyes had glazed over already. He blinked sleepily. "Yeah, okay," he mumbled.

"I will kill you if you ever touch Simone again," Jesse murmured into his ear as the other man slipped into unconsciousness.

"Do you think he'll heed your warning?" Rayne asked.

"Nope. He's stupid enough to come back around and try to take her."

"And if he does?"

He looked at Rayne. "What do you think?"

After a slight nod, she opened the back door to admit the team of mercenaries sent by Fortress to take White and detain him in the jungle.

The tall blond's eyebrows rose when he saw White. "He's dead?"

"Unconscious." Jesse tossed the used hypodermic in a hard plastic case and zipped up his mike bag. "He'll stay that way for twelve hours. When he wakes, he'll be thirsty and very disoriented."

"What do you want us to do with him?"

"Hold him until you receive word that it's safe to let him go. Watch him. He's cocky and dangerous enough to be a problem. He also loves to play with weapons and uses underhanded tactics."

"We'll take care of him. Any other instructions?"

"I want to know the minute you turn him loose." He gave the leader his number. "Same instructions if he escapes."

"Want us to hunt him down?"

"Until you get word that our op is finished, yes. Otherwise, just a notification will do. We'll be ready for him."

"Understood." Blond glanced at Rayne and gave a slight nod. "Good to see you again."

"Same. Take care of this garbage, all right? We don't need him causing trouble for Jesse's girlfriend. Their lives are on the line if White blows their cover."

"He won't get the chance." After shaking their hands, Blond signaled for his men to haul the unconscious White from the bungalow. A minute later, they were gone.

"What now?" Rayne asked.

"Search this place. I want to know who his contacts are in Sayulita."

"Why?"

"Don't ask."

They searched the bungalow and came up with a couple of names that Jesse sent to Zane for further research.

He slid his phone away and palmed White's cell phone. Didn't know if they'd come up with anything more from the man's phone but he'd let Simone check it out, anyway. "Come on. Let's get out of here. I need to see Simone."

"Unless my guess is wrong, I'd say she's waiting up for you with my teammates."

They returned to the SUV and drove from the neighborhood. Since they were in the area, Jesse swung by Joy's house. The place was still a beehive of activity with cops and crime scene technicians roaming in and out of the house.

At least the place was secure. No one in their right minds would invade a place filled with cops and techs.

Twenty minutes later, Jesse drove around behind the safe house and parked. "Thanks for the assist, Rayne."

"No problem. Let me know if I can do anything else to help." She opened the door and slipped away into the night.

He climbed from the vehicle and approached the patio. Not wanting to have his head blown off or have one of the Artemis team gut him, Jesse sent a text to tell the women he'd returned and was at the back door.

Seconds, later, Iona unlocked the door and opened it wide. "That didn't take long. Is he still breathing?"

"Unfortunately. He's a pathetic bullying worm."

"You got him to talk?"

"Not everything but I got enough to know he's down here for Simone and to make a connection in the drug trade. Seems like old Trevor wants to set himself up in business in San Francisco."

"A real nice guy, huh?"

He snorted. "Where's Simone?"

"Asleep on the couch. She did her best to wait up for you but lost the fight about twenty minutes ago. We didn't have the heart to move her."

"I'll take care of it. Thanks for watching over my girl."

"You bet. Don't lose this one, okay? We like her."

Jesse chuckled. "I'll do my best."

The two women from Artemis left the safe house and resumed their watch.

Jesse walked into the living room where Simone lay sprawled on the couch, sound asleep. His heart turned over in his chest at the sight of her. She looked totally relaxed and at peace for the first time since they'd landed in Sayulita.

Like Iona and Tegan, Jesse hated to wake her. Leaving her on the couch, though, wasn't an option. She'd wake up sore and stiff.

He bent and lifted Simone into his arms. When she stirred, he murmured, "It's okay. I'm carrying you to bed."

"You're back," she mumbled.

"Yeah, sweetheart. I'm back."

"Any injuries?"

"None."

"Good." She pressed her face to Jesse's neck. "I was worried."

"I know. I'm sorry."

"Did you get the information you wanted?"

"Most of it. We'll talk on the way to work, all right?"

"Okay."

Jesse laid Simone on the bed and draped a quilt over her. "Sleep well, Simone."

"Night, Jesse."

He watched her a moment to be sure she was asleep, then left her bedroom, leaving the door ajar in case she needed him during the night.

Jesse rolled his eyes. He was such a sap and in way over his head with the spunky computer hacker. The members of Artemis might be correct in assuming he would mess up and lose Simone. If he wanted to avoid that outcome, he'd have to work hard to convince his woman that he was worth the risk, no matter how many weeks of separation she'd have to endure while he deployed.

He went to his room and got ready for bed himself. Minutes later, he slid under the covers and drifted into a light sleep. At least he didn't have to worry about Trevor White blowing their covers. He would deal with his obsession with Simone after this mission was over.

#

Chapter Eleven

Simone woke an hour before her alarm would have gone off and sat up. Great. This was becoming a bad habit and not the way she planned to start the day. She sighed and threw off the quilt Jesse had used to cover her early this morning.

She grabbed a change of clothes and padded to the bathroom. Emerging clean and clothed thirty minutes later, she tugged on her running shoes and stood. Time to prepare breakfast and find out what happened with Trevor.

She shivered imaging all the horrible things Trevor said about her. He'd always been vocal in his opinions, especially of her. All bad, of course. Everything wrong was her fault. She'd stayed with him too long. Trevor was a bully and enjoyed belittling people, particularly women. But she'd escaped his clutches. Better late than never.

Turning on the light, Simone walked to the pantry and refrigerator to check their stock of ingredients. After careful consideration, she went with French toast, always a winner in her book.

She prepared the egg mixture, soaked pieces bread and tossed two slices on the large skillet.

"Something smells good." Jesse walked into the kitchen. "What are you fixing?"

"French toast."

"One of my favorite breakfast foods. How can I help?"

"Make coffee and let Iona and Tegan know breakfast is almost ready."

He sent a text and headed for the coffeepot. "How did you sleep?"

"Okay, I guess."

Jesse looked at her.

"It was rough, okay?"

"Something bothering you?"

"You mean besides the fact that we're hunting a traitor to the country, someone who is ruthless enough to sell anything and everything to get ahead, no matter what it costs?"

His lips curved. "Yeah, besides that."

"I've been thinking about the program and how invasive it is. Zane had asked me to save a copy for him to study before I destroyed the original. I'm thinking the only way to get rid of this virus is to wipe out all traces of it."

"So no copy for Z? I don't know how wise it is to tick off your current division head."

She laid two pieces of French toast on a serving platter, then soaked two more pieces of bread in the egg mixture. "You're probably right but I don't think it's wise." She tossed him a glance. "This virus is too dangerous to keep around."

"You realize that you and Zane could recreate this virus in a matter of hours, right?"

She glared at the medic. "Of course. Well, probably. The virus has to be pretty sophisticated to get through antiviral software which takes some work. My concern is for Fortress's systems. If this virus slips into our system, we'll be compromised in less than a minute. We'd lose everything to an enemy combatant or a competitor and compromise the identities and locations of every operative employed by Brent."

Jesse whistled softly. "Wow."

"Exactly. We can't afford to slip up with this virus. It could wipe out every piece of information we've gathered since the company started. If word of the breach leaks, no one will trust Fortress to guard a loved one or VIP much less pay us for cybersecurity when we can't protect our own systems from outside intrusion."

A knock sounded on the back door and Jesse admitted Iona and Tegan. "How are you holding up?"

Tegan gave a faint smile. "If I sit for over ten minutes, I'll be napping."

"That boring out there, huh?"

"Not even a cat walked by to ease the boredom."

"I'm glad."

"Yeah, we are, too." Iona nudged her teammate. "Aren't we?"

"Boring is good," Tegan agreed. "Just need a little more excitement to push back the fatigue. Either that, or we need a source of coffee."

Simone eyed her. "Make coffee in here."

"She's right." Jesse poured coffee into four mugs. "Use our kitchen. I know how it is on long night watches."

"If you're sure you don't mind, we'd appreciate the caffeine," Tegan said.

"We'll leave coffee supplies out for you."

Iona breathed deep. "You're going to spoil us, Simone. French toast with maple syrup? Reminds of me home during the winter months with snow on the ground. Mom always made French toast on snow days."

"Sounds like wonderful memories." Simone added two slices of toast to the growing pile and dunked more bread into the egg mixture. By the time she finished the French toast, Iona, Tegan, and Jesse had set the table and added a bowl of cut fruit as well.

She set the platter of French toast on the table. Minutes later, the platter and the fruit bowl were empty.

"You're nominated as my favorite chef," Tegan said, sitting back in her chair. "Jesse, remember what we told you early this morning?"

"Yeah."

"Goes double now."

He saluted her, mouth curving upward in a smile.

"What's on the agenda for the day?" Iona asked.

"More of the same." Jesse pushed back from the table and gathered plates and bowls. "Simone is blowing through assignments, hoping to get noticed by the special projects group. If that doesn't work, we'll have to plan some B & E at the homes of the group members. I'd rather not resort to drastic measures."

Simone didn't like that option either but the likelihood was looking more likely by the day. Her plan to get noticed was moving too slow. Every hour that passed, the programmer came closer to achieving his goal. "I'm afraid it will come down to that, Jesse."

"Maybe not."

"It's the most likely scenario."

"You need to see what kind of setup they have in the special projects division. The easiest way is for you to be invited to the fifth floor for an interview."

"Agreed. I'm doing all I can to gain attention with my work. I don't know what else to do without being obvious."

"Maybe something will happen today," Tegan said. "Jesse said you were blowing through assignments. They'll notice that kind of work ethic."

"I hope so. I don't want to break into houses. If we're discovered, they'll know why we're at DA."

"Let us know if we can help." Iona smiled. "We rock at B & E."

Jesse chuckled.

"Come on," Tegan said to Iona. "We'd better go so no one notices us leaving the house. Let us know if you need anything, Jesse."

"Appreciate it."

"Need help with the cleanup since Simone cooked?"

"I've got it."

"Thanks again, Simone," Iona said. "We owe you and Jesse breakfast." She and Tegan left by the back door.

Simone rose. "Let's clean the kitchen, then we'll head out. We need to get to the cubicle farm to check for bugs and cameras before anyone else shows up and asks what we're doing."

They washed and dried the dishes before gathering their gear. Jesse stopped Simone before she stepped outside. "Wait here while I check the vehicle."

Soon, he returned. "We're clear."

They drove to Dragon Alley without incident. From what Simone could see on the drive, no one paid attention to them. Just the way she liked it.

Inside the lobby of DA, she and Jesse signed in and rode the elevator to her floor. The cubicle farm was quiet. No one else had arrived yet. Perfect.

Jesse motioned for her to log in and start on her work while he used his electronic sniffer to hunt for any surprises.

His soft growl told her he'd discovered more unwanted electronics. Boy, looked like Dragon Alley was going to waste a lot of money on these little gadgets. Jesse dropped each one into a small bag, then rechecked for bugs or cameras. One more bug and a tiny camera later, he declared her workspace clean.

If the upper echelon had spent so much time trying to figure out what she was doing, Simone wondered if they were doing the same thing to Joy. She rose and hugged him. "Thanks. Do you have time to check Joy's station, too?" she whispered.

"Sure." He pressed a quick kiss to her mouth and straightened. "Take care today, baby. You're drawing attention like you wanted."

She grimaced. "I hope it's the right kind. We're running out of time."

He rounded the edge of the cubicle wall and disappeared from sight. Two minutes later, Jesse returned, holding a small bag filled with black discs. "Tell Joy to watch her back."

"I will. Thanks, Jesse."

After another quick kiss, Jesse left the cubicle farm to dispose of the unwanted electronics.

Simone ran a diagnostic test on her computer and scowled at the results. Some yahoo had tried to hack into her computer and failed. Good to know her program worked. Ticked her off that someone was doing their best to spy on her, though.

She double checked the results and found them the same. Well, that meant she needed to add a couple of layers to her protection.

Simone glanced at the clock. She should have enough time to set up the extra protection before anyone arrived for work. Her colleagues had dragged in just before starting time yesterday and the day before.

She downloaded two more programs to beef up her security. No one to this point had broken through the firewalls. Hopefully, this wouldn't be the first time that happened.

With that finished, she logged into her work email and culled through the assignments waiting for her. Her eyebrows rose. Nice. Definitely more her speed. This batch of assignments might keep her busy until lunch.

When Joy arrived at her station an hour later, Simone had already finished a quarter of her assignments for the day. These, however, were at least more interesting than some others. More in line with a programmer rather than grunt work.

Joy stored her stuff and walked into Simone's space. "You're here early again."

"I was hoping for more interesting tasks today."

"Did you get any?"

"A few. I'm knocking the assignments down in the order assigned."

Joy laughed. "You're going to finish before lunch again, aren't you?"

"Probably. Was everything okay last night?"

Her friend's cheeks turned a pretty shade of pink. "I was fine. Mateo checked on me several times throughout the rest of his shift."

Simone smiled. "You like him."

"Maybe."

"I'm glad. He seems like a nice guy. By the way, Jesse ran a background check on him overnight. He's clean."

Joy stared. "He did? Why?"

"We want you to be safe, Joy. He showed up out of nowhere and was instantly attracted to you. While he's smart to be interested in you, we wanted to be sure he wasn't a gold digger or something."

Simone's friend rolled her eyes. "Well, if he is, he's out of luck. I'm not independently wealthy. He's a good man doing his best to keep people under his care safe." She sighed. "I really like him, Simone. We're going on a date tonight. He's off duty."

"Good for you. I hope things work out." She hugged Joy. "Jesse checked your station this morning. You had a lot of listening devices and a couple of mini cameras hidden in your area. He said for you to be careful today."

Joy gasped and pulled back. "Are you serious?"

"I saw them myself. Just watch yourself, okay?"

"Why would they do that to me? I've been here over two years."

"Might result from associating with me. Someone is doing the same to me. Jesse has cleared out several bugs and cameras from my area yesterday and today. I also found evidence of someone trying to hack into my computer."

Joy scowled. "I'll check my computer as well. This is unbelievable. I don't get it. If they don't trust me, why don't they fire me?"

"Don't know."

"I'd better get started. You're already miles ahead of me this morning."

"Lunch at the same time?"

"You bet. See you later." Joy disappeared into her cubicle.

Simone returned to her tasks, and the morning flew by with only a small hitch in her pace. One assignment was a little tricky. She untangled the mess and finished the last of the tasks as Joy came around the cubicle wall.

"Ready for lunch?"

"You bet. Breakfast was several hours ago." Simone stretched and sent Jesse a text. "Ready. Let's find out what's on the menu."

Joy checked her phone and smiled.

Simone nudged her. "Something from Mateo?"

Her friend nodded. "He said he's looking forward to tonight." She looked up, dismay in her eyes. "What am I going to wear? I don't know if I have anything appropriate."

"Where are you going?"

"He didn't tell me, and I don't want to ask."

"Go middle of the road, clothes you can dress up or down. You know, business casual."

"Perfect. I can work with that."

"Take a jacket along if you need to dress up a little more but wear comfortable dressy flats."

"You're a genius, Simone."

"Hardly but I have some experience with dates like this."

"I guess Jesse is as bad as most men, not giving you a hint at what type of date you're going on."

That was a tough one. Simone didn't want to lie to her friend, but she didn't have experience to go on. "He's better than most at giving me hints."

"Lucky you."

"Don't worry. The longer you date Mateo, the easier you'll get at reading him for clues to what's coming for the evening."

They walked into the crowded cafeteria and headed for the line. "Wonder when Jesse will be here? He said he might be a little late."

"We'll make our selections, then you can return to get food for Jesse. That way he won't waste time in the line."

"Good idea."

After taking their trays to a table, Simone returned to the line to choose food for Jesse. Good thing he wasn't picky. To make things simple, she chose the same food she'd selected for herself.

When she stopped to pick up two bottles of water for Jesse, someone stepped up to her.

"Ms. Kenyon?"

Simone turned to face the man she'd been wanting to meet. Griffin Daley. "Yes?"

"I'm Griffin Daley, head of the Special Projects division."

She smiled. "It's nice to meet you, Mr. Daley. Please, call me Simone."

"Would you have time to stop by my office after lunch? I'd like to discuss something with you."

"Of course. I'll have to let Ms. Kirk know I'll be late returning from lunch."

He waved that concern aside. "I'll take care of it. I'm looking forward to speaking with you."

"See you soon, Mr. Daley." She watched as he strode away. Well, well. Looked like this might be a good day unless Daley planned to call her hand on removing the bugs and cameras. No doubt in her mind that the Special Projects division was responsible for the spy equipment, especially if they were suspicious of her activities.

She returned to the table where Joy waited for her and set down Jesse's tray.

"Was that who I think it was?" Joy asked, eyes sparkling.

"If you think it's Griffin Daley, then, yeah, it was."

"What did he say?"

"He wants to see me after lunch."

"Yes!" Joy pumped her fist. "I knew it. You're being tapped to go into the Special Projects division."

"We don't know that."

"Ha. Mr. Daley doesn't talk to any of the peons here unless he wants them for his division. No one else grabs his attention."

"We'll see."

"This is so exciting. I've met no one who works in that division, and now the woman I'm mentoring is being invited into the ivory tower of programming at DA."

Simone studied her friend. "You're good at the work, Joy. Why hasn't anyone tapped you for this division?"

"I'm not in your class." She shrugged. "We both know it's true. I'm not complaining, though. I enjoy grunt work. Someone has to do it."

"It's the Special Projects division's loss."

"That's nice of you to say although it's not true."

Jesse walked into the cafeteria and made a beeline for Simone. He kissed her before taking his seat. "Thanks for getting my lunch. Did I miss anything?"

"Did you ever," Joy crowed. "Griffin Daley asked Simone to stop by his office after lunch. He wants to talk to her."

His gaze locked with Simone's. "Did he say what he wants?"

She shook her head.

"Worried?"

"Why should she be worried?" Joy asked. "The Special Projects division is exactly where Simone should be. I've seen no one as fast as Simone. They'll be lucky to have her."

"I agree." Jesse squeezed Simone's hand and dug into his meal. "Let me know how it turns out. Joy, how was your night?"

"Quiet, thanks to Mateo."

His eyebrows rose. "Did he stay with you?"

Her cheeks flushed. "No, of course not. He checked on me frequently through the night."

"And?" Simone teased. "Tell Jesse the rest."

"We're going on a date tonight after work."

"That's great. Congratulations." Jesse opened a bottle of water and chugged down half of it. "I ran a background check on him. He's a good guy, Joy."

"Simone told me. Thanks for doing that. I feel better knowing you did."

"Let me know if you need me to dig deeper. I did a standard check but nothing popped up as hinky."

"I will if something feels off tonight." Her color deepened. "He messaged me twice this morning to check on me. It's sweet."

"I'm happy for you, Joy." Simone smiled at her friend. "He sounds amazing."

"Almost too good to be true." Some of Joy's happiness dimmed. "What if I'm wrong?"

"You're smart. If something is wrong, you'll know."

"I hope nothing happens. I really like him."

By the time they finished lunch, butterflies flew in Simone's stomach. This interview with Daley had to work. Simone hoped the meeting was an invitation to join his department. If not, she didn't know what else to do but engage in a little B & E to find what they needed.

After disposing of her tray and lunch detritus, Joy hugged Simone. "I have to return to work. I want to know everything when you're finished."

"You got it. See you later."

Jesse rose and disposed of their trays, then returned for Simone. He held out his hand. "Come on, beautiful. I'll walk you to the elevator."

Outside the cafeteria, he clasped her hand and walked her to a small alcove where he took Simone in his arms. "Are you ready for this?" he murmured.

"I have to be. What other choice do I have?"

"Remember to stay in character, sweetheart. You've got this."

"Easy for you to say. Everything is riding on it."

He brushed his lips over hers. "We have options. Relax and be yourself. Your cover is airtight. Zane wouldn't leave loopholes."

Jesse was right. Zane had meticulously built Simone Kenyon's credentials. He'd covered everything. As good as the Special Projects division workers were, Zane was better.

Slowly, the tension in her muscles eased. "You're right." Simone wrapped her arms around Jesse and hugged him. "Thanks for the reminder."

"You can do this. You're more than qualified." After a gentle kiss, Jesse released her and led her to the elevator. "Shoot me a text when you're finished. I'll be close if you need me."

She flashed him a smile, stepped onto the elevator, and pressed the button for the fifth floor. When she stepped out, a pleasant woman at a receptionist's desk greeted Simone. "Good afternoon, Ms. Kenyon. Mr. Daley is expecting you. Wait while I inform him you're here."

After a murmured conversation into the phone, the receptionist stood and came around the desk. "This way, please."

She followed the woman along the corridor filled with offices and conference rooms until they reached the double doors of the corner office and knocked. The receptionist opened the door. "Ms. Kenyon is here."

"Send her in. Thanks, Ms. Mulgraves."

"Yes, sir." She smiled at Simone. "Good luck," she whispered and closed the door behind Simone.

Daley rose from behind his large oak desk and motioned to the chairs in front of it. "Thanks for coming. Take a seat, Ms. Kenyon."

"Simone, please."

"Simone, then. May I get you anything? Water, coffee, a soft drink?"

"No, thanks."

"Ms. Kirk recommended I ask you to join the Special Projects division. She's impressed with everything you've done, especially the speed and quality. Your supervisor assures me you're exactly the person I need to have in this division."

"I'm flattered."

"You should be," Daley said. "Not everyone is eligible to join our division. It's an honor."

"What kind of work does your division do?"

"The classified kind. Sometimes we fulfill contracts for the government. Other times, we do something fun like create a video game. Anything is on the table."

"Expensive work?"

Daley chuckled. "Triple the going rate."

She stared. Holy smoke. No wonder the employees made seven figures each year. "Bonuses?"

"If you come in under budget and under the time limit. Ms. Kirk told me how fast you are in finishing every job she assigns you. Some tasks you completed in record time this morning came from me. They were the first part of your interview."

Huh. "I guess I passed?"

"With flying colors. I'm impressed, Simone. You're incredible."

"Thank you, sir."

"Griffin, please. We're informal in our division." He named a salary well over the seven figures she'd been expecting. "Are you interested in working with us, Simone?"

"Yes, sir. When do I start?"

He smiled. "Ms. Kirk says you're out of assignments again. What do you think about starting right now?"

"Sounds good. I need to grab my gear from my cubicle, then I'll be ready to begin."

"Excellent. Let me show you where you'll work from now on. By the time you're situated, I'll have assignments in your email." He stood and held out his hand. "Welcome to Special Projects, Simone. Let me know if you need anything. I'll take care of you."

"I appreciate that."

"I understand you're dating one of our security guards."

"That's right. Is that a problem?"

"Actually, it's perfect. Your work is classified and our security staff is carefully vetted before being hired. If you take work home, your boyfriend will be required to maintain the same amount of secrecy and discretion as you."

"Won't be a problem."

"Good." Daley circled the desk and opened his office door for Simone. "I'm looking forward to working with you. Follow me."

She trailed after the division head to one of the larger offices near the elevator. Daley opened the door and gestured for her to precede him.

"This is your new office." He picked up a set of keys laying on the desktop. "Lock any work in your desk when you leave the office. Nothing is to be left out."

"Understood. Thank you, Mr. Daley."

"Griffin," he reminded her and moved to stand a little too close for Simone's taste. "I can't wait to get to know you better," he murmured. His gaze drifted over her face and lingered too long on her mouth. "Maybe some evening we can get better acquainted over drinks. My treat."

"I don't think Jesse would like that unless you invite him as well." She smiled. The nerve of Daley. He was hitting on her. She hoped she found the target program fast. Otherwise, she might have to resort to drastic measures to fend Daley off. Simone suspected he wouldn't take no for an answer.

He blinked. "Oh, of course, I meant to include him in the invitation as well. It's always a pleasure to get acquainted with the security staff."

"Thanks for the invitation."

Daley gave a curt nod. "I'll let you get situated. When you're ready, check your email. You'll have plenty of work to keep you busy this afternoon."

After he left, Simone grabbed the keys and slid them into her pocket. Inside the elevator, she sent Jesse a text. Seconds later, he agreed to meet her at the cubicle farm.

She walked to her station and logged in to delete the programs she'd downloaded for security, then grabbed her stuff, and circled the wall to Joy's station. "Hey, I'm going to the fifth floor."

Joy spun her chair around to stare at her. "Now?"

"Yeah. Still want to meet for lunch each day?"

"You bet." She scribbled something down on a piece of paper and handed it to Simone. "My cell phone number. Text me whenever you're ready to eat lunch."

"Will do. Keep me updated about your date with Mateo, all right? Good luck tonight."

"Thanks, Simone. I'll see you tomorrow."

Jesse walked up and took Simone's backpack from her shoulder. "Ready?"

"Yeah. Let's do this."

"See you later, Joy." Jesse wrapped his hand around Simone's and escorted her from the cubicle farm. Inside the elevator, he said, "What's wrong?"

Her brows knitted. "Am I that transparent?"

"I know you. What happened?"

Why fight it? He'd find out anyway. "Daley hit on me."

Jesse scowled. "Did he put his hands on you?"

"No. I took care of it. He asked me to meet him for drinks after work one night, and I told him you would have to be invited as well or I wouldn't go. He invited you, too."

"If he gets out of line, you'll tell me." Not a question, a demand.

"Of course. I want you to check my office for bugs or cameras. I don't want anyone spying on me."

"No problem."

When the elevator arrived at the fifth floor, Simone introduced Jesse to Ms. Mulgraves. "You'll be seeing him on the floor occasionally. We're dating."

"It's nice to meet you, Mr. Porterfield."

"Call me Jesse." He walked with Simone to her office and shut the door before setting down her pack and removing his electronics detector from his pocket.

Jesse completed a slow circuit around her office, stopping six times to remove four bugs and two mini cameras. "Clear," he murmured.

He kissed her. "I'd better get back. See you after work, sweetheart." Jesse trailed a finger down her cheek and left the office.

Simone sat in her chair, logged in, and downloaded her three programs to prevent anyone from spying on her through her computer. That done, she checked her email and got to work.

Chapter Twelve

Jesse returned to his rounds, checking the perimeter of the Dragon Alley campus. The whole time he circled the property, his skin crawled. Was it the encounter Simone had with Daley, or was someone watching him with the security cameras?

Probably both. He was still an unknown element on the security staff, and as much as he tried to fit in, the other security guards didn't trust him. Neither did his boss.

After completing his check of the perimeter, Jesse started his rounds through each floor of the main building. Occasionally, he'd meet another member of the security staff. Jesse greeted other employees as they went about their business.

His comm system crackled. "Porterfield, report to my office."

His eyebrows rose. What did Boudreaux want? "Yes, sir. Five minutes."

"Copy."

He finished his check of the third floor and returned to the security division to knock on his boss's door. He turned the knob. "You wanted to see me, sir?"

"Have a seat."

Jesse did as instructed. "Yes, sir?"

"How do you like it here, Porterfield?"

What was this about? "Very much. I enjoy my coworkers and the work atmosphere at Dragon Alley."

"Not too tame for you?"

"No, sir."

"You were a military cop. You don't find the work here boring?"

"Work as a military cop is much the same as it is here. Long stretches of nothing with short, intense bursts of life-and-death situations."

His boss rested his elbows on the padded arms of his chair and steeped his fingers. "Do you want something more than this?"

Jesse remained silent a moment. "Are you asking if I want to quit, sir?"

"I want to know if you're open to a different assignment, one with more responsibility and pay."

If he was a normal employee, he'd jump at the chance to bail out of a boring job. But he wasn't a normal employee, and he didn't want to be separated from Simone. "What kind of assignment?"

"Dedicated security to our Special Projects division employees."

"A bodyguard?"

"You could classify it as bodyguard duty. It's only for a couple of weeks. After that, things will go back to normal, and you'll return to your regular duties."

"Bodyguards are assigned to one person rather than a division. How many people am I expected to protect, Mr. Boudreaux?"

"Six, including the division head, Griffin Daley. In fact, he's the one who asked for you to be assigned to this detail. I wouldn't consider assigning this to a rookie, but Daley insisted. What did you do to impress him?"

"Nothing, sir. This probably has more to do with my girlfriend. She was reassigned to that division a few minutes ago. I know they work late hours. Perhaps he wanted to keep Simone happy and willing to stay late by assigning me to protect the workers in the division."

"Ah. That makes sense. Got to keep the little woman happy or she won't put in the long hours that division demands of its workers. I thought perhaps you had done something heroic to get yourself noticed."

"No, sir."

"I understand you have been extra vigilant about security in the cubicle farm."

He shrugged. "Just looking out for Simone and her friend, Joy. But you know that, don't you?"

"Why do you say that?"

"Come on, sir. You're the one who slipped microphones and cameras into their work spaces each night."

"How do you know I'm responsible?"

"Are you saying someone else has more authority and power in matters of security than you? You're monitoring all the employees to make sure they follow security protocols. How many people are you employing to watch the camera feeds and listen to the audio information you're gathering?"

Boudreaux's lips curved. "You're too smart for your own good, Porterfield."

"Am I wrong?"

"No. I have fifteen employees keeping track of everything going on."

"Where are they stationed?"

"In the red building on campus." He chuckled. "You're wreaking havoc over there, my friend. The guys have been complaining about the lack of information coming from your woman's area and now her friend's area."

"Tough. I don't want anyone spying on Simone or her friend. I'll keep removing bugs and cameras from their areas. Either stop spying on Simone or Dragon Alley can let both of us go."

"Drawing a line in the sand, huh?"

"It's a hard line, Boudreaux. Dragon Alley recruited Simone. If they don't trust her to do the work, she has better offers on the table. Your company is lucky to get her."

"What about you?"

He shrugged. "I'll go wherever Simone is. I can get a job anywhere. She's the brains. I'm the muscle. As long as she's happy, I'm happy."

"Noble of you. Doesn't bother you that your woman is brainy?"

"Are you kidding? I love it. She's amazing, and I'm blessed to have her in my life."

"That's nice to hear."

Nice. Jesse held back a wince. He hated that insipid word. "Should I expect a pink slip, sir?"

"No. I'll leave Ms. Kenyon's space free of unwanted devices and Ms. Walters' space."

"I appreciate it, sir."

"Don't clear my devices from other spaces, all right? You'll cost me too much money."

"Yes, sir. Do you still want me to serve as security for the Special Projects division, Mr. Boudreaux?"

"I'd be a fool not to take advantage of your keen interest in that area, wouldn't I? Report for duty on the fifth floor immediately. I'll let you know if I need to change your assignment."

"Yes, sir."

Jesse left the office and rode the elevator to the fifth floor. He checked in with Ms. Mulgraves before he went to Simone's office.

She glanced up, surprise on her face. "Something wrong?"

"Daley asked for me to be assigned to the Special Projects division for a couple of weeks."

"Interesting."

"Isn't it? I'll be around if you need me." He walked the hall, introducing himself to those he encountered on his rounds.

When he finished, Jesse stationed himself near the receptionist's desk and assessed each visitor to the floor. Most he recognized from other parts of the company. A few were outsiders.

As the afternoon progressed, Jesse continued to do rounds on the floor every half hour, varying the time by a few minutes for each round. By the time his shift ended, he wondered why he'd been assigned. Was Daley expecting trouble or was he monitoring Jesse?

A few minutes after their shift ended, Simone emerged from her office with her backpack draped over one shoulder and locked her office door.

Jesse took the pack. "Ready to go?"

She nodded. "I'm starving. I hope we have something quick to prepare."

"We'll come up with something."

Daley intercepted them on the way to the elevator. "Well, how was your first afternoon in our division?" he asked Simone.

"Fun."

He stared. "Really? You enjoyed your work?"

"I love an enjoyable challenge, Mr. Daley. Today's assignments were more in line with what I'd been expecting at Dragon Alley."

"Did you finish everything?"

"Of course." She smiled. "Did you expect me not to?"

"Frankly, yes."

"Guess this is your lucky day."

The division head looked thoughtful. "I believe you're right." He glanced at Jesse. "I trust your day was uneventful."

"Yes, sir. Thanks for asking me to protect your division. It's an honor, sir."

"I read your background file. Very impressive, Mr. Porterfield. You're exactly who we need to watch over us for two weeks."

"I appreciate the vote of confidence, Mr. Daley."

After a curt nod, Daley stepped aside. "I won't hold you any longer. Good job today, both of you. See you tomorrow."

Jesse escorted Simone onto the elevator and rode to the first floor. They signed out with the receptionist. As they walked toward their SUV, Jesse said, "Since we're both tired today, would you like to go out for dinner?"

"As long as I don't have to dress up, I'm all for it."

"We'll stop at a restaurant I saw at the edge of town. I asked Joy about it earlier today. She recommended the food."

"Sold."

He unlocked the SUV and set Simone in the passenger seat. Jesse leaned over and kissed Simone, slow and sweet. "I'm considering this our first official date," he murmured.

Simone kissed the hollow behind his ear.

Jesse shivered, goosebumps of pleasure racing over his body. "You're potent, baby."

She laughed. "I have the same reaction every time you touch me." Simone buckled her seatbelt. "Come on. Let's go eat."

Jesse climbed behind the wheel, drove to the outskirts of Sayulita, and parked in the lot beside La Cocina de Siempre.

When they entered the restaurant, the scent of the spicy food sent his taste buds into overdrive. At his request, the hostess escorted them to the back table in the corner. He seated Simone and took his own seat with his back against the wall.

He scanned the menu, made his selection, and turned his attention to the other occupants of the restaurant. The place was packed with people eating their meals with gusto, all except for the occupants of one table toward the front of the restaurant. Jesse recognized three members of the Special Projects division. Beckett Francen, Wyatt Hatcher, and Allison Norbert. Allison, obviously upset, was being comforted by Francen. Hatcher kept shoveling in food like he was afraid someone would take away his plate before he finished.

"What's wrong, Jesse?"

He turned his attention back to Simone. "Francen, Hatcher, and Norbert are sitting at a table near the front. Norbert looks pretty upset."

"Wonder what's wrong?"

"Don't know but she seemed uptight all afternoon. I passed her twice in the hall. The rest of the time she stayed in her office or Francen's."

"If they're still here by the time we leave, we should say hello."

They gave the server their orders and soon were digging into their own meals. "Joy was right," Jesse said. "The food here is amazing. I'll have a hard time eating Tex-Mex food after this."

"We should get original Mexican recipes and try to make the food ourselves."

"Might be a lot of work."

"Worth it if the food tastes this good."

Near the end of their meal, Allison left her table and headed for the restrooms.

"An opportunity just dropped in my lap," Simone said. "I'll be back in a minute."

"Be careful."

"Yep." She rose and followed Allison at a distance to the women's restroom.

While she was gone, Jesse monitored Allison's companions. The two men immediately got involved in a heated argument.

Five minutes later, Allison returned to the table and Francen and Hatcher left the restaurant with her.

Simone dropped into her seat.

"How did it go?" Jesse asked.

"Interesting. Allison is feeling the pressure of not being able to find a solution to a programming issue at work, one she can't talk about. I offered to help, but she said the program was top secret and she couldn't accept any help."

"I'm wondering if she's been getting help from Francen off the books."

"Same. Whatever the problem is, Allison is afraid she'll get fired if she can't come up with a solution."

He hoped that was the least of her worries. Allison was a security risk. She knew too much about the project, whatever it was. If the person who commissioned her to write this program felt the risk was too great to leave her still breathing, Allison could be in big trouble.

If she was working on the target program. She could be working on something else highly classified but not related to the program he and Simone wanted to prevent from being finished and sold.

"I think I'll stop by her office tomorrow and check on her," Simone said. "Hopefully, I can form a friendship with her."

"She'd appreciate the gesture, especially since you're the only two women in the division besides Ms. Mulgraves." He finished the rest of his water. "Are you ready to go?"

Simone nodded. "Thanks for thinking of this restaurant. We'll have to come back before we leave town."

"If we can."

"Well, if not, we'll find those authentic recipes and try some new dishes ourselves."

"Deal."

After paying their bill, Jesse escorted Simone from the restaurant.

"Help! Somebody help," a man shouted.

Jesse scanned the parking lot and saw Francen and Hatcher standing over a figure sprawled on the ground. Wrapping his hand around Simone's, they ran to the two men. "What's the problem?"

"Allison collapsed on the way to her car," Francen said. "I don't know what's wrong with her."

Jesse dropped to his knees and checked Allison's pulse.

Nothing.

He glanced at Simone. "Can you do CPR?"

"Yeah." She hurried to kneel on Allison's other side.

Jesse said, "Francen, call for help. Tell the dispatcher Allison might have been drugged."

"Drugged?" The man looked distraught. "How? We were with her the whole time."

"We'll figure that out later. Call for help right now." He started chest compressions with Simone forcing air into Allison's lungs every few seconds.

When Simone wavered a few minutes later, Jesse looked at Francen. "Take over for Simone. Did you call for help?"

"Yeah, I did. They said it would be ten minutes or more. There's a big accident on the other side of town tying up all their resources."

Too long. "Simone, grab my mike bag in the back of the SUV."

She rushed off and returned seconds later with his medical supplies.

Hoping he wasn't making a huge mistake that might land him in jail, Jesse said, "Hatcher, take over for me."

"What? I don't know how to do that," the programmer protested.

"On-the-job training. Get down here."

With reluctance, Hatcher knelt beside Jesse. "Show me."

He demonstrated, talking through his compressions for a few beats, then said, "You try." When he was positive Hatcher had gotten the hang of it, Jesse thrust his hand into his mike bag and pulled out Narcan.

Before he administered the drug, Jesse checked Allison's pupils. When he tried to rouse the woman with no success, he felt he didn't have a choice. He sprayed the medicine into her nose and waited.

In less than a minute, Allison moaned.

"Hold the CPR," Jesse snapped as he watched the woman on the ground. "Allison, can you hear me?"

Another moan.

"Come on, sugar. Time to wake up and show us your pretty eyes."

She blinked.

"There you are." He smiled at her. "How do you feel?"

"Like a truck ran over me," she said, voice raspy. "Why does my chest hurt?"

"That's quite the story. Your friends saved your life."

Her eyes widened. "I don't understand."

"You went into cardiac arrest and collapsed. Your friends administered CPR and saved your life."

Her eyes filled with tears as she looked up at Francen. "Thank you, Beckett. You, too, Wyatt. I don't understand what happened. I just had a physical last week. Everything was perfect."

"What you do in your off time isn't my business, but you almost died. I need you to answer my question honestly. I'm not a cop so I can't arrest you."

"For what?"

"Taking drugs."

"What?"

"Did you take any drugs, Allison? Be honest. The doctors at the hospital will have to know in order to treat you properly."

"I don't take drugs. I barely take medicine at all, just for the occasional headache."

"What did you give her?" Francen demanded. "She woke up almost immediately."

"Narcan."

Shock filled the other man's gaze. "Are you serious?"

"Afraid so. Based on the symptoms Allison exhibited, I think she overdosed on a drug, maybe fentanyl or cocaine."

"But I don't do drugs," Allison protested. "I swear."

"If you don't, then someone close to you in the past few minutes deliberately dosed you with fentanyl. The drug is so powerful, it wouldn't take much."

"I took nothing. I swear." Tears leaked from her eyes.

"I believe you. Listen, when the ambulance takes you to the hospital, you need to tell the paramedics and the doctor that you might have been exposed to fentanyl or cocaine, and you had one dose of Narcan."

"How did you have Narcan on you?"

"Besides being in security, I'm also a medic. I always carry a mike bag wherever I go, and Narcan is standard equipment."

Sirens sounded close by. Jesse breathed easier. Excellent. As long as the hospital wasn't too far away, Allison had a good chance. "I need to get going, Allison. You should be fine now."

"Thanks, Jesse. I can't thank you enough for what you did."

"It was a group effort." Jesse squeezed her hand briefly. "See you later."

When he stood, Francen shook his hand. "Thanks, man. I owe you."

"Just take care of her, all right? If the doctor releases her tonight, don't let her go home alone. She needs someone with her tonight."

"I'll take care of it myself."

"Good. Do me a favor?"

"Anything."

"Don't mention my role in this, all right? I'd rather not have to spend most of my night at the police station."

"You got it."

Jesse clapped him on the shoulder, nodded at Hatcher, snagged his mike bag, and ushered Simone to their vehicle. He lifted her to the passenger seat and jogged around to the driver's side. He didn't want to be here to answer awkward questions by the cops.

"Are you sure we should leave them?" Simone asked. "What if Allison needs your help again?"

"The EMTs should be able to help her. Besides, if we stay, we'll end up at the police station answering questions all night. With the drugs and ammunition I've got in my bags, I will more than likely end up in jail."

She blew out a breath. "That wouldn't be good."

"We have to stay out of the hands of the local police, Simone." If they didn't, the authorities would toss them in jail and throw away the keys.

Jesse drove squares for 30 minutes to be sure he didn't lead anyone back to the safe house. When he was satisfied they didn't have a tail, he turned the last square and headed for their temporary house.

After parking in the back, he entered the house and searched for signs of intrusion. Nothing. He breathed easier as he returned to the vehicle for Simone. "Clear. Let's get inside."

"Worried?"

"Oh, yeah. I don't like that someone tried to kill Allison Norbert."

"Do you think she's the one assigned to create the virus?"

"I'm not sure if it's Allison or Beckett."

"That's why you told Beckett to stay with her. Protection for both of them."

"Can't think of a better way other than assigning someone to guard their six, and we don't have the resources available to keep them safe."

"Maybe we should encourage them to go on a long, extended vacation to a tropical island."

"If I thought they would go, I'd do it. Unfortunately, if one of them is working on the computer virus, they won't be allowed to leave if the work is unfinished."

He grabbed his bags from the back of the vehicle and escorted Simone to the house and locked the door.

After storing the bags in his room, he returned to find his girl already booting up her laptop. "What's the plan for the night?"

"Checking the results from the bots. We're running out of time."

Before he could reply, his cell phone rang. Jesse glanced at the screen and frowned. "It's Jesse. What's wrong?"

"That little weasel Trevor White has escaped."

Chapter Thirteen

Simone's eyes widened. "Trevor's missing? I thought the mercenaries had him locked down."

Jesse looked disgusted. "Yeah, so did I. Turns out he's as slippery and sly as you said. He got his hands on a knife, stabbed one mercenary in the chest, and escaped. They were so busy saving their teammate they didn't stop Trevor from bolting into the countryside."

She groaned. "Will the mercenary be all right?"

"The doc at the hospital said he'd be fine, but he's in for a two-week hospital stay."

"Good grief. The damage must have been extensive."

"Your ex punctured this mercenary's lung and nicked his heart."

Her stomach twisted into a knot. "Man, I hope Trevor stays away from us. He could cause major trouble if he finds us."

"Yeah, he could. We'll have to come up with a plausible excuse for your name change if he shows his face in Sayulita."

She thought about the possibilities and decided the simplest explanation might be the best. "I changed my name and left San Francisco to get away from Trevor."

"I'll call Zane so he's aware that he might receive a phone call to verify the information. Need coffee?"

"Water."

"Coming right up." He grabbed two bottles of water and handed one to Simone. "I'll be back in a minute."

She dove into her research, pulling up data on Griffin Daley first. Her eyebrows rose at the number of classified projects he'd headed over the years. The man had a knack for being in the right place at the right time to snag prime government contracts. He'd been recruited away from a think tank in Seattle, Washington five years earlier and hadn't looked back.

Of all the computer programmers, Daley was the one to draw the largest salary and sweetest benefits package. Her temporary boss would never have to worry about his retirement. He had money stashed in various countries in several accounts. No scuttlebutt about him or his work except many sources reported that he'd sell his own mother for a buck.

She switched to reading the results gathered on Patrick Meyers. Nothing raised a red flag except he begged for overtime and moonlighted to pay for his children's Ivy league education.

Trouble in paradise, though. His wife had recently returned to the States with no return date.

She moved on to Wyatt Hatcher. He was ambitious and angry to be passed over for promotion to the head of the Special Projects division. He felt as though the job had been snatched away from him and given to Daley. Definitely not a team player. Simone frowned. Was he angry enough to undermine the targeted project, or the programmer assigned to that task?

Not the project itself, she decided. Hatcher was the type to wipe out the competition and leave the way clear for him to sail in and take all the glory. What better way to thumb his nose at Daley and the Dragon Alley executives?

Nothing in Hatcher's information said he was the culprit responsible for Allison's collapse but Simone wouldn't be surprised if it was true. If he was guilty, he must have been angry that Jesse forced him to help save Allison.

She blew out a breath. Speculation without proof was pointless. She could lead herself and Jesse down the wrong path. For the moment, she stuck Hatcher at the top of her suspect list and moved on to Allison Norbert.

Simone scanned the information on the other woman, her brow furrowing. She was good but nothing to write home about. Why had Allison been tapped to join the Special Projects division?

A good track record at five big-name tech companies but she wanted to get away from a terrible relationship, a familiar problem. Five months into her employment contract with Dragon Alley, her divorce from her husband of ten years was finalized.

As she read further, Simone ran across an interesting fact about Allison and Bastien Boudreax. The two had dated until two months ago when Allison broke up with him and moved on to Beckett Francen.

"Got something?" Jesse said. He dropped into the seat across the table from her.

"Allison and Bastien Boudreax dated until two months ago when Allison dumped him for Beckett."

"Interesting. Wonder why Allison and Bastien broke up?"

"Don't know. Maybe you can find out."

He snorted. "Don't bet on it. Boudreax isn't my biggest fan."

"Why not? You're good at your job."

"He only knows what my cover story shows, and he didn't select me to be an employee. The CEO of Dragon Alley foisted me on him. Besides, Boudreax was Special Forces. He's not impressed with a former military police officer with no special skills. He won't make me his best friend and confidante."

"His loss."

"That leaves digging into Allison and Bastien's relationship up to you. Should be relatively easy to talk to her. You have a reason to ask her how she's feeling."

"Wonder if she'll be at work tomorrow?"

"I hope not," Jesse said. "Her body needs time to recover."

"How did you know she was drugged?"

"Restricted pupils, slower heart rate, acting drunk although she hadn't consumed alcohol. All are classic signs of drug poisoning. She responded immediately to the Narcan as well."

"She said she doesn't take drugs except for the occasional headache. Do you believe her?"

"I didn't see evidence of drug abuse but I only did a quick assessment."

"Well, if she didn't take a drug herself, then someone poisoned her. If you hadn't been there, she would have died. Wyatt and Beckett didn't know what to do for her. Jesse, I think you're right. Someone tried to kill her."

"The question is, why?"

"To get rid of a weak link."

"If so, they'll keep trying until they succeed. Did you find out anything about her that raises a red flag?"

"Allison is good at her job but she's not exceptional."

Jesse glanced up. "DA hires the top in their field."

"There has to be some connection in her background to one of the upper echelon people at Dragon Alley. Otherwise, Allison would have washed out in the applicant pool. She doesn't stand out enough to grab the attention of human resources or Griffin Daley."

Simone went to the refrigerator for another bottle of water. "What did Zane have to say?"

"First, he'll be ready for an inquiry about the name change. Second, he found a street camera that glimpsed the vehicle speeding out of the restaurant's parking lot last night."

She settled behind her computer again. "Anything come of it?"

"About what you'd expect. The plates were stolen from another vehicle, and the vehicle itself was reported stolen a few hours before the incident."

"So we have nothing."

"I'm afraid so." He booted up his computer. "The only thing Zane could tell me was the driver wasn't drunk."

Simone's blood ran cold. "The driver deliberately tried to run us down?"

"Looks like it. After he drove from the restaurant parking lot, the driver's skills improved dramatically."

"Someone knows about us."

"Maybe. So far, the incidents are spread out. Not everything is pointed directly at you or me."

"This might be farfetched, but is it possible Trevor was the driver? We didn't know he was in town but someone told him where I was. Maybe he followed us to the restaurant."

Jesse frowned. "It's possible. I didn't see anyone who stood out, but I wasn't looking for a tail either. I didn't think it mattered if someone from DA followed us to the restaurant."

"I'll keep looking through the information I found on Allison and do the same with Beckett. After that, I think I need to turn my attention to the person who's been ratting me out to Trevor."

"Have any ideas?"

Her gut clenched. Simone hoped she was wrong. "A few. I'll let you know when I confirm."

She returned her attention to her computer screen and read more on Allison. Nothing out of the ordinary popped up except for one interesting bit of information. Allison was friends with Sophie Westlake, the vice president of Dragon Alley. "Got something."

"What is it?"

"Sophie Westlake and Allison are friends. I bet that's why she was hired for the Special Projects division."

"I'll run a background check on Westlake. Keep working on Allison and Beckett."

"Are you working on something else?"

"Trying to find your ex-boyfriend."

She grimaced. "Good luck. He knows how to hide."

Jesse grabbed his phone and sent a text. He received a reply seconds later. "Zane will work on cleaning up the image of the driver, then run a comparison to Trevor's photo."

"Think he'll be able to do it?"

"It's a long shot."

If Zane cleaned up the image enough to identify the driver, she and Jesse might have an idea who was targeting them.

When she finished reading the information on Allison, Simone switched to Beckett Francen. Single, no ties to family, all about gaming. A genius according to his friends, coworkers, and former employers.

Huh. Sounds like he would have been a good one to tap for the program Simone was targeting. Had she been wrong? Perhaps Beckett was the one writing the program, not Allison.

No criminal activity in Beckett's official background check. Time to check the dark web for the unofficial check. Five minutes in, her eyebrows rose. So, Beckett had hacker tendencies even back in high school. She shook her head, recognizing the same tricks she'd used at that age. The interesting thing was Beckett didn't change his own grades. He changed the grade of his girlfriend so she could graduate on time with him.

No, Beckett hadn't needed to change his own grades. The man had made straight A's from the time he started school at age five.

She rolled her eyes. Must be nice. She'd earned every A the hard way, through hours and hours of study. The only thing she'd been good at was computers. Knowing she needed scholarships to afford college, Simone had applied herself to her studies and her part-time job while her friends were out partying. No surprise that she'd lost touch with all but two of them.

Beckett had skated by with a one-week suspension and a reprimand from his principal for the grade-changing incident, but he'd been allowed to graduate, anyway. A week later, he left for college and never looked back.

Three of the best tech companies in the world hired him, and he'd resigned the last job to take on his present role in Dragon Alley.

As she continued to read, Simone caught hints of some unrequited love for Allison while she dated Bastien. When she wised up and dumped him, she turned to Beckett who broke out of the friend zone. If he was a good guy, good for them.

According to the dark web scuttlebutt, Beckett was the go-to guy for unique projects at Dragon Alley.

Simone's gut twisted. Did that mean he was the programmer she and Jesse were looking for? And if so, did Allison know about the project? Would they have discussed the details, making her a loose end to snip off because she was skittish?

She sat back, studying the screen. Looked like she needed to talk to Allison as soon as possible. "Have you looked into Bastien's background?"

Jesse glanced at her. "Not yet. He's next on my list. I'm still looking into Sophie Westlake's background."

"I'll do a preliminary run on Bastien while you finish your check on Sophie."

Twenty minutes later, Jesse's cell phone signaled an incoming message. He checked the screen and surged to his feet. "We've got company."

Chapter Fourteen

Jesse turned out the lights in the kitchen and went to the back door, easing aside the curtain over the window and peering into the darkness.

Who could be here at this time of night? For that matter, who knew where they were living? He'd been careful not to tell anyone where they were staying. No sign of movement out in the backyard.

"Who's here?"

"Iona couldn't tell anything except that it's a man. He's wearing a baseball cap pulled low over his forehead. Monitor the backyard."

Simone closed her computer lid and took Jesse's place.

"Don't open the door for anyone, sweetheart. If someone shows up back here, let me know but stay out of sight."

He walked to the living room and tugged aside the curtain just enough to see out. Their visitor was walking up the walkway to the front door, cap pulled low enough so his face was in shadow. His walk, though, was familiar.

With a scowl, Jesse unlocked the door and opened it. "What are you doing here?" he demanded.

Sawyer Chapman's eyebrows rose. "Some greeting. Why are you so grumpy?"

Jesse stared at his teammate. "You're supposed to be on vacation."

"So are you." Sawyer stepped inside and closed the door. "Why aren't you sunning yourself on some beach and watching the babes in bikinis?"

"Simone is here."

"And?" Sawyer's eyes twinkled.

"She's the only babe I want to watch in a bikini."

"Does she know that?"

"She does," Simone said as she walked into the room. "And she appreciates his excellent taste." She hugged Sawyer. "What are you doing here?"

"Came to lend a hand. Brent told me you were undercover. Figured Jesse wouldn't let you out of his sight. Mind if I stick around to keep the two of you out of trouble?"

"You didn't answer our question," Jesse said. Something was wrong. Sawyer had big plans for his vacation time. He shouldn't be back in the States yet much less here in Sayulita. "Sawyer, you know you're always welcome but why aren't you still on vacation."

"A long story for later." He set his Go bag by the door. "Bring me up to speed."

Yep, something was up. Later, Jesse would dig into it and find out what brought Sawyer home early. "Coffee?"

"Thought you'd never ask. Who's on watch?"

"Iona and Tegan from Artemis."

"No kidding. Didn't they make me coming up to the house?"

"How do you think I knew you were here before you rang the bell?"

A curt nod. "Glad to hear you have backup."

"Come to the kitchen," Simone said. "We'll make coffee and talk."

"Thanks." Sawyer glared at Jesse. "At least someone appreciates me being here."

"Did I say I didn't want you here?" he protested. Sheesh. Question a guy over cutting his vacation short, and look at the reaction he got? "You needed the vacation, Sawyer. I feel bad that you cut short your time away on our account."

"I'm fine. I told Brent as much. Although he didn't believe me, the boss agreed to let me come down here to give you a hand."

Simone finished prepping the coffeemaker and turned to lean her back against the counter. "How will we explain your sudden appearance in Sayulita?"

Sawyer shrugged. "Easy. If someone sees me and questions you, tell him I'm Jesse's brother or his best friend from his military days."

"The latter works better," Jesse said. "Why is my best friend visiting me now?"

Sawyer's expression grew grim. "After a nasty breakup, I needed to get away for a while."

Yeah, definitely trouble in paradise. He'd see what he could get out of his friend after Simone went to bed.

When the coffee finished its brewing cycle, Simone poured steaming liquid into two mugs. She opted for another bottle of water.

"Tell me what's been happening."

Jesse and Simone spent several minutes recounting what they'd learned and heard. "That's about it," Simone said, running her fingers through her hair.

"You have almost nothing."

"Except someone is targeting us, and now he's gone after Allison."

"Assuming it's the same person." Sawyer cradled the mug between his palms. "With Simone's ex-boyfriend in the area, I wonder if he might be responsible for the scare at the restaurant."

Jesse nodded. "Zane is working on the photo he captured of the vehicle and driver. However, the picture is poor quality."

"Doesn't have to be crystal clear, just enough to identify him."

"And if it was Trevor?" Simone asked. "What then? He's out there somewhere, waiting to get back at me for his prison time."

"I'll find him, Simone," Jesse said.

"We'll find him," Sawyer corrected him. "You're not alone in this now."

"I appreciate the help."

His friend inclined his head. "So, you going to tell the lady assassins outside that I'm a friendly so I don't have a knife in my gut when I least expect it?"

"Good idea." Jesse slid out his phone and sent a text to Iona.

Simone's eyebrows rose. "They wouldn't do that, would they?"

"In a heartbeat." Sawyer shook his head. "Those women are as tough as anyone I've ever met or worked with. If they believed I posed a danger to you or Jesse, they'd slip in here and cut my throat before I knew I was being stalked."

She stared. "You're serious."

"Very."

"Wow."

Jesse's phone signaled an incoming text. He glanced at the screen and snorted. "Iona said the only reason they didn't follow you inside was because Tegan thought she recognized you and you owe her dinner. She expects you to pay up soon."

Sawyer laughed. "Pass the word to Tegan that I haven't forgotten. I'm making plans."

Well, now, this was interesting. "Why don't I know about this?"

"Contrary to your own belief, you don't know everything, Jesse."

He rested a hand over his heart. "I'm shocked. Hasn't Brody told you repeatedly that I know all and see all?"

His friend rolled his eyes. "Dream on. Our team leader can't pull the wool over my eyes like that."

"Are you going to tell the class why you owe Tegan dinner?"

"None of your business."

Jesse pointed at him. "That's a challenge. I accept."

"Waste of time." Sawyer turned to Simone. "Who do you think is writing the program we're hunting?"

"I thought it was Allison. Now, I'm not so sure."

"Why?"

"Although Allison is good at her job, she doesn't stand out in the field and never has. Yes, she worked for high-powered tech companies but she didn't make a name for herself. Every job she landed was because she knew someone in the company, not because she was exceptional at her job. I can't find a reason for her to snag the attention of Griffin Daley or the human resources department at Dragon Alley. Based on credentials alone, she shouldn't be making as much in salary as she is."

"Who's your top candidate for the programmer?"

"Beckett Francen, Allison's boyfriend. Unlike Allison, Beckett is brilliant and has raked in accolades in the tech field since he was in high school. He's gotten better each year." Simone frowned. "I like Beckett. He seems like a good guy."

"That's what the friends and neighbors of serial killers say, too."

She glared at him. "I can't see him as a traitor. Nothing in his background or the things I found on the dark web show his loyalty to the US is for sale."

"He also appeared genuinely upset about Allison," Jesse said. "He was the one calling for help in the parking lot and willing to do anything to save his girlfriend. I had to force Wyatt Hatcher to help Beckett do CPR while I used Narcan on Allison. Wyatt wasn't happy about it."

"Maybe he's squeamish," Simone said.

"Maybe he didn't want Allison to survive," Sawyer said. "All right. Let's say you're right about Beckett being our target programmer. How do we prove it? How do we find out if he's doing the work under duress? That will be the game changer for law enforcement."

"We should talk to him and Allison," Simone said.

"If he's been willing to write the program, then what?" Jesse asked. "Once we tip our hand, our cover is blown. Francen won't keep that information to himself."

"We could ask Artemis to sit on the couple for the duration of our mission." Sawyer finished his coffee and rose to pour himself another mug of the brew. "Or ask Fortress to send a team to pick them up and take them to the States for further interrogation or for their own protection, depending on their roles."

"I believe Beckett is doing this because he's being forced," Simone insisted. "No proof, just a gut feeling."

Sawyer shrugged. "Only one way to find out."

"What are you suggesting?" Jesse asked. Unfortunately, he had a good idea.

"You said Allison is in the hospital."

"As far as I know, that's correct."

"You have access to Dragon Alley's employment records. Get Beckett's cell number and call him to find out where they are."

Simone returned to her laptop. "I'll look it up." Less than a minute later, she rattled off the numbers.

Jesse made the call.

Beckett Francen answered on the second ring. "Francen."

"It's Jesse Porterfield. I wanted to check on Allison."

"She'll be fine, thanks to you. I owe you. Anything you need, I'm there." His voice cracked with emotion.

"What was she drugged with? Do they know yet?"

"They think it was cocaine but the blood tests haven't come back yet and won't for a while. They're keeping Allison overnight to be sure she has no more problems."

"You're staying with her?"

"If someone tries to kick me out, he'll have a fight on his hands."

"Are you at Hospital Angeles?"

"Yeah. Allison is in Room 234."

"Mind if I stop by?"

"Of course not." He gave a short laugh. "Maybe you can help me figure out what the doctor and nurses are saying. I'm not the best at speaking Spanish."

"No problem. See you in a few minutes." He ended the call and glanced at Simone. "You want to come with me?"

"Definitely. I might convince Beckett to talk if he clams up on you."

"We should go now. We might have to sneak into the room. I'm not sure what their visiting hours are."

Sawyer rose and helped Simone to her feet. "This should be interesting."

Jesse hoped this visit would net them the information they needed. Simone was right. They were running out of time, and Beckett and Allison might not survive the next attempt to kill them.

#

Chapter Fifteen

Simone walked into the hospital with Jesse and Sawyer. No one stopped them when they crossed the lobby and stepped onto the elevator.

On the second floor, they walked down the corridor to Allison's room and knocked lightly on the door.

Seconds later, Beckett Francen opened the door. His eyes widened at the sight of the three of them standing in the hallway. "Hey."

"We brought our friend Sawyer with us," Jesse said.

"Come in. Allison, it's Simone and Jesse from work, and their friend." He motioned them inside the room.

Allison opened her eyes to look at the trio. She focused on Jesse. "Jesse, thank you. The doctor said you saved my life."

He walked to her bedside and took her hand. "No thanks needed. Are you feeling better?"

"Some. The doctor said I would be better in a couple of days. Right now, I'm tired, weak, and nauseated."

"When did he say you could return to work?"

Tears filled her eyes. "Not for three or four days. I'm afraid I'll be fired."

"You can't help what happened, baby," Beckett said. "It wasn't your fault. I'll tell Griffin what happened. He'll understand."

"You know how he is. He's driven by deadlines, and you can't turn in anything late without serious repercussions."

"I'll take care of it." Beckett leaned down and kissed her. "Trust me, okay? I'll make sure you don't lose your job."

"I didn't realize Griffin was such a bear," Simone said lightly. "Maybe I should have passed up the promotion to the Special Projects division."

Allison wiped tears from her face. "Don't let my experiences color your own. I heard Griff talking to your former boss about you. They have nothing but high praise for you and your work."

"That's nice to know. Listen, I heard you tell Jesse at the parking lot you don't take drugs."

"No, I don't. I swear. That isn't my thing. I don't even drink alcohol much less take illegal drugs."

"Same here. Since you didn't take the drugs voluntarily, do you have any idea who could have drugged you and why?"

Allison shook her head. "It makes little sense. Who would hate me so much that they would try to kill me?"

Beckett clasped her hand in his. His expression was grim. "You know who it is."

"Who?" Jesse asked. "I can help."

"How?"

"I'm in the security business, Beckett. Not only that, Boudreax assigned me to the Special Projects division as security today. I need to know what's going on, and I think you can give me information to help me protect you, Allison, and Simone."

The other man's eyes narrowed. "You were assigned to our division? Like as a guard to keep the prisoners in?"

"More like a bodyguard to keep you safe."

"You work for Griff, then," he said flatly.

"My job is to keep you and Allison safe. Daley requested me for the assignment but I don't work for him. I work for the division."

"Will you report this incident to him?"

"Should I?"

He shrugged.

"You'll have to tell him something when Allison doesn't show up for work."

"Or me. I'm not leaving Allison alone."

Time to push her coworkers a little more. "Beckett, do you think Griffin is responsible for what happened to Allison?" Simone asked. "If so, Jesse and his friend, Sawyer, can help you."

He looked miserable. "I don't think anyone can help me. All I care about is keeping Allison safe. She's innocent. I don't want her to suffer because she's dating me."

"You need help," Jesse murmured. "Both of you. I think Allison's poisoning was deliberate."

Allison gasped. "What?"

"If I'm right, the people responsible won't stop until you're dead."

"I don't understand why anyone would want to kill me. I haven't made enemies. You must be wrong."

"He's not," Beckett said flatly.

"Explain," Jesse demanded.

"It's my fault."

"How?" Allison clenched the blanket draped over her. "You have done nothing wrong."

"You know, Allison."

"You're wasting time," Sawyer snapped. "Do you want our help or not? If you don't, we'll leave you to face the enemy on your own."

"They're threatening Allison to keep you in line, aren't they?" Simone said. No other explanation fit because she didn't want to believe that Beckett was working for the wrong side.

Beckett gave a curt nod, his fingers threading through Allison's. "How did you know, Simone?"

"I looked into your background. Nothing shows you would resort to serious criminal activity to get ahead. Changing a grade is child's play compared to what you're working on now."

He stared. "You know about the project, don't you?"

"Yeah, we do," Jesse said.

"How? It's classified, and I have told no one." Beckett looked at each of them. "How do you know?"

"Anonymous source inside the company hired outside help to find and stop the program from being completed."

Beckett and Allison exchanged glances. "We're in over our heads," he said finally, turning back to Jesse. "I didn't know what they intended to do with the program. When I found out and wanted to quit, they threatened Allison. I didn't think they'd follow through."

"There's a lot of money riding on this program," Sawyer said. "They're serious."

Beckett closed his eyes a moment. "I wish Daley hadn't assigned the program to me."

"Is he the one coming after Allison?" Simone asked. She couldn't see Daley doing his own dirty work.

"He's behind it but I didn't see him at the restaurant tonight. He couldn't be the one who poisoned Allison."

"But he has plenty of people who would take care of it for him," Allison said. "What are we going to do?" she asked Jesse. "If you're right, Daley won't think twice about killing me or hurting Beckett to force him to finish the program."

"It's not finished yet?" Simone asked.

Beckett shook his head. "I've been dragging my feet, trying to think of a way out of this mess."

"What were you doing?"

"Deliberately making mistakes, fixing part of them, then having to go back and fix the rest." He looked unhappy. "Unfortunately, I'm out of ideas. If I don't think of some new bug to plant in the programming fast, I'll have to finish it in the next couple of days."

"Why did they ask you to write the program?"

He scowled. "Daley said I'm the most qualified programmer he has and the one he trusts the most."

"Do you know who the program will target?" Jesse asked.

"I didn't until a few days ago. I overheard one of Daley's phone conversations and almost lost it when I realized the program was going to be used against the US military and our contractors." Beckett sounded bitter. "By then it was too late to back out. I tried, and you see the result right here. I don't want Allison at risk because of me."

"Do you want help?"

Beckett's head whipped toward Jesse. "Are you serious?"

"Answer the question."

"Yes. A thousand times yes. But what can you do?"

"My job is to protect you and Allison, Beckett. Saving you both will require a relocation that might be permanent."

"Quitting our jobs?" Allison's eyes widened. "Is that really necessary?"

"How much do you want to live?" Sawyer asked.

"We'll do anything," Beckett said. "I want to have a life together with Allison."

"How much does your job matter to you?"

"Not enough to sacrifice the woman I love. I can find a job anywhere."

"Right answer." Sawyer looked at Jesse. "Artemis?"

"Until we arrange transport back to the states. Beckett, if Simone was in Allison's place, I'd leave this hospital as soon as she was stable and take her to a safe house until I arranged an escape from Mexico. Are you willing to go when and where we tell you?"

"The sooner, the better. I don't think Allison is safe here."

Alarm bells rang in Simone's mind. "Why do you say that?"

"I've seen the same orderly several times on the floor but he doesn't appear to be doing anything. How many times do you have to wash the same stretch of floor before it's clean and sanitized? Every time I leave the room, he's around and appears to be watching the door, almost like he's looking for a chance to get into the room."

"Describe him," Sawyer said.

"About five foot eight, medium build, dark hair and eyes, a Caucasian."

"Clothes?"

"Scrubs with running shoes."

"Any distinguishing features? No offense, but the guy you described could fit half the population of Sayulita."

"He has a scar on the right side of his neck, like someone tried to slice his throat and missed."

Sawyer left the room.

"Where's he going?" Allison asked.

"To find the orderly."

"He shouldn't go alone. What if the orderly is dangerous?"

"He can handle it," Jesse said.

"Who are you three? Why do I have the feeling you're not working for Dragon Alley just to have a job?"

Simone glanced at Jesse. How far could they trust Beckett and Allison? Believing the best of them was one thing. Trusting them to protect her and Jesse and the other operatives already involved in the case was another matter.

"We're not," Jesse admitted. "The three of us work for another company. Someone hired us to find the programmer and stop him from completing the job."

Beckett stiffened. "I shouldn't have talked to you. Please, don't hurt Allison. Do whatever you want with me, but don't hurt her. I'm begging you."

"I meant what I said earlier. I'm going to protect you. The best way to do that is to get you out of the line of fire."

"What does that mean for us?"

"A new job in another location."

"Dragon Alley has a long reach," Alison said. "If Daley and his cronies don't eliminate us, they'll blackball us. How will we make a living?"

"You let us worry about that. Your job is to get better and escape Mexico. We'll handle the rest."

"They won't give up," Beckett said. "They're tenacious."

"So are we. We'll create new identities for you."

"A fresh start." Allison pressed Beckett's hand against her cheek. "That's what we need. Please, say yes. We can't do this alone."

"How do we know we can trust them?"

Simone had the answer for that one. "If we wanted you dead, Jesse wouldn't have saved your life tonight, Allison. Jesse and his teammates are professionals. Killing you and your boyfriend would have been easy and accomplished in a matter of seconds. Jesse and his friends saved me a few weeks ago. I would trust them with my life any time."

"What choice do we have, Beckett?" Allison looked up at him. "I believe them."

Beckett watched Jesse for a beat, then said, "If you're lying to us, I will hunt you down and kill you."

Jesse inclined his head. "I understand. You won't have to resort to anything so drastic." He grabbed his phone and sent a text. He received a reply seconds later. "It's arranged."

"What do we do now?"

"First thing to do is get you and Allison out of here and into the safe house. From there, we'll work out the logistics to transport you from the country."

"We'll need our passports."

"You'll need new passports with false identities. I'll arrange for that as well." Jesse walked to the computer at the small desk near the bed and scanned the information on the screen. "You're being held overnight as a precaution, Allison. You aren't to receive any more medication. The doctor is satisfied with your progress and your prognosis. Leaving the hospital now won't affect your recovery."

"Are you sure?" Beckett asked. "I don't want to risk Allison's health."

"I'm positive. Besides, if she has a problem, I'll be less than five minutes away. I have the medication on hand that Allison needs if she has a relapse."

"How do we get past the orderly?" Allison asked. "I'm not strong enough to run."

"We'll carry you. Leave the orderly to us. We'll handle him."

Simone patted Allison's hand. "This is what Jesse and his friends do. You can trust them to handle any crisis."

Sawyer returned. He shook his head. "Didn't see the orderly on the floor. He left behind his mop and bucket, though."

"We're taking Allison and Beckett to Artemis."

His eyebrows shot up. "You think that's wise?"

"Have a better idea until we fly them out of Mexico?"

"Got me there. How will we do this?"

"Monitor the hallway while we get Allison situated. Beckett, be honest with me. Can you carry your girlfriend from the hospital to our SUV in the parking lot? If you can't, it's no shame. Once we leave this room, we may not have time for someone else to take her from you."

"I can do it."

"Can you carry her on the run?"

He hesitated. "I've never tried that."

"We need two armed people just in case," Sawyer said from the doorway. "Safety protocol."

Simone tugged away the blanket covering Allison, thankful she still wore street clothes. "Come on. Let's see if you can sit up. We need to go before the orderly returns."

She and Beckett helped Allison sit up on the side of the bed. The other woman swayed a moment, then steadied. "Ready to get out of here?"

Allison nodded. "Let's go. I feel like my skin is crawling. Something is going to happen. I know it."

"Then let's not linger and give the enemy a chance to target you again," Jesse said. "Sawyer?"

"Clear for the moment. I'm with Allison. My gut says trouble is coming."

Beckett bent and scooped Allison into his arms. "Ready."

Sawyer took the lead with Beckett and Allison behind him. Simone and Jesse brought up the rear. Instead of heading for the elevator, Sawyer led them to the back stairwell. He held up a fist when he reached the door. "Wait," he whispered and opened the door a crack. When nothing happened, he slipped into the stairwell and returned seconds later. "Clear."

As they followed him into the stairwell, Simone couldn't help but think they were sitting ducks if the orderly appeared with a gun in his hands. Good thing they were only on the second floor.

Sawyer went through the same procedure at the exit door except he disabled the alarm so it wouldn't ring and alert the hospital staff that the outer door had been opened.

He led the way out into the parking lot. Halfway to the SUV, a couple of men dressed as orderlies barreled from the exit door and raced toward the small entourage. Two more men ran from the front entrance and spread out while racing toward them.

"Keep moving," Sawyer said.

"Simone." Jesse handed her the key fob. "Get them inside the SUV as fast as possible. Stay focused."

"Got it. Come on, Beckett. This way."

"What about the orderlies chasing us?"

"Jesse and Sawyer will handle them. You'll be safer inside the SUV. It has several safety features normal cars don't."

Gunfire broke out.

Allison pressed her face to Beckett's neck but didn't scream.

Although Simone longed to help Jesse and Sawyer, her presence would be a distraction, and she had a job to do.

When they were a few feet from the vehicle, she unlocked the doors. "Into the back, Beckett."

Sirens sounded in the distance. Oh, no. Being detained by the local police was out of the question. She could imagine the questions because of the weapons Sawyer and Jesse carried. They couldn't use Fortress's name to help smooth the way so they needed to get out of here before the police showed up.

Simone climbed behind the wheel and cranked the engine. She backed from the parking space and headed toward Jesse who was the closest of the two men. Bullets plunked against the vehicle but none of them penetrated the doors. She skidded to a stop beside Jesse.

He yanked open the door and jumped in. "Go to Sawyer," he said as he lowered the window and aimed at the closest gunman. Jesse pulled the trigger. A second later, the gunman flew back and hit the ground. He didn't move.

Simone raced through the parking lot toward Sawyer, praying no one else was in the parking lot. Bullets flew everywhere. Windows in cars shattered. A few tires went flat. Car alarms screeched, adding to the cacophony.

She slammed on the brakes beside Sawyer who climbed into the back with Allison and Beckett. "Go, go, go!"

Simone floored the accelerator pedal and raced for the closest exit. "Where to?"

"Turn left onto the street," Jesse said as he dropped the empty magazine from his Sig and loaded a fresh one. He and Sawyer aimed at the two remaining gunmen. Four shots later, the gunmen were no longer a threat. "Drive the speed limit. We don't want to be seen racing away from the hospital."

"Do we have to worry about those gunmen tailing us?"

"No," Sawyer said, his voice grim. "They won't be going anywhere except to the morgue or to surgery."

"As soon as I'm sure we're safe, I'll have you pull over so we can check the vehicle for trackers," Jesse said. "Right now, though, it's better to be sure we have firepower available in case of another ambush."

"I hope not. I don't want to drive through a hail of bullets again."

Jesse chuckled. "Didn't like the excitement?"

"Not a fan. How do you guys deal with this all the time?"

"Training and experience," Sawyer said. "Want to join the black ops arm of our company?"

"No, thanks. I'll stick to being a keyboard warrior. You can have all the adrenaline rushes you want."

"Chicken."

"You bet."

Simone drove for another thirty minutes, taking turns as Jesse directed until she didn't know where they were.

"I don't think we have a tail," Jesse said. "Pull over at the hotel and park around the back. I need to check the SUV for trackers."

She did as instructed and gladly handed the key fob to Sawyer. "It's all yours with my blessings."

"You did good, kid. Thanks for saving my bacon out there."

"All part of the service." She hopped out of the vehicle and took Sawyer's place in the back with Beckett and Allison.

Jesse climbed in the passenger seat again. "All clear. Let's get out of here, Sawyer."

He drove from behind the hotel and onto a side street. For the next few minutes, Sawyer took turn after turn. Finally, he drove toward the safe house.

Finally, Sawyer drove around the back of a small villa and parked. "End of the line," he announced. "Stay put until we return." He and Jesse climbed out and closed the doors.

"Why can't we go inside?" Allison asked.

"Jesse and Sawyer will make sure it's safe. They won't take long."

"Aren't you afraid?"

"Terrified," she admitted. "But I've seen Jesse and his teammates in action. They know what they're doing."

"You know what will happen when Allison and I disappear," Beckett said.

"I have a good idea."

"Don't take the job, Simone. These guys mean business."

"This is the only way to stop them from finishing the program and selling it to our enemies."

"I hope you know what you're doing."

So did she.

Chapter Sixteen

Soon, Jesse returned, opened the door, and helped Simone from the vehicle. "Straight to the back door. Rayne is waiting for you."

"What about you?"

"I'll come in as soon as Allison and Beckett are safe." He kissed her lightly and nudged her toward the villa.

As she approached, Rayne smiled. "Welcome to our villa."

"We got a bungalow. How did you rate a villa?"

The other woman laughed. "Luck of the draw."

"Or maybe we scared the tech geek at Fortress enough that he gave us a really sweet safe house," another woman said.

Simone walked into a warm, welcoming kitchen. She glanced at everything. "Wow. This is amazing."

"Pretty sweet, isn't it," said the second woman. "Hi, I'm Violet."

"I'm Simone. Thanks for helping us out tonight."

Violet shrugged. "It's what we do."

"Where's Riley?"

"Outside, protecting your friends from Dragon Alley."

Beckett walked inside the villa, carrying Allison.

"This way," Rayne said. "The living room has a comfortable couch."

Jesse and Sawyer walked in and locked the door behind them.

Simone trembled. She knew what it was, but that didn't make the adrenaline dump less annoying.

Jesse wrapped his arms around her and eased her against his chest. "You okay?"

"I will be."

"Adrenaline dump?"

She nodded.

"You were amazing tonight, sweetheart. You kept your head when things were chaotic outside the hospital."

"Ha. If you were inside my head, you would have heard me screaming in terror."

"But you didn't freeze. You did what had to be done and saved all of us."

Uncomfortable with the praise, she changed the subject. "How long will this adrenaline dump last?"

"Not long. You'll want a flat surface to sleep on in about 30 minutes."

She wrinkled her nose. "Lovely." Simone shuddered again.

Jesse pulled her closer and trailed a hand up and down her back. "We'll return to the safe house soon. You need to sleep as much as you can. Tomorrow will be interesting."

"Is that a low-key way to say tomorrow will be tough?"

"Caught me." He gazed into her eyes. "You know what will happen when Daley realizes Allison and Beckett have disappeared."

"He could turn to someone else in the division."

"He'll want the best. That's you."

"If he taps someone else in the division, we'll be able to pinpoint the computer being used for the work." She smiled. "Maybe I'll get to practice my B & E skills."

He laughed. "I should have known you'd see it as a challenge. Come on." Jesse nudged her toward the living room. "I need to check on Allison before we leave."

When they joined the others, Jesse crouched in front of Allison. "How are you feeling now?"

"A little shaky but glad to be out of the hospital." She reached for Beckett's hand. "Those guys meant to kill me, didn't they?"

"Either that or they intended to take you as a hostage to force Beckett to finish the work."

"What's the next step?" Iona asked. "We can keep your friends under wraps while your mission is ongoing. However, that doesn't solve the problem of what to do when we're deployed again."

Jesse stood. "I've already communicated with Zane. One of our jets will be at the airstrip before dawn. We're sending Allison and Beckett to Nashville where they'll be placed in another safe house with bodyguards until this operation is complete and they're safe."

"What about our jobs?" Allison asked.

"Do you really want to keep working for Dragon Alley?" Simone asked. "People who work for them are trying to hurt you."

"Are you open to jobs with a different company?" Sawyer asked the couple.

"We want to work at the same place," Beckett said. "Otherwise, we're open to a change. Do you know of an employer needing to hire two computer geeks?"

He smiled. "As a matter of fact, I do. Let me make a call. No guarantees, but by the time you land in Nashville, both of you may have a job interview lined up."

Minutes later, Sawyer, Jesse and Simone drove back to the safe house, again taking a circuitous route to make sure they didn't lead the enemy to their doorstep.

"Do you think Allison and Beckett will be safe back in the states?" Simone asked.

"Zane has already asked Wolf Pack to watch over them," Jesse said. "They'll be fine. Jake Davenport is their medic. He'll watch Allison to be sure she doesn't have any problems physically."

Simone relaxed. "That's good. What about the job interviews?"

"Already arranged," Sawyer said. "Brent and Zane will interview them late tomorrow afternoon."

"Do you think Brent will hire them?"

"As long as they pass their security checks, he'll offer them contracts. If he's not satisfied with their background checks, Zane will offer them jobs at Game Theory. Don't worry, Simone. They'll land on their feet without a problem."

"That's great." Even if neither of the job opportunities worked out, at least they would be alive which is more than Simone could say if they'd remained in Mexico, working for Dragon Alley. "Thanks for arranging the interviews, Sawyer."

"Can't let outstanding talent go to waste. Besides, Brent always needs more computer techs. While I don't think Allison would be a good fit as the tech support for a black ops team, I think Beckett would enjoy the challenge."

She hoped everything worked out for the couple. They deserved a break after the raw deal they got at DA.

So, what did that mean for her? No question, Griffin Daley would be desperate to find another programmer at the same skill level as Beckett. Hopefully, he'd give her the job so she could end this mission sooner than later. As much as she loved the weather and the people she'd interacted with in Sayulita, Simone hated working at Dragon Alley. Even though Jesse swept her work space for bugs and cameras every day, she still felt as though someone watched over her shoulder while she worked.

They arrived at the safe house a few minutes later, and Sawyer remained with her in the SUV while Jesse checked the house. When he returned, he opened Simone's door and held out his hand to her.

The men escorted her inside the house. After checking in with Iona and Tegan, Jesse said, "Do you need anything before you get ready for bed? A drink, a snack?"

Simone shook her head, fatigue crashing down on her now. Definitely adrenaline dump. "Like you said, I just need a flat surface."

He chuckled. "Come on, then." Jesse walked her to the main bedroom and stepped inside with her, closing the door. "I'll be taking the first watch tonight. After that, I'll be in the room across the hall. If anything happens or you feel uneasy, come get me."

"Thanks, Jesse."

He moved closer and captured her lips with his own.

Heat and fireworks exploded inside Simone at his touch. Unable to help herself, she burrowed closer to him and reveled in the heat and sizzle of Jesse's kiss. Boy, she could get used to this in a hurry. No doubt in Simone's mind and heart that no other man would measure up to Jesse. How did she get to be so lucky?

Finally, he broke the kiss and rested his forehead against hers. "I have to go, baby," he murmured. "My control is in shreds."

"Good to know I'm not alone in this. I feel like I'm burning up with a fever."

He chuckled. "Same." Jesse released her and opened the door. "I'll be close." He left without looking back.

The medic was fast becoming an addiction. As the adrenaline rush of his kiss waned, Simone's energy level dropped. Yeah, time to go to sleep while she could. The next day's work might begin earlier than usual.

Four hours later, she woke to the alarm blaring in her ear. Simone groaned and rolled over to turn off the blasted thing.

She sat up and swung her feet to the floor. After dragging her way through a shower and getting dressed, Simone put on her running shoes and went to the kitchen.

Sawyer handed her a mug of coffee. "You look like you didn't sleep well."

She frowned. "Thanks a lot. Some friend you are."

He grinned. "Just stating the obvious."

"Is Jesse up?"

"In the shower. He should be ready in five minutes. What's your pleasure for breakfast?"

"Omelets." She went to the refrigerator. "We've been feeding Iona and Tegan every morning, too."

"Got it. Want to be sous chef?"

"Glad to help."

They got to work. By the time Jesse arrived, they had finished prepping for the omelets and Sawyer was heating the skillet.

"Good morning, sweetheart," Jesse said as he bent to kiss her. "What are we having?"

"Omelets. Tell Iona and Tegan breakfast will be ready in ten minutes."

"Is the coffee ready?"

"Just made a fresh pot."

Jesse sent a text as Sawyer plated the first omelet.

With her part of the omelet prep finished, Simone washed pieces of fruit, cut them into bite-size chunks, and mixed them in a bowl.

A knock sounded at the back door. Tegan entered the kitchen followed by Iona.

"Quiet night?" Jesse asked.

"What there was of it." Tegan dropped into the nearest chair. "Please tell me you have coffee strong enough to peel paint off the walls. I need a big dose of caffeine."

"Same," Simone said as she set omelets and fruit in front of Tegan and Iona.

"I'll pour the coffee," Jesse said. "Did your teammates get Allison and Beckett to the airstrip?"

Iona nodded. "No issues. This thing is heating up pretty fast. Will you need backup inside Dragon Alley?"

"Shouldn't."

"If you do, let us know."

Sawyer scowled over his shoulder. "Hey, what about me?"

"You're busy with another task," Jesse said as he set the mugs in front of the Artemis team members.

"Trevor?"

"We need to find him before he blows our cover."

"Do I have a starting point?"

"I can find out where he disappeared but I don't see the point. White will make his way back to Sayulita if he hasn't already reached the town limits. He's obsessed with Simone."

She rolled her eyes. "He's interested in payback because I sent him to prison. Trevor doesn't want me."

Jesse shook his head. "I believe you're wrong about that."

"How do you know?"

"You're the one who got away. He's all about control, and you slipped the leash."

"Good for you," Iona said. "I hope you're not even considering taking him back."

Simone smiled at Jesse. "I had a better offer."

"Excellent." Tegan pointed at Simone with her fork. "Good job. I wondered when someone would snag Jesse's interest."

When they finished eating, Jesse and Simone sent the others back to their tasks while they cleaned up the kitchen.

Minutes later, they were on the road to Dragon Alley. "Last chance to back out," Jesse said as they neared the gate. "No one will think less of you for changing your mind."

"I will. I have to finish this, Jesse. Too many innocent people will die if I fail."

He stopped by the guard shack and showed their credentials, then headed for their assigned parking space.

Jesse came around to open Simone's door. "I'll be close all day if you need me. If I'm not available, don't forget you have an emergency button on your watch so you can speak to someone at Fortress."

She nodded.

He bent his head and captured her mouth with his. A long minute later, he came up for air. "Let's go. We have someone watching us on the fifth floor."

"What else is new?"

Jesse helped Simone to the asphalt and locked the vehicle.

They walked into the building and checked in at the receptionist's desk. Together, they rode the elevator to the Special Projects division.

As soon as they stepped onto the fifth floor, Bastien Boudreax and one of the other men who worked security met them. Boudreax's eyes glittered. "Mr. Daley wants to speak to you both."

Cold seeped into Simone's bones as she and Jesse were escorted to Griffin's office. Had they been found out? Did Trevor hook up with someone from Dragon Alley and break their cover?

"What's going on, Boudreax?" Jesse asked.

"You'll find out soon enough. Grant, get the door, will you? I'll just hang back here with a gun pointed at the pretty programmer until this business is resolved. Don't try anything funny, Porterfield. You won't like the results." He chuckled. "Your girlfriend definitely won't."

Grant knocked on Griffin's door, then opened it wide. "Kenyon and Porterfield are here."

"Good. Bring them in."

Grant stepped into the office and motioned them inside. Boudreax shoved Jesse who stumbled forward. Simone followed him.

"What's going on, Daley?" Jesse glared at the Special Projects division head. "You're the one who asked me to take on the role of bodyguard for the division. Why were we met with an armed escort?"

"I have a new project in mind for your girlfriend, and I wanted you to hear about it firsthand."

"You could have asked me to the meeting," he said dryly.

"This was more expedient." Daley turned his attention to Simone. "Take a seat, Simone. You, too, Porterfield."

Another hard shove in the back sent Jesse careening into one of the empty chairs. "Knock it off, Boudreax."

"Sit down and shut up."

Oh, man. This wasn't good. Simone looked at Griffin. "This better be good or Jesse and I will be resigning effective immediately. No one treats him like that and gets away with it."

Griffin's mouth curved upward. "I do. You'll do exactly what I tell you to do starting right now."

"And if I don't?"

Boudreax rested the barrel of his gun against Jesse's temple. "I'll kill your boyfriend, and you'll do the work anyway." He leered at her. "You might even find yourself with a new boyfriend before the end of the project. After all, I have to make sure you cooperate, don't I?"

"Touch her, and you die," Jesse said.

"Who's got the gun and the power, Porterfield?" He sneered. "It ain't you."

"You're threatening Jesse?" Simone demanded, her gaze locked on her boss. "What kind of crazy joint is this place?"

"The kind making pots full of money, my dear, and you're going to finish a very special project for me with a time sensitive deadline."

"How soon does it need to be finished?"

"Tomorrow at noon."

She blew out a breath. "You don't ask for much, do you?"

"You don't know the half of it." He chuckled. "I had someone else working on the project, but you'd know that, wouldn't you?"

Simone remained silent. What could she say to that? She didn't know how much Griffin knew about their role in Allison and Beckett's escape.

"Thought I might get a response out of you. I'm disappointed. What sob story did Allison and Beckett tell you?"

Jesse's knee pressed against her leg in silent warning. A warning not to say too much, but how much was that? "Someone poisoned Allison last night at a restaurant. She was understandably upset."

Their boss scoffed. "Poisoned? Get real. Who would poison a little nobody like Allison? I can't believe you bought into her drama. What did you do?"

She shrugged. "We got them out of the hospital like they asked."

"And then?"

"We dropped them off at a hotel on the edge of town," Jesse said. "Where they went from there, we don't know."

"What hotel?" Boudreax demanded.

Jesse stared at him.

The security chief shifted the gun from Jesse's head to aim it at Simone. "Answer the question, Porterfield."

He snorted. "You won't hurt my woman. You can't afford to lose a programmer with her skill."

"Back off, Bastien," Griffin snapped. "I don't want to frighten my prize employee unless it's necessary." His gaze shifted to Simone. "I'm sure it won't be necessary, will it, my dear?"

"But, sir...," Boudreax protested.

"Later. What do we care if Allison and Beckett are in the wind?"

"They know too much."

"By now they're too afraid to talk. Don't worry. We'll find and eliminate them."

"Too late if they talk before we get to them."

"I said I'll handle it. Simone, Jesse, come with me." He led the way from the office.

"Where are you taking us?" Simone asked. "People on the floor will notice if we don't show up for work today." Joy would notice, especially since she'd promised to give Simone details about her date with Mateo.

"Don't worry. I already have an explanation for your absence. No one will dare question me about it."

Inside the elevator, Boudreax used his key card to access a subbasement floor that no one could enter except with special authorization. She supposed Boudreax was one of those allowed onto the floor.

A minute later, she and Jesse were forced out of the elevator and herded toward the right. Concrete floors and no windows made the place resemble a bomb shelter or a bunker. She shivered from the damp, chilled air permeating the place as they trekked toward the end of the hallway and yet another door with access only by authorized key card.

Once through that doorway, they were led along another corridor. Each steel door was closed. This felt like a prison, and Simone supposed that's what it would be until she finished the program or they escaped.

If they escaped.

#

Chapter Seventeen

Jesse stayed close to Simone, furious at this turn of events. Although he knew the people in power who commissioned the program would be desperate for to finish it on time, he never expected to be taken hostage to force Simone to work for them.

Worse, unless he and Simone gave an Oscar-worthy performance and convinced Boudreax and Daley they were one hundred percent on board with the program and motivated by the payday associated with it, Daley was likely to instruct Boudreax to get rid of them and dump their bodies where they would never be found.

Grant stopped in front a steel door and used his key card and an access code to unlock the door.

Boudreax and company shoved Jesse and Simone into a cold, windowless room filled with computers and chairs. One couch was pushed against the wall along with a mini fridge. Although the room was carpeted, the floor underneath was concrete.

He scanned the room. No exit other than the door they came through. Several things to use as weapons after Boudreax searched him. If he didn't do a search, the security chief was more of a fool than Jesse thought.

Daley grabbed Simone's arm and looked at the security chief. "Search Porterfield. He's a military cop. He'll be armed. No tricks, Porterfield, or your woman will pay the price."

Jesse remained still and silent as Boudreax searched him and removed several knives and two weapons before shoving Jesse into the closest chair.

"Hands behind your back."

Gaze locked on Daley, Jesse complied. Boudreax cinched his wrists together and secured them with a zip tie. "Is this really necessary?"

"Until beautiful Simone finishes her work, it is." Daley propelled Simone to a chair in front of a bank of computers. "This is your new workstation. You won't leave this room until the program is complete."

"What program?" Simone snapped. "All I've heard from you is how important this program is but I know nothing about it."

"Francen and his girlfriend didn't give you details?"

"They only told us they needed to get away because Allison was in danger. They didn't stick around to give details."

"We helped them escape," Jesse said. "That's all."

Daley and Boudreax exchanged glances. "Interesting and surprising," Daley said. "I'm not sure I believe you."

"Doesn't matter," Boudreax snapped. "We have a deadline to meet."

The Special Projects division head glowered over his shoulder at the security chief. "I'm aware." He handed Simone a piece of paper. "Beckett's login and password. The name of the project is Death Wish."

Simone made a face. "Lame name."

Daley's handed fisted. "Log in and get to work. You have eighteen hours to complete the program. If you don't, your boyfriend dies first, then you'll die whenever I tire of keeping you for myself."

Jesse stiffened. "Leave her alone, Daley. She'll do the work faster if you don't threaten her."

"We'll see, won't we?" Daley grabbed Simone's hair and jerked her head back. "How much do you love your boyfriend?"

She scowled. "What kind of question is that?"

"Just wondering how much suffering he'll endure on your account."

Simone stared. "I love him, Griffin. I don't want him to suffer at all."

"Keep that foremost in your mind to help you finish the job as fast as possible. If you delay, Porterfield will pay the price." He looked at Boudreax. "I think our beautiful Simone needs a demonstration."

"No!" Simone tried to leap from the chair. "Don't."

Daley yanked her back and clamped his hand around her throat. "What did you say to me?"

"Simone," Jesse said, voice low.

"Jesse." Her voice broke, sending a spear of pain through his heart.

"Trust me."

She said nothing more, gaze locked on him.

He gave her a slight nod of approval. Any weakness she gave away to these men, they'd use against her.

"Do it," Daley ordered Boudreax. "My prize programmer needs a demonstration of the serious consequences of disappointing me."

"My pleasure," the security chief said from behind Jesse.

He heard a familiar snap and a split second later, an electric current ripped through his body, locking every muscle and sending pain cascading through him.

As Jesse's vision went dark, Daley gave the order to stop. Boudreax took his sweet time obeying the command.

Man, being Tased sucked big time. Worse, he was paralyzed until his system rebooted itself. If anything happened to Simone, he wouldn't be able to help her until he could move, and that might be too late.

"Each time I think you need a reminder, Porterfield will be the recipient of Boudreax's special attention."

"This is nothing," Boudreax bragged. "Just wait until you see what I have in store for your boyfriend the next time."

"Why are you doing this?" Simone asked. "You need me to help finish a program. That's my job, isn't it? You don't have to threaten us for me to do my job."

"This is a special project that will sell for millions of dollars."

"Every computer program I develop has a high price tag. What's new about that?"

Daley smiled. "This one is not for Dragon Alley."

"I'm writing a program off the books?"

"That's right. You're working for me on this project."

"Don't your superiors have a problem using company resources for your own purposes?"

He laughed. "You're so fast at everything assigned to you, no one will say a word. You've already finished your assigned tasks well into next week. No one's going to notice your absence from the office for a couple of days."

"How will you explain it?"

"Easy. I'll tell people I encouraged you to take two days off to become familiar with the area." Daley released her hair. "Get to work, Simone."

"Wait. What is this program supposed to do? I can't work blind."

"Hack into databases, gather information, and leave a virus behind."

"Blackmail?"

"What do you care? You'll be rewarded handsomely for your success or castigated for your failure."

"I won't fail."

"We'll see." He gestured toward the bank computer screens. "Get busy. I'll be back in two hours. If I don't see significant progress, your boyfriend will suffer."

"What about me? Am I going to suffer, too?"

"Can't harm the golden goose. No, I'll deliver your punishment later." Daley trailed a finger down Simone's cheek and neck. "I'm looking forward to it." With that last threat, he left the room followed by Grant and Boudreax. The door locked behind them.

Simone leaped up and ran across the room to Jesse. She cradled his cheek with her palm. "Are you all right?" Tears glimmered in her eyes.

Although Simone had created a lengthy distraction to give him time to recover, Jesse struggled to speak. "Cameras, bugs," he whispered.

"I don't care about that," she whispered back fiercely. "Are you okay?"

"Takes time."

"This is terrible, Jesse. It's not right." She pressed a gentle kiss to his mouth. "Does this constitute an emergency?"

"Yes. Go. Be fine soon."

Another kiss, and she returned to the computer station, pressed the emergency button on her watch, and went to work.

How soon would help arrive? Jesse had no way of knowing. Even if help arrived in time, how would the operatives find them in this subterranean maze?

He looked at the concrete walls again and wondered if the signal from Simone's watch would reach Fortress. No matter. If it didn't, Artemis and Sawyer would alert Fortress when they didn't show up tonight. They just had to survive the day.

Jesse handled the muscle spasms in silence, again surveying the room and pinpointing places with items to use as weapons.

Simone stared at the computer screen for long minutes, scrolling down lines of code. Once in a while, she scribbled something on a pad of paper, muttered to herself, and continued reading the screen.

Ninety minutes later, Simone stood and stretched. She walked to the mini fridge and peered inside. She removed two small bottles of water. Opening one, she knelt in front of Jesse. "Want a drink?"

"Was the cap sealed?"

She nodded, then raised the bottle to his mouth so he could drink. When he finished, she set the bottle aside and wrapped her arms around his neck. "How are you?" she murmured.

He nuzzled his face against hers. "I'm okay for now."

"Hurting anywhere?"

"Shoulders."

She stood and massaged his shoulder joints. "I wish I could do more. I'm sorry, Jesse."

"I've had worse pain in the past. How's the work going?"

"The program is complicated and Beckett set up a lot of error codes to slow down his progress. I'll have to undo each trap and correct it before I move to the next. At last count, I saw one hundred error codes, and there may be more. I won't know for sure until I fix the ones he added in and run the program."

"Come here." He needed to prepare her for what was to come. The punishments he'd endure as a spur to Simone's speed and willingness to work would increase in intensity. She might not be aware of the time but he was. He also knew how much of a sadist Boudreax was.

Simone knelt in front of him again. "What is it?"

"We have 30 minutes until Daley and company check on your progress."

She paled. "I have nothing finished. I just completed the first read-through of the program." Tears glittered in her eyes.

"It's all right, baby."

"No, it isn't. Boudreax will hurt you because I'm not working fast enough."

How could he help her understand? "Simone, Boudreax wants to hurt me. He'll take every opportunity he can find to test my mettle."

"What can I do to help?"

"Do absolutely nothing. Every time you give away a weakness, Boudreax will take advantage and push you to your limits. Daley wants you to succeed. He's only using me as a way of gaining your cooperation. Do your job, sweetheart, and I'll do mine."

"Tied up like a Christmas turkey?"

"Told you. You're the brains of this outfit. I'm the muscle. I'll endure whatever they dish out. Stay focused on your job."

"When I fix the error codes, there's no guarantee the program will work. I don't know how many hours this will take."

"Just do your job."

Tears streaked down her cheeks.

"We'll make it," he murmured and kissed her gently. What he wouldn't give to take her in his arms and hold her against him. He could break the zip tie but Simone needed to do what she could to fix the program, then sabotage it first. Someone else besides Daley and Boudreax was involved in this conspiracy, and he wanted the name of that person before he worked on freeing himself and Simone.

He broke the kiss. "Anything from Fortress?" he murmured against her ear.

"They know we're in trouble and are working on a plan."

"Stay focused. The rest will work out."

She kissed him again and returned to her station. After wiping the tears from her face, Simone focused on the screen. "For the record, I hate this."

He chuckled. "So do I."

She sighed. "All right. Now that I've completed the first walkthrough of the program, I'm going back to the beginning and working my way down from the top."

Jesse watched her in silence, marveling at the speed and concentration she brought to bear on the problem at hand.

When 30 minutes had passed, Jesse said, "Simone."

She glanced up and looked at the clock, scowling. "Maybe they'll be late."

"Fat chance, baby."

Sure enough, two minutes later, someone unlocked the door and stepped inside.

Daley, Boudreax, and Grant walked in, locking the door behind them. "How much progress have you made?" Daley demanded from Simone.

She glared over her shoulder. "Do you know the mess Beckett left behind?"

"Mess?" He frowned. "What are you talking about? He said there were bugs in the program but he was working them out. You shouldn't have any problems."

Simone laughed. "Have you looked at the program?"

He flushed. "Of course."

Jesse's eyebrows rose. Daley was a terrible liar. He'd either totally ignored the program or he wasn't capable of understanding it.

"Then you should know how many traps he laid in here."

"Traps?" Boudreax narrowed his eyes. "What does that mean?"

"Beckett set up booby traps and if I don't dismantle them in order, the program will be destroyed and I'll have to create the program from scratch. I'm good but even I can't recreate this program by noon tomorrow."

"You're lying." He strode to Simone and clamped a hand around her throat. "I don't like liars."

Jesse's muscles bunched as Simone gagged. "Boudreax, get your hands off her."

The security chief laughed. "What are you going to do about it? You're trussed up like a turkey."

Daley shoved Boudreax back. "Enough. I need her."

"You won't always."

"Long enough." He turned back to Simone. "Show me some traps."

Jesse relaxed a fraction as Boudreax let go of Simone. The security chief would pay for hurting her. Even if Jesse had to come back to Sayulita to get the job done, he'd do it.

Simone walked through the program with Daley leaning over her shoulder, too close for Jesse's peace of mind.

When she finished showing him a sample of the traps Beckett had laid, Daley cursed. "I can't believe he did that."

Jesse couldn't believe the Special Projects head hadn't recognized what was in front of him, and that made him wonder at what level Simone and Zane operated. Were they that good or had Daley been promoted beyond his ability?

Daley straightened and dragged a shaking hand down his face. "Just fix it, all right? You still have a deadline of noon tomorrow. We have to meet it."

"I'll do my best. What's the big rush?"

"The client wants the program operational by that time. You'll do it or else." He turned his head to glare at Jesse.

"Keep it up, Daley, and you'll be fixing this yourself," Simone snapped. "I know what's at stake. You continuing to threaten my boyfriend doesn't get the work done faster. Go away and leave me alone so I can concentrate."

After a glance from Daley, Boudreax sneered at Jesse and palmed his Taser as he approached.

Simone gasped.

Jesse sent her a warning glance, and she closed her mouth, hands fisting in her lap. Although he wanted her to look away, he didn't blame her for not cooperating. He wouldn't have turned aside if she was the one being Tased.

He endured two rounds of torture without uttering a sound. Barely conscious when Boudreax stepped away from him, he shuddered as his muscles spasmed over and over. Yeah, he hated this, hated especially that Simone was being forced to watch it.

"Get the job done," Daley said. "Otherwise, we'll move to more drastic measures to spur you along."

"Get out and leave me alone." She turned back to her keyboard, ignoring the other two men until they left the room.

As soon as the door locked behind them, Simone sprang to her feet and ran to Jesse. "Hey, you still with me?"

He nodded before another spasm racked his body. When it subsided, he said hoarsely, "Go."

She pressed a kiss to his mouth and dashed back to the bank of computer screens, dropped into her chair, and resumed her task.

Every 30 minutes, she checked on him, gave him water, then returned to her work. Her fingers flew over the keyboard so fast Jesse was amazed the thing didn't catch fire.

At one point, she shoved her hands through her hair and growled.

"What's wrong?"

"At this moment, I hate Beckett with a fiery passion."

"Can you fix it?"

She blew out a breath. "Yeah, I can. I could work faster with food and a supply of caffeine."

"No guarantee they'll feed you."

"Us." She turned to him. "They better feed us if they want this program fixed by the deadline."

Who was pulling the strings on this? Maybe Daley, but based on his inability to understand the program Beckett had created, Jesse doubted he was the decision maker. He was greedy enough to force another programmer to do what he couldn't and take credit for the work.

The more Jesse thought about it, the more certain he felt that he'd stumbled upon the truth. If Daley wasn't the decision maker behind the program, then who was?

As he pondered the question, he monitored the clock. Fifteen minutes before Daley and his cronies returned for another round of torture to pressure Simone. If they weren't careful, one of two things would happen. She would crack under the pressure or she'd rebel and refuse to work at all unless Daley backed off on torturing Jesse.

The latter possibility concerned him the most. Daley was worried. Otherwise, he wouldn't be pressuring Simone so hard to finish the job unless he had someone else pressuring him. If she rebelled, Jesse feared Daley would resort to drastic measures to force her cooperation.

Suddenly, Simone shoved back from the desk and did a little victory dance. "Yes!"

"Finished?"

"Ha. I wish. However, I figured out Beckett's pattern, and I'm halfway through this maze. Another two hours and I should have cleared out all the traps Beckett set. After that, I'll have to run the program to see if it works."

"And if it does?"

She sobered. "Then the genuine work begins. Adding my special touches. I never let a program leave my hands without a little something with pizazz."

He smiled, understanding that she planned to set her own traps for Daley. "Good for you." Jesse glanced at the clock. "Ten more minutes."

Simone kissed him before massaging his shoulder joints, then moving down to his elbows and what she could reach of his wrists.

"Thanks, sweetheart."

"Hang in there for me. It won't be long now."

Amazing. Here she was trying to comfort him when she was the one who had so much riding on her skills.

She leaned down and hugged him from behind, her mouth against his ear. "Zane said five more hours."

"Time it so your work conclusion coincides with the breach of the compound."

Daley and his cronies unlocked the door again and strode inside. The boss scowled at Simone. "Why are you away from your station? Get back to work."

"Not happening without lunch and caffeine."

"You don't get to dictate. You do as you're told."

"You want the program fixed? You'll do as I say. I need food and coffee. If you drug me, your work won't be finished. Period. All bets are off because I don't respond well to drugs of any kind and they take forever to leave my system."

He cursed and looked at Grant. "Go to the cafeteria and get food."

"For two, Grant," Simone added. "Plus coffee. I need caffeine to keep moving at this pace." She left the threat hanging in the air.

More cursing from Daley. "Do as she says." After Grant left, Daley said, "Progress report."

"I'm halfway through dismantling the traps Beckett set."

A scowl. "Is that all? What have you been doing in here? Mooning over your boyfriend?"

"You have cameras and listening devices in here. If you can't tell I've been working, that's not my problem. The traps are complex, and each one is different. They're taking a long time to find and dismantle."

"We don't have a long of time," Boudreax snapped. "Do you need another demonstration of how important it is to work fast?" He removed a capped syringe from his pocket. "Maybe another deadline to save your boyfriend's life will finally convince you we're serious."

Jesse's muscles tightened. No telling what was in that syringe but he didn't want his reflexes hampered. Not only that, he knew without a doubt that if he was drugged, Boudreax wouldn't give him the antidote. He'd be content watching Jesse die.

Dying wasn't on the agenda because it would leave Simone alone and vulnerable to Daley and Boudreax. Neither one would let an opportunity pass to abuse Simone.

Simone shifted to stand between Jesse and Boudreax. "No more abuse, Daley. You want the program ready? I'll do it but only if you leave Jesse alone. Touch him again and I'm done."

Boudreax stalked closer. "I could switch the torture sessions to you. In fact, I'd enjoy it."

"Go for it, you jerk." Simone crossed her arms. "Then you can do the programming work when you're finished.

#

Chapter Eighteen

Simone's heart rate skyrocketed as she waited for Boudreax and Daley to decide if her threat to stop working on the program was serious or just her blowing smoke to spare Jesse pain. She'd do anything to stop these clowns from hurting Jesse.

Daley watched her a moment. "Back off, Boudreax."

"But, sir...."

"Zip it. Simone, show me what you've accomplished so far. If it's not significant progress, I'll turn Boudreax loose on your boyfriend."

She walked up to Boudreax. "Not one bruise, needle prick, scratch, or shock. Am I making myself clear?"

The security chief glared down at her. "Don't push me, little girl. You don't know how dangerous I am."

Although sheer terror weakened her knees, Simone glared at Boudreax. "A few taps on my keyboard, and I can ruin you financially and every other way I can find. You'll never recover. Keep pushing me, Boudreax, and I'll show you the power of a few keystrokes."

Daley snorted. "You heard the lady. Stay away from Porterfield." He shifted his hard gaze to Simone. "For now."

With a bravado she didn't feel, Simone said, "Come with me." She led Daley to the bank of computer screens and sat down in front of the keyboard. A few keystrokes later, she pulled up a copy of the program with all the traps in place. After splitting the screen, she showed her progress in dismantling Beckett's traps. "As you can see, each trap is unique and has to be taken apart in a different manner."

"Beckett sabotaged the program," he muttered.

"From the very first line of code," Simone agreed. "He was working under duress?"

"Not at first," Daley admitted. "He was on board until he realized what we were doing with the program."

"The buyers, you mean?"

A curt nod. "He had too much of a conscience. All he had to do was finish a program, and he'd walk away with a million dollar bonus. How hard is that?"

"He must have felt the price was too high for the victims."

"How much longer until you're finished?"

"Hopefully, about six hours. Depends on what I find when I finish removing the traps and run the program." She spun around in her chair to look up at him. "So, we never talked about my reward for fixing this mess Beckett left behind. I want his bonus."

"Naturally."

"Good. You'll also deposit the bonus into my account before I hand you the completed program."

Daley glowered. "Are you crazy? I don't have that kind of money."

"Find it. Is this program worth the money to you? If not, well, I'm sure I can sell it on the open market without a problem."

"It's my program. You aren't selling it out from under me."

Simone laughed. Stall, stall, stall, she reminded herself. "Yours? Get real. If this computer program was yours, you would develop it yourself. But you aren't, are you? Makes me wonder if this is above your skill level."

Still cuffed to the chair, Jesse frowned at her.

Yeah, she was pushing Daley hard but her skill was the only leverage she had to keep Jesse and herself safe.

"You don't know what you're talking about. I'm too busy for grunt work like this."

And that's when she had confirmation she was right. Daley wasn't capable of writing this program. "Remember the bonus money, Daley. I get it first or you don't get the program."

"What's preventing me from killing you after you finish it and sending myself a copy of the program?"

"You could but you won't."

"Why not?"

"You'll never figure out my passwords in time to access the program and send it to the buyer." She smiled. "They change every time you log into the computer."

"You think you have me over a barrel, don't you?" Daley jerked her out of the chair by grabbing the neck of her shirt and hauling her up against him. "I could replace you with dozens of programmers who are several cuts above you."

"But you won't. One, you don't have time. Two, you'll be hard pressed to find someone with my skill set. Suck it up, Buttercup. Get the money to pay me off and you can have your vicious little program on time."

"You'll pay for this," he vowed.

"Not as much as you will if you don't deliver the program to the buyer."

Grant returned with two to-go boxes and two cups in a carrier. "Lunch."

"Great. I'm starving. Let me go, Daley. You're delaying me."

The Special Projects division boss released Simone and shoved her away from him. "Go. Hurry."

"Cut Jesse loose."

Boudreax scowled. "Who died and made you queen?"

Simone raised one eyebrow and waited.

Daley caved first. "Do it." He looked at Jesse. "One move to harm any of us, and Simone will suffer the consequences. Understood?"

He nodded.

"This isn't a good idea, boss," Boudreax protested. "He's dangerous."

"So are you. Watch him on the monitor. If he acts suspicious or threatening, you know what to do."

The security chief brightened as his gaze slid to Simone. "Oh, yeah," he crooned. "I know exactly what to do. I'll make Porterfield watch."

Eww and barf. Simone watched as Boudreax pulled a knife and cut the zip ties from Jesse's wrists. "Watch yourself, Porterfield. I won't hesitate to take you out."

"Yeah, yeah."

Boudreax walked toward the door. Grant set the food and drinks on a nearby table. The two security men left the room followed by Daley who again muttered a threat before he exited the room, locking the door behind him.

Simone circled behind Jesse to be sure Boudreax had severed the plastic ties and was pleased to see the tie on the ground. "You're free."

He slowly moved his arms to his sides, growling. Sweat popped out on his forehead as his breath gusted in and out.

"What can I do to help?" Simone asked. She hated to see him suffer like this.

"Eat while the blood flow in my arms and hands returns to normal. I'll be fine, baby. Promise."

He was right, she realized. If she didn't wolf down her lunch and get back on task, Daley would make a reappearance. That, she didn't want. The longer she kept Daley and company away from Jesse, the better.

She crossed to the table and opened one container. Simone rolled her eyes. Grant was such a guy. He'd stacked pizza slices on top of a cheeseburger. He'd also dumped French fries in one section and chocolate cake in another. At least he remembered to add the eating utensils so she wouldn't have to eat chocolate cake with her fingers.

A few minutes later, Jesse grabbed the other box and sat beside her. "How are you holding up?"

"I want this to be over. I want to go home, Jesse." She nudged him. "We have some dating to do before I say yes to your proposal."

His head whipped toward her. "But you're thinking of saying yes."

"I am."

"Good, because I will ask before long." His intense gaze locked on hers, a silent message in his eyes.

What was that about? "You'll have to work for it."

"I'll do anything for you."

"So noted." She leaned over and kissed him before returning to her lunch. Minutes later, Simone tossed her empty food container in the trash, then took her coffee to the workstation. Spotting a door to the right of the console, she opened it. A bathroom. Excellent.

After using the facilities, she returned to work, sweeping through the remaining booby traps laid by Beckett. As she worked, Simone considered and discarded several options for laying her own booby traps that wouldn't trigger until Daley tried to open the program without her help. If the traps sprung too soon, she and Jesse would be caught in the crossfire.

Jesse polished off his lunch and took up a position on Simone's left with his back to the bank of screens.

"Eyes on the door?"

"That's where the enemy will be."

Silence remained between them until Daley returned three hours later to check on her progress.

"Out," she snapped. "I'm busy."

"Progress?"

"Getting there. Leave me alone, Daley."

"Don't push me. You won't like the consequences."

She lifted her hands from the keyboard and rested them in her lap as she stared at him. If he wanted to play rough, she would push back harder. "One sequence of keystrokes will wipe out this program. Don't tempt me."

He cursed viciously and took a step toward her.

Jesse was on his feet in an instant, standing between her and the Special Projects boss. "No."

Boudreax swaggered closer. "You can be tied up again, Porterfield. Don't threaten the boss."

Daley waved the security chief off. "Out. You have two hours, Simone. If you're not finished by that time, I'll turn Boudreax loose on you."

"I'll be ready. Go."

The other men left the room and locked them in again.

Jesse settled back into his chair. "You don't want to push them any farther, Simone."

"I won't have to. My sweep is finished. Now, I'm going to run the actual program to see if it works as Beckett wrote it. If it doesn't, I'll have to diagnose the problem."

"And if it does?"

"I'll add my special touches."

She ran through the program and watched the result on her screens. Nope. Beckett had made a couple of mistakes near the end.

Simone corrected them and ran through the program again. No problems this time. Excellent. Satisfaction swept through her.

She rubbed her hands together. Now, to set up the program so it would work until it was transferred from this computer to any other device, including a flash drive or the cloud, and accessed without her help.

Simone went back to work, frequently checking the clock. Occasionally, she received an update from Fortress through her watch. Most of the time, Fortress didn't disturb her.

Finally, she wrapped up the final finishing touch and sat back. "Done," she murmured.

"Fifteen minutes to spare."

"Maybe they'll let us go when Daley gets the program."

"You know better."

She sighed. "Yeah. Figured. What will we do?"

"They won't shoot us here. Too messy and they'd have to clean up evidence of the deed. My guess is they'll take us off site."

"Daley must pay me or he won't get the program. Nonnegotiable, Jesse."

"Why do you care?"

"The money isn't going to my account. It's going to the account of my favorite charity. They can use the extra donation."

He squeezed her hand. "I should have known you'd do something selfless."

Simone shrugged. "I don't want tainted money but the literacy fund will use it well. They won't care where the money came from."

"You're doing a good thing, baby." He tugged Simone into his arms, holding her close. "I'm proud of you."

"Why? I'm a programmer. This is what I do."

"But you don't normally write computer programs under such heavy duress. You did an outstanding job."

"Let's hope it passes muster with Daley." She looked up at him. "We have to find a way out of here. Without a key card, we won't be able to accomplish that unless you have a magic trick up your sleeve I don't know about."

"We'll do what's necessary to survive until help arrives."

The door unlocked, and Daley and his cronies strode into the computer lab. "Well?" Daley demanded. "Is it finished?"

"Come look." Simone booted up the program for Daley and set it to run with a few taps of the keyboard. When the program ended, she said, "Satisfied?"

"Run it again."

She did as he requested. The program gave the same result.

"Very good." Daley straightened and looked at her with a speculative gleam in his eyes. "I might keep you around a little while longer. You're more useful than I thought."

"Good to hear." Simone turned back to the keyboard and tapped in her code. The screen went blank.

"What did you do?" Daley sounded panicked. "Where is it?"

"You owe me $1 million." She brought up the bank account of the charity foundation. "Transfer the money or I won't bring it back."

Daley looked at Grant. "Go. Bring her to the lab."

Her? Simone glanced at Jesse. Were they about to meet the person commissioning the program to sell to outsiders?

Grant left and returned five minutes later with Sophie Westlake.

Simone's eyes widened. The vice president of Dragon Alley was responsible for this? Wait. Was Dragon Alley creating programs to sell worldwide to the highest bidder, even to terrorists?

"Well? Is Death Wish finished?" Sophie asked, her gaze shifting to the computer screens.

"It's finished," Daley said. "I checked the program myself. It works just as I told you it would."

What a liar he was.

"What's the holdup, then? Why did you call me down here? I told you to send it on to the buyer immediately."

"Simone is demanding the reward money up front before she'll release the program to me."

"Is she?" Sophie smirked. "Very enterprising of you, Simone. I'm surprised. I heard you were a straight arrow."

"You heard wrong. Make the deposit in the account I've queued up, and the program is yours."

After a long moment of chicken, Sophie must have decided Simone wouldn't budge on her demand. She strode to the computer, tapped in a long string of numbers.

Simone checked the charity foundation's balance before she closed out that screen and brought up the prized computer program. "Here you are."

"Show me that Death Wish works." She slid a cool glance toward Simone. "You better not be lying to us, Simone. Lying wouldn't be good for your health or that of your handsome boyfriend."

She did as instructed, keying in the codes for the program to run without activating the traps.

"Beautiful work, Simone. I'm impressed." Sophie beamed at her. "I brought Allison on for projects such as these. However, she disappointed me until she started dating Beckett. He was a jewel. You're in a different category altogether. I think we can work with this arrangement and with you. Are you interested in a very lucrative partnership?"

"Hey, wait a minute," Daley protested. "You said nothing about cutting her in. I'm the computer expert here. I'm the one you should offer a partnership."

Sophie laughed. "Oh, please, Griffin. Don't be ridiculous. I know exactly how much you've done on this project. Nothing. You pressured Beckett Francen into creating the program when Allison proved useless, and when he found out what we were going to do with it, he balked. You had to bring in outside talent to finish the job because you couldn't handle the work yourself."

"You don't know what you're talking about," Daley snapped.

"Oh, you'd be surprised exactly what I know." She looked at Boudreax. "Take care of this for me, will you, babe?"

Simone's eyebrows rose. *Babe*? Man, she hadn't seen that coming. No wonder Boudreax strutted all over the building like he owned the place.

"With pleasure, honey." Boudreax pulled his weapon and pointed the barrel at Daley who paled. "Grant, cuff him."

"You can't do this to me." Daley glowered at Boudreax and Sophie. "You won't get away with it."

"Don't whine, Griffin." Sophie shook her head. "You had a good ride but now you're a liability instead of an asset. I know when to cut my losses."

"You can't just shoot me. I'm too important to go missing. People will notice and ask questions."

"Get real. All I have to do is tell people we fired you for embezzling company funds. No one will question your absence. They'll all be relieved to not have the microscope turned on them."

"Take him," Boudreax said to Grant. "You know what to do. Make sure it's done right."

"Yep. My pleasure. Let's go, Daley. You cause me trouble, and I'll shoot you where you stand and haul your body out of here." Grant shoved him into motion and propelled him from the lab.

"You're next, Porterfield." Boudreax aimed his weapon at Jesse.

Ice water ran through Simone's veins. She couldn't let Boudreax kill Jesse. "You want me to work for you, Ms. Westlake?"

"I think we can make a lot of money together."

"I'll work for you on one condition."

Sophie's eyes narrowed. "What condition?"

"Jesse remains unharmed."

"You, I need. Jesse, I don't."

"I love him. If you want me, I get Jesse alive and unharmed."

"And if I refuse?"

She tapped a few keys on the keyboard, and the program disappeared. "No Jesse, no program."

Boudreax clubbed Jesse on the back of the head with the butt of his pistol and shoved him to his knees. He grabbed a fistful of hair and jerked Jesse's head back, shoving the barrel of his pistol against Jesse's temple. "You sure you want to play hardball with us?"

He jammed the barrel harder against Jesse's temple. Blood trickled down his cheek. "We don't need her or Jesse, baby. The job's finished. We'll find a replacement for Simone. She's already been more trouble than she's worth."

"You have nothing without me," Simone warned.

"What does that mean?"

"I saved the program in my cloud. Only I can retrieve it. You'll never break the code in time to meet your buyer's deadline."

Sophie studied her a moment before shifting her attention to Jesse. "He means that much to you, Simone?"

"I love him."

"There's no ring on your finger."

"Jesse has had a ring for months. I've been leading him on a merry dance while he tries to convince me to marry him." Simone frowned. "You're messing with my plan, Sophie."

The other woman's mouth curved. "Sorry about that." She leaned back against the computer console. "We have a bit of a problem here, Simone."

More than one. "What's that?"

"We don't need your boyfriend. In fact, he's a security risk."

"He would do nothing to cause me harm."

"See, that's where I have a problem. I met a friend of yours a few days ago."

Uh oh. "What friend?"

"Trevor White."

Chapter Nineteen

Simone scowled, trying to come up with an idea to get them out of this mess. Trevor, The Jerk, had screwed up the operation after all. "What about him?"

Sophie's eyebrows winged upward. "You don't deny knowing him?"

She snorted. "No. Why should I?"

"He says your name isn't Simone Kenyon. It's Simone Kent."

"For once in his life, he told the truth."

Sophie looked amused. "I guess there's no love lost between the two of you."

"Not a drop. That man has caused me nothing but grief since I've known him."

"You lied to us about your identity," Boudreax said. "Why should we believe you now?"

"What lie? I told you the truth. My name was Simone Kent. It's now Simone Kenyon. There's no crime in changing your name if you do it legally."

"Why the change?"

"Two words. Trevor White. He's also the reason I jumped at the chance to come to Mexico. The man is a menace, and I want nothing to do with him."

"But you dated him."

"Yeah, and I regret every minute I wasted on him." She let the anger she felt over Trevor's treatment boil over. "Do you know what he did to me? Good old Trevor beat me to within an inch of my life. I was in the hospital for more than a week."

The other woman looked sympathetic. "How did you handle it?"

"How do you think? I reported him to the cops. He was arrested and convicted of assault and battery. As soon as the cops didn't need me anymore, I left California and never looked back. Once he was free, he pursued me all over the country and now to Mexico."

Boudreax snorted. "Quite a story, Simone. It's not good enough to spare your boyfriend or you."

Simone's heart sank. She and Jesse needed a few more minutes for Fortress to make their move, then this mission would be over and they could go back home. But she feared that would never happen. "You think you can access the program without me, Boudreax? Go for it." She folded her arms. "I dare you. One wrong move, and the program will destroy itself."

At that moment, Simone's watch vibrated. She glanced at the screen. Fortress was ready. Thank goodness.

"You don't have a chance of accessing the program without my cooperation." She rose from the chair and walked toward Boudreax. "Let Jesse go."

"Or what?"

"No payday for either you or your lady friend. Jesse's mine. I don't need a partnership with either of you, but I need Jesse." She held out a hand to the man of her dreams.

After a moment's hesitation, Boudreax released Jesse and backed away, his attention shifting to Sophie. "What do you want to do, baby?"

Simone helped Jesse to his feet and steadied him when he swayed. His face was pale aside from the streak of blood down his cheek. "You okay?" she murmured.

He gave a slight nod.

Right. Why didn't she believe him? Perhaps because he looked like death warmed over. This wasn't good at all. If Jesse wasn't up to handling these two, their chances of survival plummeted into the basement.

Oh, yeah. They were already in the basement. Guess their survival outlook was ten notches below lousy.

Simone slid her arm around his waist and hoped he didn't go down. If he did, Jesse would take her with him.

"We might work something out," Sophie said. "Simone, you have your money. You verified it's in your account. Now, let's talk about our partnership."

"My price for continuing to work with you is Jesse. Nonnegotiable."

An alarm went off, followed by the overhead lights flashing red.

Simone edged closer to Jesse who tightened his grip around her.

"What's that?" demanded Sophie. "Bastien, what's happening?"

Boudreax glanced at his smart watch and cursed. "The compound is under attack. We have to get out of here."

"What about them?" Sophie gestured to Simone and Jesse.

"They're coming with us. We'll take care of them when we're out of town."

"I need the program, Bastien."

Boudreax aimed his weapon at Jesse. "Give Soph the program, Simone, or I'll shoot Porterfield, then turn the gun on you."

"You're going to kill us, anyway."

"You can both die now or you can die later. Choose," he shouted.

Jesse squeezed her briefly. When she looked at him, he gave a slight nod while keeping his gaze locked on Boudreax.

Although Simone didn't like it, she couldn't see another way out of this dilemma. Also, she'd promised Zane to listen to Jesse.

She released him and walked to the computer. "How do you want the program?" she asked Sophie. "Do you have a flash drive or do you want me to send it as an attachment to your email?"

"Send it to my personal account." Sophie rattled off the email address. Once Simone sent Death Wish to her email account, Sophie beamed. "It's mine, Bastien. Finally, the program is complete, and it's mine. I'll be able to broker deals on this program for a long time, thanks to you, Simone." She patted Simone's shoulder. "I'm sorry we have to end our partnership before it's really begun but you must understand my position. I can't have a security leak, and you, my dear, are a tremendous threat to my security."

Simone tapped a few keys and started a system dump onto one of the Fortress servers reserved for her use on this mission, then blanked out the screen.

"What did you do?" Sophie demanded.

"Wiped my presence from the system, of course. I don't want either of my names associated with you and your crony."

"Soph," Bastien warned. "We need to go." He handed her his weapon which she trained on Jesse. "I'll cuff them, then we'll get out of here. If the attackers are their friends, we'll use these two as hostages to escape."

"Where will we go to kill them?"

"I know a place out in the jungle. No one will find their bodies before the wildlife takes care of the evidence. But we need to move fast."

Boudreax used a zip tie to secure Jesse's hands behind his back, then jerked Simone to her feet and did the same to her. "Let's go. Sophie, bring up the rear. If Jesse so much as sneezes, shoot him." He bent and grabbed a gun from his ankle holster. "But I don't think he will. If he does, I'll shoot his girlfriend, and I don't think he wants me to do that."

Simone flinched as Boudreax jammed the barrel of his gun into her side and propelled her to the door.

He unlocked the door and dragged Simone from the room. "You give me any trouble, and you'll regret it," he muttered.

"Wow. I'm shaking in my shoes over that one."

"You should be. I can make your death easy or hard. I'd prefer hard."

"Of course you would."

"Simone," Jesse murmured.

Yeah, yeah. She needed to quit antagonizing the security chief. They needed him off his guard so she and Jesse could escape.

Would they be able to accomplish that with Jesse injured? He said he was all right but Simone knew he was more hurt than he'd admitted.

She remained silent, waiting for a sign from Jesse or for an opportunity to make a move.

Boudreax marched her along the hall to another doorway. After a card swipe, the door opened to reveal an underground garage with several SUVs parked in a row.

The security chief unlocked the first vehicle and shoved Simone into the backseat. A moment later, Jesse joined her.

Boudreax and Sophie climbed into the front with Boudreax behind the wheel. After pressing a button on the vehicle's dashboard, a large door opened in front of them.

Simone's eyes widened at the large black opening. A tunnel. Someone had planned for every eventuality. "Why does Dragon Alley have an escape tunnel?"

Boudreax drove into the tunnel. "This area is rife with cartels and their soldiers. We had to make contingency plans in case they turned on us."

Each section lit as they approached, then the lights went out as they passed. They drove for about half of a mile before they emerged onto a dirt road outside the compound.

He navigated over rough terrain until he reached a road a good distance away from the compound. Boudreax sped away from the area, navigating around the outskirts of Sayulita. When he reached the countryside, he floored the accelerator.

Did anyone from Fortress realize they weren't in the compound? If so, would they be able to track them?

She blinked. Of course. Their watches had GPS chips in them. Hopefully, someone at Fortress was tracking their movements.

A spot in Simone's back tingled and turned warm. She looked at Jesse. "Zane activated my tracker," she mouthed.

He nodded. "Mine, too."

Excellent. That meant Fortress was aware of their location. Now if one operative reached them before Boudreax shot them, they were in business. If not, Simone hated to think she'd lose out on getting to know the man who had her heart.

She rested her head against Jesse's shoulder. Why had it taken her a month to realize Jesse was every dream she'd had for a boyfriend and potential mate? Simone wanted time to know Jesse better, to make him feel as special as he'd made her feel.

Resolve stiffened her spine. She wouldn't allow Boudreax and Sophie Westlake to take Jesse from her. Simone didn't know how to stop them, but she'd work something out. Jesse Phelps was too special to let him die. She had a substantial reason to live besides being furious at the two jerks in the front of the SUV.

"This will be close," Jesse whispered in her ear. "Be ready."

She kissed his jaw.

"Aww. Aren't you sweet?" Sophie looked at them, amusement in her gaze. "Too bad you don't have more time together."

"You could fix that for me." Simone glared at her. "After all I did to finish the program, and this is the thanks I get?"

"Sorry, Simone. My safety is more important than yours. Programmers are thick on the trees. You can be replaced."

Not news to her. She'd already discovered that truth long ago. However, Simone was well aware her skill set was unique and would be harder to replace than Sophie realized. Poor comfort after she was dead and gone.

No, she reminded herself. She wasn't giving up. If she did, Jesse would die, and that was unacceptable. "Where are you taking us?"

"To a clearing in the jungle. Very peaceful," Sophie added. "It's beautiful and quiet, so no one will disturb us. A great spot for you to disappear."

"Don't expect me to be grateful."

The other woman frowned. "I could have let Bastien do away with you in the subbasement at Dragon Alley. You should be thankful I didn't."

Simone stared at her. Seriously? She might be grateful to have a few more minutes with Jesse, but she wouldn't be telling Sophie as much.

"Keep watch behind us," Boudreax muttered. "I don't think we have a tail but I'm not positive."

Jesse's arm muscles flexed.

Although Simone kept her face toward Sophie, she watched Jesse from the corner of her eye. What was he doing?

She and Jesse remained silent throughout the rest of the drive. As the miles passed, the countryside morphed into untamed land, gradually changing until the SUV stopped at the edge of a dense jungle.

"End of the line," Boudreax said. "We walk from here."

"How far is this clearing?" Sophie kept her weapon aimed at Simone. "I'm not dressed for a hike in the jungle."

"Worried about your shoes?" The security chief rolled his eyes. "You'll be fine. I need weapons trained on both of them."

"No problem," Sophie said, fire in her eyes. "I'll hold on to Simone. You can hold a gun on her boyfriend."

"Whatever," Boudreax muttered. "Let's go. I don't want to be out here after dark. Too hard to find your way out. Once these two are dead, we'll go to dinner. I'll treat you to a night in an exclusive hotel."

Sophie's mouth gaped. "Are you crazy? We need to leave the country and broker the deal for the computer program. Whoever attacked the compound must know about the program."

"Now who's crazy? No one identified the attackers. Maybe one cartel took over Dragon Alley. We're in the middle of cartel territory."

"Why would they want the company?"

"We make money hand over fist. What a lucrative way for the cartels to break into another line of work and make a ton of money. We should go back to town, lie low until we find out what went down at DA, and sell the program like we planned but from a hotel room. If we're in danger, we can always leave in the morning. No one will know where we are."

"Why shouldn't we leave tonight?"

"Think about it, baby. If the cartels are responsible, they wouldn't believe we'd stick around Sayulita."

"We shouldn't," she argued. "It's foolhardy."

Boudreax's face reddened. "I'm the one with an inroad into the cartels. We have a good working relationship. I'm telling you, I haven't seen or heard anything that shows they were ready to make a move against us."

"I don't like it."

"Trust me, all right?" Boudreax nodded toward the backseat. "Let's take care of these two, then go back to civilization where we can find out what's going on for ourselves."

He and Sophie yanked open the doors of the backseat. Boudreax hauled Simone out while Sophie waved the gun at Jesse and ordered him to climb from the SUV on his own.

They met at the front of the vehicle. "March, Porterfield. You, too, Simone."

"Where?" Simone scanned the wall of jungle ahead of them. "There's no path."

"Straight ahead."

"This would be easier if you cut the zip ties. Our balance will be terrible out here with so many exposed roots and foliage."

"Forget it," Sophie snapped.

"We'll slow you down if you keep us tied like this."

"Tough," Boudreax said. "Move." He shoved Jesse and Simone into motion.

Simone stumbled and almost went down. "Hey, knock it off."

"Worried about a few new bruises? Who's going to see? The wildlife won't care. Quit whining, Simone."

Jesse paused a second to allow Simone to walk ahead of him. "Keep going," he murmured.

Was he planning something? He must be. Otherwise, he wouldn't place himself between her and the couple holding guns on them.

She hated it, though. Simone didn't trust Boudreax not to shoot Jesse in the back to get rid of him before they reached the clearing, and Sophie wasn't that comfortable holding a gun. Plus, with her walking through the jungle on three-inch heels? That wasn't a good setup for her or Jesse.

Simone walked in front of Jesse, shouldering her way through thick foliage and brush and tripping over exposed tree roots. She stumbled over rough terrain for what felt like ten miles before she reached a small clearing.

Her breath gusted in and out as she trudged toward the jungle on the other side. Man, how much farther was Boudreax going to make them walk? Between the heat, humidity, and sheer terror, Simone was ready to sink onto the dirt and take a nap. If she did, she'd be taking a permanent one. Something told her the security chief wouldn't hesitate to pull the trigger.

"Hold it right there, Simone," Boudreax said.

She turned, eyebrows soaring. "You need a break, Boudreax? How out of shape are you?"

"Shut up, you little twit. You've walked far enough. This isn't the clearing I wanted to take you to, but you're too slow and I don't want to be stumbling around in the dark."

Jesse stepped in front of Simone as he faced Boudreax and Sophie. He backed up one step at a time, forcing Simone closer to the jungle.

Didn't take a genius to know his plan. Duck and run. But would they be fast enough to evade a barrage of bullets?

"That's far enough, Porterfield." Boudreax raised his gun and aimed at Jesse.

"Come on, Boudreax. No chance to say goodbye to the woman I love? Have a heart, man."

Sophie sighed. "Hurry, Jesse. This is taking too long, Bastien. This place is creepy, and I want to go to the hotel and take a long, hot shower."

"Not much longer, Soph. Get on with it, Porterfield or I'll shoot you and your woman and walk out of here with my woman for a nice steak dinner while the wildlife chomps down on you."

Jesse pivoted and crowded against Simone, nudging her back until she was only one step from the jungle foliage. He bent his head and brushed his lips over hers. "Ready?" he murmured.

"Any time you are."

He raised his voice. "I love you, Simone Kent."

"I love you, too, Jesse Porterfield. I'm sorry I kept you waiting for my answer."

"Oh, yeah?" He smiled, a teasing glint in his eyes. "So, what is it? Yes or no?"

How could he smile at a time like this? What if his plan didn't work and Boudreax fired multiple rounds into both of them? Where was Fortress?

She tilted her chin up to look at Jesse. Would his face be the last one she would see on this earth? "My answer is a resounding yes. I'd love to marry you."

The words settled into her bones and felt right. He was the right one for her. Too bad she'd just discovered the truth.

Shock filled his eyes. "You would? Seriously?"

Simone smiled. "I would."

He huffed out a laugh. "Your timing could stand some improvement."

"I've been told that."

"I really love you, you know," he murmured.

She captured his mouth with hers. "Then we better stay alive to do something about it."

"Deal. I'm looking forward to dating you and learning everything about my future wife."

"Same."

"When I tell you to run, take off. I'll be right behind you."

"Enough sap, Porterfield," Boudreax said. "Turn around or I'll shoot you in the back like the coward you are."

Jesse ignored the security chief. "Ready, sweetheart?" When she nodded, he winked at her and said, "Run."

She spun and took off like a rabbit.

Boudreax shouted for her to stop.

Simone kept running, stumbling every few steps. The jungle floor was a carpet of traps. If she fell, they'd be on her like white on rice. If she twisted her ankle, she and Jesse would be caught.

She veered to the left, then to the right a few yards later, keeping to the thicker foliage and bushes even if it slowed her down. She and Jesse needed the jungle coverage to prevent Boudreax from having a clear shot at them.

One of the Gruesome Twosome fired multiple shots into the jungle. Boudreax cursed viciously. Sophie screamed.

Simone heard the foliage rustle behind her.

"It's me," Jesse said. "Go to the thick stand of trees on the right."

She dodged to the right as another barrage of bullets tore off leaves and tree bark to her left. When she reached the trees, Simone darted behind them.

Jesse was right behind her. He bent, slapped his wrists hard against lower back. The zip tie broke, and Jesse was free. He spun Simone around, slipped his fingers into her zip tie, broke it, then clasped her hand and led her through the jungle.

How long they ran Simone didn't know. Long enough for her to develop a stitch in her side.

Jesse tugged her toward a thick bank of bushes. They pushed their way through to the other side where a fallen tree lay on the jungle floor. "Perfect. Get on the ground as close to the log as you can."

She crawled over the tree and dropped to the ground.

"Flat, sweetheart," he murmured.

Eww. Simone wrinkled her nose as she obeyed. "What will you do?"

"Take care of Boudreax and Sophie."

"They have guns."

"Not for long. Stay here. Arm yourself with whatever you can find in case they slip past me. Above all, no matter what you hear, do not move from this tree."

"Be careful."

"Always. I love you." And he was gone.

Chapter Twenty

Although Jesse hated to leave Simone alone, he had no choice. If he didn't take care of Boudreax and Sophie, the couple would track them down. Even though Jesse hadn't left signs for Boudreax to follow, Simone didn't have the same skill. She'd left a trail obvious enough for even the worst tracker to follow.

Time to protect his woman and get out of this jungle. Once they were safe, Simone could delete the program in Sophie Westlake's email.

He circled to the right and followed a parallel path to the location where he heard Boudreax cursing. At the moment, the security chief was the bigger threat to Simone's safety. He'd go after Sophie after he dealt with Boudreax.

Minutes later, Jesse spotted Boudreax tracking Simone's prints on the ground and the signs of her passage through the foliage. His mouth curved. Yeah, he'd have to teach Simone how to walk or run over the terrain without leaving signs of your passage. He hoped they'd never be in a situation like this again.

Boudreax swore as he batted aside thick jungle foliage that seemed to cling to him like a second skin. He paused and crouched beside a scuff in the jungle floor where Simone had slipped in her haste to flee from Boudreax and Sophie.

The other man chuckled. "Gotcha. I always said women were more trouble than they're worth." He stood and resumed his tracking.

Jesse waited for the other man to pass before he made his move. He tackled Boudreax from behind, taking the security chief down hard.

Boudreax cursed as he threw Jesse off and shoved to his feet. He spun to face Jesse in a crouch. "You should have kept running, Porterfield. I'm going to kill you and your woman, too."

Jesse said nothing as Boudreax spouted more threats. He simply kept moving, waiting for an opening to take down his opponent.

"You got nothing to say?" Boudreax snorted. "Figures. You really are a coward, aren't you? Some military cop you are. Bet the Army was glad to be rid of you. Where's your woman? Hiding in the jungle?" He laughed. "Doesn't matter, Porterfield. I'll find her. Might spend some time with her before I kill her."

The security chief gave a come on gesture. "Let's see what you're made of, Porterfield. I don't have all day. I want some time with your woman before I escort mine from the jungle. Then we'll really celebrate, thinking about you two being dead and gone." He lunged forward.

Jesse sidestepped. When Boudreax stumbled past him, Jesse slammed the side of his fist into the back of the other man's neck.

Boudreax fell to his knees but scrambled back up to his feet before Jesse could finish the job. Shaking his head as though to clear it, Boudreax glowered at Jesse. "Think you're so clever, don't you?" He grabbed a knife from his boot sheath and brandished the weapon. The metal gleamed in the waning daylight as the blade caught light from a ray of sunshine. Boudreax charged and took Jesse to the ground.

Jesse caught Boudreax's knife hand as he plunged the wicked-looking blade in a downward strike. With a quick twist, he disarmed Boudreax, and planted his foot on the outside of the man's right leg. He wrapped his arm around Boudreax's neck and used his index finger like a fishhook, and yanked the other man's head to the right, forcing him to roll.

Reversing their positions, Jesse plowed his fist into Boudreax's jaw, followed up with a left hook, then a right cross, and his opponent was out.

Breathing hard, Jesse rose and flipped Boudreax onto his stomach. He used zip ties to secure the security chief's hands and ankles, then used two more ties to secure his hands and feet together, hogtying him. Although the ties wouldn't hold permanently, killing Boudreax wasn't necessary. If he got loose and came after them, Jesse would kill him without regret to protect Simone.

He stripped the security chief of his weapons, confiscating the Glock and extra magazine, and tossing the other weapons far enough away that Boudreax would have to be on top of them to see them. The jungle growth was thick in this area, and the sunlight was waning by the minute. Soon, the area would be pitch black.

Jesse headed back to the location of the fallen tree. About halfway to his destination, his watch vibrated. He glanced at the screen and grabbed his phone to call Fortress.

"Yeah, Murphy."

"It's Jesse."

"Simone's in trouble."

Jesse broke into a run. "Sit rep."

"Sophie Westlake found her and is forcing Simone to walk toward a waterfall. It's a steep drop, Jesse."

"On it. Backup?"

"They just arrived at the edge of the jungle. They're heading your way."

"I left Boudreax trussed up like a calf." He rattled off the coordinates. "I don't want him coming up on my six, Z."

"I'll pass the word and send Simone's GPS signal to your phone. Watch your back. Westlake sounds like she's desperate."

"Copy that." Jesse ended the call, brought up Simone's tracker on his phone, and picked up his speed.

His gut churned. He'd screwed up by leaving Simone alone. Now, Dragon Alley's vice president had the woman he loved in her clutches.

He leaped over the fallen tree, seeing signs of a fight between the two women as he passed. How had Westlake found Simone? She must have stumbled across her by pure chance. Westlake was not a woman comfortable in such an untamed environment.

Jesse bulldozed his way through thick plants and undergrowth, shoving past large leaves, and startling wildlife in the area.

As he ran deeper into the jungle, the sound of a waterfall grew louder and louder. Jesse pushed himself harder, sweat running down his back. The humidity was dense enough to slice with a knife. Every breath was a fight. Just one reason he enjoyed living in middle Tennessee rather than this close to the equator. Plus, he enjoyed the change of seasons.

A gunshot broke the silence.

Jesse's heart skipped a beat. Despite the heat and humidity, ice water flowed through his veins. No. He prayed Simone was safe. If he lost her now, he'd never forgive himself.

He sprinted toward the waterfall, the roar of the flowing water so loud he couldn't hear anything else.

Finally, he broke free of the jungle and skidded to a stop. In front of him stood Sophie Westlake and Simone. Sophie had a gun pointed at Simone who was bleeding from a gunshot wound to the shoulder.

"Get going, Simone." Sophie took two steps closer to Simone. "Move or I'll shoot you again."

"Why are you doing this?"

"You're a loose end I'm snipping off. Jump. Now." She fired off another round.

Jesse broke into a run as Simone cried out, clutched her right side, and stumbled backward. She tumbled over the edge and into the water. "No!"

Sophie spun, panic on her face, and fired her weapon again. This time, the shot went wild.

Jesse tore the gun from her hand and punched her in the jaw.

The woman crumpled to the ground and didn't move.

Still clutching her weapon, Jesse ran until the earth fell away. He peered over the side and saw Simone floating face down in a large pool of water. Without hesitation, he threw Sophie's weapon into the water and leaped in after Simone.

The warm water closed over him as he plunged into the depths. He kicked his way to the surface, grabbed a breath and sped toward Simone's prone body.

When he reached her a minute later, she wasn't breathing. "Simone. Come on, baby. Don't do this. Don't leave me."

He turned her over and forced air into her lungs as he kicked to keep them both afloat. No response.

Jesse breathed for her again, then set out for the edge of the pool where he could perform CPR on Simone.

When his feet touched the bottom, Jesse scooped Simone into his arms and scrambled from the water. He laid the woman he loved on the muddy ground and prayed as he forced her heart and lungs to work.

One minute. Two. Three. When at last despair threatened to tear him apart, Simone gasped and coughed.

Thank God. Jesse rolled Simone to her side and held her while she expelled the water in her lungs. When she finished, he rolled her onto her back and smiled down at her. "Hey, beautiful."

Simone's smile might be faint, but he'd take it. "Hey, handsome," she murmured, voice raspy.

"Any more bullet holes I need to know about?"

"Two aren't enough for you?"

He chuckled. "Just checking."

"Jesse!"

He glanced over his shoulder to see Sawyer running toward him with Jesse's mike bag.

"What do you need?"

"Pressure bandages and alcohol pads. We'll start with that until I can see what I'm working with." He looked down at Simone. "I'm going to patch you up until I can treat you in better conditions, okay?"

She nodded. Her face pale, Simone shivered.

"You'll be okay, kid," Sawyer said as he handed Jesse supplies. "Jesse is the best medic in the business."

Right now, he wanted to spirit Simone from this jungle and onto the jet to fly her to the best medical facility. As much as he wanted to do so, he couldn't take Simone to the hospital in Sayulita unless he wanted to end up in jail. The hospital officials would report the gunshot wounds to the cops.

"Is a mug of coffee in my near future?" she asked. "I'm freezing."

Sawyer glanced at Jesse. "Mylar blanket?"

He nodded. "Over her legs for now. Simone, I hate to do this but I need to lift your shirt. I have to see your injuries and treat them."

"Do it." She glared at Sawyer. "No comments from the peanut gallery."

"No, ma'am. Never. Jesse, what do you need me to do?"

"Get behind Simone. When I tell you, help me lift her to a sitting position. Sweetheart, I'm going to check you for broken bones first, then we'll take care of your gunshot wounds."

She nodded.

He wasted no time checking her extremities, then her ribs. No broken bones he could feel although she might have a few cracked ribs from the fall.

Excellent. Could have been a lot worse. In fact, Simone was very lucky she had hit no rocks when she went into the water.

He lifted the bottom of her bloody shirt just enough to see the wound on her side. A through-and-through. Looked like the bullet cut a path through tissue and muscle but missed hitting anything vital. "Help me roll her to the left, Sawyer." When he did, Jesse examined her back. Yeah, definitely an exit wound. At least he wouldn't have to dig out a bullet on the jet. "Let's raise her to a sitting position."

Sawyer slid his hands under Simone's shoulder blades to lift her up.

Blood drained from Simone's face, leaving her sheet white. She went limp. Sawyer caught her as she slumped to the side.

Jesse used Boudreax's knife to cut Simone's shirt far enough to check her shoulder. Another through-and-through. "Nasty wounds but barring complications she should heal well." He'd make sure there weren't any complications. Simone wasn't leaving his sight until she was out of danger.

He hoped Simone meant what she said in front of the Gruesome Twosome because he planned to make a pest of himself until he felt comfortable enough to leave her. The way his emotions were running riot, Jesse was positive he'd never want to leave Simone's side.

Since she was out and wouldn't feel his next actions, Jesse cleaned the wounds and applied pressure bandages to both the entrances and exits to stop the flow of blood. Once he got her on the jet, he'd stitch her wounds, pump her full of antibiotics and pain meds, and monitor her as they flew to Texas, the first stop for wounded Fortress operatives and principals once they reached the US.

He sat back as Simone stirred. "You with me, Simone?"

She moaned.

He'd take that as a yes. "You ready to get out of this jungle?"

"Oh, yeah."

"Sawyer, grab my mike bag. Sweetheart, I'm going to carry you out of here."

"I can walk," she muttered.

He smiled. "Not this time. I'm carrying you. Get over it."

She wrinkled her nose. "Don't get used to me giving in all the time."

Jesse slid his arms beneath Simone's back and knees and lifted her from the mud.

Simone hissed, her body arching as pain shot through her. "Hurts."

"I'm sorry. I'll take care of the pain as soon as we board the jet."

"My computer. Can't leave my computer here. We need our stuff from the house, Jesse."

"We have everything in the vehicles," Sawyer said. "Someone from Artemis gathered all our gear before we converged on Dragon Alley."

"The five of you mounted an assault on DA?" Jesse asked as they walked. "That's impressive. Boudreax has at least 20 security guards around the DA campus."

"We had a little help. Shadow Unit was back in the area."

"Nice." Shadow Unit was the best of the best as far as Jesse was concerned. They worked in the shadows and focused on freeing human trafficking and kidnapping victims. They ran into their share of terrorists as well. Their missions were the most difficult and gut wrenching of all the Fortress black ops teams.

Simone rested her head against Jesse's shoulder and nuzzled his throat. "I might get used to being carried around like this."

"Fine with me. Let me know when you want a lift."

She laughed, then moaned. "Oh, man. Hurts. Don't make me laugh."

"Sorry." He kissed her temple. "Rest. We'll be out of here before you know it."

Sawyer walked ahead of them with his weapon at the ready and Jesse's mike bag slung over his shoulder.

They finally made their way to the top of the gorge and saw Iona keeping watch over Sophie Westlake who sat on the ground with her hands secured behind her back with a zip tie.

Iona's eyes flicked to Simone. "She okay?"

"She will be, no thanks to Westlake. Simone has two gunshot wounds. I need to get her to the jet."

Her eyes went cold and hard as she turned her attention to Westlake. "What do you want me to do with her?" Iona's voice said it all. She would end Sophie Westlake without batting an eyelash if Jesse wanted her to take care of the problem.

"She's coming with us."

Sophie glared at them all. "Forget it. I'm not going anywhere."

"You'll come with us or you'll die right here in the jungle," Iona said flatly. "Your choice."

"You can't do this. I'm an American citizen. I have rights."

"Yeah, you do," Sawyer said. "You'll have your day in court. Once we land on US soil, you're no longer our problem."

"You're planning to kill me?"

"Don't tempt me, Westlake," Jesse said. "For what you did to Simone, I wouldn't shed a tear if you were no longer breathing. Get up."

Iona yanked Sophie to her feet. "Let's go."

"What about Bastien? Did you kill him?"

"As long as he didn't attack one of my teammates, he's still alive." Iona paused. "For now."

"You're all terrorists. I'll have you sent to prison for this."

"Good luck with that, lady." The female operative gripped Sophie's arm and propelled her forward.

"You'll regret this. I swear, I'll kill you all."

Iona snorted. "If you think we're intimidated, you're dead wrong."

"You won't get away with this."

"Watch us," Sawyer snapped as he took the lead.

"You'll pay," she vowed. "All of you."

When they finally reached the SUVs without incident, the rest of Artemis was waiting for them. Tegan straightened. "What happened to Simone?"

"Shot twice by Ms. Westlake," Jesse said. "You got our gear?"

She glared at Sophie as she nodded. "Even brought your vehicle. We didn't want to leave it at the safe house."

"Where's Bastien?" Sophie demanded. "What did you do to him?"

"Not what we wanted," Riley said. "He's in the back of the SUV." She smiled. "He's not a happy camper."

"If you've hurt him, you'll all die."

The operative rolled her eyes before turning Iona. "Orders?"

"Load Ms. Westlake into the backseat and stay with her. If she so much as twitches, kill her."

"What?" Westlake looked from one woman to the other. "Are you out of your mind? You can't kill me."

"Don't give us an excuse," Riley said and shoved the executive toward the SUV. "Get inside or we'll make you."

"I hate you."

"My feelings are hurt." Riley guided her to the back of an SUV, opened the door, and helped her inside. She followed her in and closed the door.

Tegan tossed a key fob to Sawyer.

"Where's Shadow Unit?" Jesse asked as he carried Simone toward their vehicle.

"Making sure no evidence is left at the safe houses. They'll meet us at the airstrip."

"What about Dragon Alley?"

"Once we determined you had been driven away from the site, we vacated the premises as the Federales descended on the compound. No injuries on either side."

"Excellent news." Sawyer opened the door for Jesse. "You leaving with us?"

Tegan nodded. "Boss's orders. He has another assignment for us. This one is stateside."

The operatives climbed into their vehicles and drove toward the airstrip. Sawyer activated the Bluetooth system to make a call.

"Yeah?" came Jordan's masculine voice over the cabin speaker.

"It's Sawyer. We're coming in hot. Have the jet ready to go wheels up as soon as we arrive."

"Copy that." The pilot ended the call.

Simone pressed herself closer to Jesse. "Cold," she muttered.

He arranged the Mylar blanket around her to help hold in the heat. "We'll be on the jet soon and we'll crank up the heat in the bedroom at the back."

Jesse unzipped his mike bag and pulled out a chemically activated hot pack. He shook it, then slipped the hot pack under the blanket. "Hold this. It will help."

When she took the hot pack, her eyes widened. "Oh, this feels wonderful."

He smiled. "Better than me?"

"Everything is a distant second to you."

"Oh, man," Sawyer complained. "Lighten up already. I'm working up here."

Jesse chuckled.

Thirty minutes later, they drove onto the tarmac and parked near the jet's stairs. Another SUV was parked close by. Artemis pulled in behind the first SUV.

Three operatives from the Shadow Unit descended the jet's stairs and helped Artemis escort the prisoners inside the cabin.

Nico Rivera, Shadow Unit's leader, turned to Jesse. "How do you want us to handle the prisoners?"

"Knock them out. I don't want to hear a peep out of them until we're on the ground in Texas."

"Any injuries to your team?"

"The female prisoner shot Simone twice."

Nico scowled. "Do you want Sam's help when she's finished with the prisoners?"

"I'll let Sam know if I need an extra hand."

A curt nod. "Let's get out of here. We've picked up chatter in the past two minutes. We'll have company soon. I'd rather not be here when the Federales arrive."

"Good plan. Let's go." He carried Simone up the stairs and to the bedroom at the back of the jet. Sawyer followed them inside, placed the mike bag on the floor by the bed, and spread a plastic sheet over the top to protect the mattress. "Thanks, Sawyer."

"What do you need?"

"Bottles of water. Tell the pilot we need a smooth ride."

Sawyer flashed him a grin, then left the room. When the operative returned, he carried four bottles of water. "Anything else?"

"Stick around. I can use a hand treating her injuries."

"You sure you don't want Sam in here?"

"No one else but you for now," Simone said. "Suck it up and deal, Sawyer."

He chuckled. "Yes, ma'am."

Jesse pulled equipment and supplies from his mike bag and laid them on a cloth-covered rolling table and locked the wheels.

He cradled Simone's hand in his. "I need to flush out your wounds, baby. The process is painful but necessary to get rid of foreign matter still inside the wound. After that, I'll have to close the wounds with stitches, then start you on antibiotics and IV fluids."

She flinched. "Doesn't sound fun."

"It won't be." He squeezed her hand. "I can take the edge off the pain with Lidocaine, but you'll feel everything I'm doing."

"What's the other option?"

"Knock you out with a drug that will put you to sleep for a few hours."

Simone studied him. "But you don't want to do that."

"I'd prefer you stay awake and alert so I can monitor you better."

"Then we'll go with the Lidocaine. Make it fast, all right? I'm not a glutton for punishment."

He kissed her palm. "You got it."

Jesse prepared the hypodermic, used an alcohol pad to clean the skin close to her wounds, and injected the medicine near her entrance and exit wounds.

When the areas were numb to the touch, Jesse prepared the saline. He brushed his mouth over Simone's. "Ready?"

She gave a curt nod.

"I'll need to remove your shirt. Are you okay with that?"

"Do it."

"Would you like me to ask Sam to take my place?" Sawyer asked. "It's your choice, Simone. I understand if you'd prefer another woman in here."

Simone bit her bottom lip and glanced at Jesse.

"Your choice," he murmured. "We'll do whatever you're comfortable with."

"Ask Sam to come in, Sawyer."

"You got it, kid." He patted the top of her head and left the room.

A minute later, Sam poked her head in. "Need me, Jesse?"

"Yeah. I need to cut off Simone's shirt and flush out her wounds."

Sam grabbed the scissors, cut away the shirt, and tossed the bloody remnants into a lined trash can. "How can I help?"

Jesse eyed Simone. "I can either do this myself or Sam can work with me. She can take one wound while I take the other."

Sam squeezed Simone's hand. "If we work together, we'll finish in half the time."

"Sold."

"We'll make this as fast as possible." He glanced at Sam. "Ready?"

She tugged on a pair of gloves and nodded.

He handed her one bag of saline and took the other for himself. "Do your best to hold still, sweetheart."

Her hands gripped the rubber covering.

"Let's do this, Sam."

Ten minutes later, the wounds were flushed, and Simone shuddered, her face dotted with perspiration.

Sam patted Simone's knee. "You're doing great, Simone. Hang in there a little longer."

After checking to be sure Simone was still numb, Jesse handed Sam one of this stitch kits. He looked at Simone. "Here comes the fun part."

She wrinkled her nose. "More fun than flushing saline through the wounds?"

"Afraid so. You'll feel tugging but you shouldn't feel pain. If you do, tell me and we'll give you more Lidocaine. Ready, Sam?"

"Yep."

"Front first, then we'll turn Simone to her side."

"Got it."

They worked in tandem to stitch the entrance wounds together. When they finished, Jesse looked at Simone. Tears streaked her cheeks. "Do you need more Lidocaine?"

She shook her head. "Just finish it."

Taking Simone at her word, Jesse nodded at Sam and together they rolled Simone to her side. They quickly stitched the exit wounds and covered both sides with bandages.

After rolling Simone to her back, Jesse and Sam propped her up on an incline and covered her with a sheet and blanket.

"Need me for anything else?" Sam asked.

"No, thanks. Appreciate the extra hands, Sam."

"Any time. I'll check on you after a while, Simone, but you're in excellent hands with Jesse."

Simone gave a wan smile. "I know. He's the best."

When Sam left, Jesse grabbed two packets of capsules from his bag and opened one of the remaining bottles of water. He handed Simone two capsules from each bag. "Antibiotics and pain meds."

She swallowed the capsules without argument and settled back against the pillows. "Will you stay with me?"

"Absolutely. Rest now. I'll be here."

Jesse cleaned up the medical detritus while Simone drifted to sleep. After he finished, Jesse pulled up a chair beside the bed, wrapped his hand around Simone's, and settled down to watch over her.

Chapter Twenty-One

Simone woke to pain and heat. Although she could do without the pain, thank you, the heat was a welcome change from the chills she'd had after being shot.

She opened her eyes and glanced around the jet's small bedroom. No Jesse. Had he stepped out for a moment?

What was the unfamiliar weight across her middle? Simone glanced down to see a muscular arm wrapped around her and realized Jesse was behind her.

"How do you feel?" he murmured in her ear.

"Warm."

Jesse chuckled. "How's the pain level?"

She considered downplaying the pain and knew she wouldn't get away with it, so why bother? "Aggravating. That's what woke me."

He pressed a kiss to the side of her neck and rolled away from her. A moment later, he presented her with two more capsules. "We'll land in another hour," he said as he handed her a bottle of water. "Do you want to sleep more?"

"I don't think I'll be able to."

Jesse checked the IV and changed out the bag for a fresh one.

"You do this all the time for your teammates?" she asked.

"Not all the time."

"But a fair amount."

He nodded. "We're in a dangerous business. That's why most of our black ops teams have medics. All operatives have field medicine training but medics are trained to a much higher level."

Jesse sat in the chair beside the bed and wrapped his hand around hers. "Can you handle it, Simone?"

She studied him, ignoring the throbbing in her shoulder and side. He was worried. Why? When she made a commitment, she didn't back down. "It's your job, Jesse."

"I can get another job. I don't have to work for Fortress."

Stunned at the sacrifice he was willing to make for her, Simone turned her hand and threaded their fingers together. "You love your job and your team. I would never stand between you and what fulfills you. I'll deal with the fear and loneliness."

"Why?"

She blinked. "I love you. Your job makes you happy. I want what's best for you."

"Even if I'm out of the country for six months out of the year?"

Simone shrugged her uninjured shoulder. "It's better than what military families deal with when their loved ones are deployed. Besides, I have Sage, Poppy, and Willow to keep me company while you're deployed. However, if it's safe, I expect text messages or phone calls while you're gone."

"Deal." He kissed the back of her hand. "You might even have a few special deliveries."

"While that would be fun, I'm more interested in communicating with you daily and you coming home to me."

He squeezed her hand. "You said you love me."

Simone smiled. "I did. It's true, you know."

"Enough to marry me and spend the rest of your life with me?"

"Yes."

Jesse's eyes widened. "You said yes?"

"Need your hearing checked?" She brought his hand to her face and nuzzled her cheek against his palm. "I said yes earlier, I said it again just now, and I'm not taking it back."

"Good, because I won't let you back out now. I love you, Simone Kent. I don't know what I did to deserve you, but I swear I'll spend the rest of my life making you happy."

"As long as we're together, I'll be happy."

He watched her a beat. "There's something else we need to talk about."

"What?"

"Trevor White."

Simone scowled. "What about him?"

"Sawyer couldn't find him. He disappeared after he escaped from the mercenary group."

Great. So, her problem with Trevor was on hold until her ex-boyfriend found her again. Only a matter of time, she realized.

So be it. She'd be ready for him. All she had to do was find the little weasel and give the information to Jesse and his teammates.

She paused. She might be better off telling her boss instead of Jesse.

Simone thought about that for a few seconds, then rejected the idea. If she followed through on that plan, her husband-to-be would believe she didn't trust him. She was no expert on marriage, but that didn't seem like a good foundation to build their relationship as husband and wife. "I'll see if I can find him online."

"When you do, I want the information."

"No problem."

"You won't argue with me?"

"Why would I? I want Trevor out of my life, and I don't have the skills to make him leave me alone. If I did, I'd have already kicked him out of my life permanently. As it is, he's like a bad penny, turning up when I least expect or want him. He won't take no for an answer."

"He will when I finish with him."

She narrowed her eyes. "You won't do anything against the law?"

"Do you care about him so much?"

"About him? No. I care about you, and I don't want to visit you in prison for the next few years."

His lips curved. "I'll try not to get caught."

"Trevor's vindictive enough to press charges if he gets a chance."

"He won't."

Hmm. Jesse had a plan. Good. Simone would leave the details to him. She didn't care what happened to Trevor as long as he left her alone.

That reminded her. She had another problem to track down. Simone frowned.

"What's wrong? Is the pain worse?"

"I have a leak to trace."

"A leak?"

"It's the only explanation for how Trevor keeps finding me. The most I've ever been able to escape his notice is a month."

"And he found you again in Mexico after you'd only been there for a day. That's a significant problem."

"Especially since I didn't tell anyone I was going to Mexico with you. How did he find me down there when I used a fake name?"

"Good question."

"As soon as I'm back on US soil, I'm going hunting."

"Not so fast. You can get back to your computer as soon as the doc gives you clearance. Not one minute before."

She scowled. "It doesn't take much energy to scour the Internet, Jesse."

He snorted. "I've seen you work. You burn a lot of energy every time you sit behind that keyboard. I've seen no one so focused except Zane."

"We'll see."

"Yeah, we will. Nobody argues with Doc Sorenson and lives to tell about it."

Her eyebrows soared. "Seriously?"

"No joke." He shuddered. "None of us want to see the inside of his clinic. He's a tough bird."

That didn't sound good. "I need a shirt before I see this Sorenson."

"I'll find you something. We don't want you to move your shoulder unless it's necessary. I'll be back in a minute." He left the bedroom and returned with a shirt that buttoned up the front and a pair of black cargo pants.

Perfect. "Are those yours?"

"Partly. The shirt is mine. The pants belong to Sam. My shirt will be big on you but easy to put on and remove for the doc to check your wounds."

"Can't we just go home? You and Sam did a great job fixing me up. I'm sure I'll be fine now."

"I'm not. You were shot twice. One of our doctors must sign off before we take you home."

She sighed. "This will be a pain."

"Yep. Join the party."

That caught her attention. "Wait. You were hit on the head by Boudreax. Were you injured?"

"I have a concussion and a large knot on my head. The boss will insist I get checked out before I'm cleared for duty."

Concerned, she said, "If you have a concussion, how long will you be out of work?"

He shrugged. "Depends on the severity. Maybe a week or two." Jesse squeezed her hand. "Long enough to buy an engagement ring and start dating you."

She chuckled. "We're getting married. Why do you want to date now? Isn't that backwards?"

"I'll be dating you for the rest of our lives, Simone. My goal in life is to spoil you and treat you like a princess."

Tears stung her eyes. "I don't need to be put on a pedestal. I just want to be with you."

"You deserve to be treated like the special woman you are."

Stubborn was indeed Jesse's middle name. Simone could see that nothing she said would change his mind. Fine, then. She would do her best to reciprocate. Jesse was a prince among men. She'd treat him like one.

Jesse opened the door and said, "Come in, Sam."

Shadow Unit's medic walked inside and smiled when she saw Simone sitting up. "Look who's awake. How do you feel?"

"Not as bad as I did when you saw me earlier. Still rough, though."

"That's to be expected. Jesse, why don't you step out now? I'll give Simone a hand getting dressed."

Jesse laid Simone's clothes on the bed. "I'll be outside the door."

Sam easily helped Simone change her clothes and use the facilities with a minimum of discomfort or embarrassment.

"I thought you might want a change of clothes before you get off the jet," Sam said.

"I appreciate it, Sam. I didn't want to climb back into my pants." They were stained with blood, dirt, and pond water. Not a wonderful combination when you were trying to protect a gunshot wound.

"I know you have Jesse to talk to, but if you need a female listener, I'm available." She handed Simone a card. "Here's my contact information. Like Jesse, I'm deployed every other month. Text me. I'll get back to you as soon as it's safe if I'm on a mission."

"Thanks, Sam. I might take you up on the offer."

The medic smiled and left the bedroom.

Jesse returned. "We'll land soon. Do you want to sit in the cabin with the rest of the teams or stay in here?"

"What about Boudreax and Sophie?"

"They're sleeping. Sam gave them meds to knock them out. They won't bother us."

Ridiculous to be so skittish about the couple since she was flying with twelve operatives. Even if Boudreax and Sophie were awake, they wouldn't be a threat to her. Still, Sophie had attempted to kill her twice. "All right. Let's go."

Jesse took the IV bag from the pole and handed it to Simone, then he slid his arms behind her back and knees and picked her up. "If you need anything, tell me. Don't suffer because of modesty or anything else. Understand?"

"Yeah, I got it." Uber protective. Another wonderful phrase to describe Jesse Phelps. She kissed his jaw.

He carried her to the cabin, set her on a seat against the back wall, and hung the IV bag on the hook on the wall.

Sawyer made his way to them. "Look who's up and around. How do you feel, Simone?"

"Like I've been shot."

He chuckled. "I know exactly how that feels. Do you need anything?"

"Water."

"What about you, Jesse?"

"Same."

"No coffee? You must be feeling ill."

He shrugged as he settled into the seat next to Simone's. "Boudreax pistol whipped me before we left the compound."

The amusement faded from Sawyer's expression, and his gaze slid to where the security chief slept. "No kidding. Not very sporting of him, was it?"

"Leave him for the feds. We don't need the headache of explaining to the boss why one of our prisoners disappeared."

"Yeah, yeah. You take all the fun out of these missions. Might be worth the hassle." He went to the front of the jet and returned with two bottles of water.

"Thanks, Sawyer."

"Yep. I'll get your gear when we land. You take care of your girl."

"Appreciate it."

Twenty minutes later, the jet landed at the airport in Texas. As soon as they taxied to a stop, three black SUVs drove onto the tarmac.

"Who is that?" Simone asked, watching men exit from the vehicles and walk toward the jet.

"Some of them are part of Doc Sorenson's crew. The rest are FBI agents. They're here to collect Boudreax and Westlake."

"FBI?"

"Boudreax and Westlake have been dodging their tax obligations and selling out our country to the highest bidder with earlier programs."

"Death Wish wasn't the first program they commissioned?"

He shook his head. "It's the third one. The first two were developed for military use. They made copies of the programs before they delivered the originals to the military, made a few changes and sold the program to our enemies. The programs were classified. Now, the feds will have to fight it out among themselves to figure out who gets first crack at Boudreax and Westlake."

"Huh."

"One thing I know for sure."

"What's that?"

"They'll never get out of prison with all the crimes the feds have on them."

"Good." Didn't hurt her feelings. They were a menace to society.

"The program Sophie uploaded can't be used?"

"Without my authorization codes, the program will self-destruct and wipe out the computer to which the program is downloaded. I have a copy in my cloud so the feds can use it as evidence. I also sent copies of the program and all Dragon Alley's computer files to Zane."

"You covered all the bases."

After everyone else exited the jet except for Sam and her husband Joe, Jesse stood and scooped Simone into his arms.

"Need a hand?" Joe asked.

"I've got it. Thanks, Joe."

"Listen to Doc Sorenson," Sam advised Simone. "He's cranky but the best trauma surgeon around. You're in expert hands with him and Jesse."

"I will. Thanks for everything, Sam, especially the card."

"I look forward to hearing from you."

Jesse descended the stairs with Simone cradled in his arms. "What was that about?"

"Sam gave me her contact information in case I wanted to talk."

"She doesn't offer that information to many."

"Why not?"

"Security, and she's protective of her privacy."

"That's nothing new. You all guard your privacy. I'm honored that she trusts me with her phone number."

One of Sorenson's men opened the back door to a large SUV. "Need help?" he asked Jesse.

"I've got her."

A nod. "Your gear is in the back."

"Boudreax and Westlake?"

"In the hands of the feds."

Simone breathed easier. At least they didn't have to worry about the DA vice president and her boyfriend anymore. Now, if her ex-boyfriend was that easy to deal with, life would be grand.

The journey to Dr. Sorenson's clinic didn't take long. Jesse carried her into the clinic.

Simone glanced around as he took her down a long, well-lit hallway to a treatment room. Along the way, she heard dogs barking and cats meowing. Even a few birds talking and chirping.

Puzzled, she looked at Jesse. "Animals?"

He chuckled. "Not only is Doc Sorenson a trauma surgeon, he's a practicing veterinarian. Better watch it. If you ask too many questions about the animals in the clinic, he might saddle you with a pet. He also treats animals from the local animal shelter and is always on the lookout for a potential pet owner."

"I wouldn't mind a pet."

"Don't say that unless you mean it." He set her on the exam table and helped her recline, then slid a pillow under her head.

"Would you like a pet?"

"Although I'd love to have a dog, my schedule is too erratic for a pet. I'd have to leave him with a boarding place or a friend every time I deployed."

"Maybe we can adopt a pet after we're settled." Simone could hardly wait. She loved dogs and had longed to have one of her own since she left San Francisco. Like Jesse, she never stayed in place long enough to have a pet. It would have been unfair to the dog to be constantly on the move. Now, perhaps, things would change and she could have the life she'd always dreamed about.

Soon, a man with a scowl on his face and dressed in a white coat walked into the room. "Back again, Phelps?"

"Not just me, Doc. My injuries are minor. You need to check my girlfriend. This is Simone Kent. A perp shot Simone twice on this mission."

"Should have protected her better."

His face flushed. "Yes, sir. I should have. I promise you, she won't be injured like this again."

Sorenson shifted his attention to Simone. "Let's have a look at you, my dear. Phelps, out."

"Yes, sir." He brushed his mouth over Simone's. "I'll be outside the door if you need me." He straightened and stared at the doctor.

Sorenson rolled his eyes. "Yes, yes. I've got her. Go."

After a squeeze of her hand, Jesse left the room, closing the door behind him.

"Where were you shot, Ms. Kent?"

"Simone, please. Right shoulder and right side."

"The shooter tried to kill you twice?"

"And missed."

He grunted.

The examination took a while but finally Sorensen stepped back and folded his arms. "Phelps left little for me to do. I'll give you a stronger antibiotic. The meds the medics carry are mild and generic. With two gunshot wounds, I'd rather be on the safe side. When you finish the prescription I give you, see your regular physician. It's important, Simone."

"I just moved to Tennessee to work at Fortress. I don't have a doctor."

"Doctors are on staff at the headquarters. Just go down to the infirmary. They'll make sure everything has healed. If you notice any swelling, heat, red streaks or oozing from the wounds, see the doctor immediately."

"Yes, sir. Will you check Jesse now?"

"In a moment. First, I want you to be absolutely honest with me. Will you do that?"

"Of course. Ask me anything."

"Were you sexually assaulted on this mission?"

"No, sir."

"Are you sure?"

"Positive. I was never unconscious except when I fell from a waterfall into a deep pool of water. Jesse is the one who pulled me out and saved my life."

He gave a curt nod. "Good. Second, you're on leave for the next two weeks."

"But Dr. Sorenson...."

"No arguments. Your body needs time to heal."

"I'm a computer tech at Fortress. I don't have a stressful job."

"With those injuries, I would sideline an operative for a month. I considered your job."

"I've only worked for Mr. Maddox for a month. I don't have any time built up for vacation or sick days."

"Leave that to me. I'll deal with Brent. Focus on your recovery." He patted her shoulder, then went to the door and opened it. "Your turn, Phelps. Get in here."

"Yes, sir." Jesse entered the room and walked to Simone's bedside. "How is she, Doc?"

"She'll be fine. You did a good job with her injuries."

"Thanks. Treatment plan?"

"I prescribed stronger antibiotics and two weeks away from work."

"I'll see to it."

"What about you? You said you were injured."

"Pistol whipped."

"Where?"

Jesse pointed to the area where Boudreax had struck him.

The doctor examined the back of Jesse's head, poking and prodding. "Any light sensitivity, blurring vision?"

"Yeah."

"How severe are the symptoms?"

"Enough to be annoying but not debilitating."

"We'll do a scan of your head to be sure but you probably have a mild concussion. Although you have a cut, the bleeding has stopped and you don't need stitches. I'll clean the cut for you, then we'll set up you and Simone in the recovery room. You will stay overnight so I can monitor you both."

Jesse grimaced. "Yes, sir."

"Scan first, then I'll tend to your cut." Sorenson opened the door. "Reggie, take Phelps for a scan of his head."

"Yes, sir." The linebacker-size man motioned for Jesse to follow him.

After the two left, Sorenson turned back to Simone. "Well, young lady, the recovery room is across the hall. Do you think you can walk on your own? If not, I'll have one of my assistants carry you."

"I can walk." She didn't want anyone other than Jesse to carry her. Weird, but it's how she felt.

"Let me help you sit up, and we'll walk across the hall."

Five minutes later, Simone lay on the recovery room bed with a blanket draped over her body. She glanced around the room as Sorenson's assistant set up a new IV bag for Simone. Even though this was a recovery room, the furniture and decor were surprisingly pleasing and comfortable.

When the man finished, Simone thanked him.

"No problem. Need anything before I head back to our four-footed patients?"

"I'm fine. Do you think I could see the dogs and cats later?"

He smiled. "Of course. They love to have visitors. If you're feeling up to it, you and Phelps can take a dog out to the play area. We have benches out there so you can sit and watch the dog play. Best to do it after we close the vet side down for the day. We don't want too many questions about your presence here."

"No problem. I feel like I ran a marathon, and I only walked across the hall."

"You'll be back on your feet soon. Doc Sorenson is the best." He pointed to the nurse call button. "If you need something, ask. One of us will take care of it for you."

"Thanks."

After a nod, he left Simone and returned to his duties.

Man, she was so tired. Who knew being shot took your strength down to nothing? Simone scowled. The timing couldn't be worse.

What would Brent and Zane say about her needing time off this soon?

Since she didn't have an answer, Simone settled deeper into the pillow and closed her eyes. She'd rest for a minute while she waited for Jesse to return.

When she woke, the sun was close to setting, and the animals were pretty quiet. She looked to her right and saw Jesse sprawled on a recliner that he'd pulled close to her bedside and wrapped his hand around hers.

He stirred as though he felt her gaze upon him and opened his eyes. Jesse smiled. "Hey, beautiful. Have a nice nap?"

"I feel better. What time is it?"

"Almost six. Someone is here to see you."

She blinked. "Who?"

Instead of answering her question, Jesse lowered the chair footrest and opened the door. "She's awake."

Seconds later, Brent Maddox walked inside the room.

She stared. "Sir, what are you doing here?"

"I always help guard my people when they're injured. Artemis and Shadow are away on other missions. Jesse is injured and should rest so he can't share guard duty with Sawyer. Zane would have come but someone has to mind the store. He's more crucial than I am at the day-to-day running of Fortress."

"I don't believe that for a minute."

He smiled.

"Thank you for coming, sir," Jesse said.

"No problem." Brent turned back to Simone. "Sorenson tells me you're worried about taking the recommended time off."

"I've only been working for a month."

"Doesn't matter. You were injured in the line of duty. If the doc says you need two weeks off, you'll take the time he's recommending with pay. It's the perks of the job, Simone."

"I'm a computer tech. I'm not as important as the operatives."

Brent pointed at her. "You're dead wrong. We need your skills as much as we need boots on the ground. Without you, our teams wouldn't be able to operate in the field as well as they do. Zane told me how many rave reviews the teams are giving you. You're doing a vital work, Simone. Never underestimate your value to our teams and our company."

Tears burned her eyes. "Thanks."

He inclined his head. "You'll take the time off with our blessing and the thanks of the military and the government. Because of you, they could prevent hundreds of deaths to military personnel and their civilian contractors."

"I had help."

"You had the lion's share of the load, and you did well, Simone. You'll find a bonus in your next paycheck."

"But I didn't do it for the money."

"I'm aware. Doesn't mean you didn't earn the bonus." He smiled. "Take the money and use it for your honeymoon."

Her cheeks flamed. "Jesse told you?"

"It was the first thing he said after giving me a report on your condition. Have you set a date yet?"

"Six months," Jesse said. "Not one day longer. I'm dating Simone, then we're taking off on a one-month honeymoon."

Brent chuckled. "Sounds like Logan and Poppy."

"Where do you think I got the idea? However, I'm not going to Europe." He glanced at Simone. "How does a beach honeymoon sound to you?"

"Like heaven."

"Good. It's settled. I'll take care of the arrangements when we return home."

"Rest, Simone, Jesse." Brent stepped to the doorway again. "I have your backs. You're safe with me." He left the room and closed the door.

Simone blinked. "He thinks I did a good job."

"The boss doesn't give idle compliments, Simone. In fact, they're scarce. I've only received two since I started working for Fortress. I've received plenty of dressing downs. He's not shy about doling out reprimands. When we get them, they're well deserved. Brent doesn't suffer fools. If we screw up, he lets us know."

"Six months, huh?"

He squeezed her hand. "Too soon? I can wait a little longer. Probably."

She laughed, wincing as her side stitches pulled. "Six months is fine. I always wanted to be a June bride."

"Good. We'll choose a firm date after we're home. Just so you know, I'm beefing up the security at your place. We do our best not to bring our work home with us, Simone. Sometimes, despite all our precautions, things slip through the cracks and one of our target's families or friends get a bead on our locations. You need to lock the doors and windows and activate the alarm even when you're home."

"No problem."

"Always keep your phone with you and your watch, even inside the house, in case someone breaches your security."

She nodded. All sensible orders that Jesse was couching as suggestions. "All right. What else?"

"Wear the tracker jewelry we provide for family members of operatives."

Simone shrugged. She had worn the jewelry on this mission. Whatever helped Jesse keep his mind on his task. The last thing she wanted was her safety to be a distraction to him. "Fine."

"You don't mind?"

"Nope. If you need me to wear them when we're at home, I will."

He leaned over and kissed her. "Thanks."

"One of Dr. Sorenson's assistants said we could take a dog to the play area. Do you think now is a good time to go?"

"I'll find out." He left the room and returned minutes later. "We're all set. Sorenson just sent the last client and her pet home. He says he has the perfect dog for you. Did you tell him we wanted a pet?"

"No, why?"

"The smile on his face when he told me about the dog. Sorenson has something up his sleeve." He handed Simone the IV bag, slid his arms under Simone's back and knees, and carried her down the hall to an exit.

Sawyer was waiting for them. "All set?"

"We're ready."

"How are you, Simone?"

"Curious about this dog. Have you seen it?"

He grinned. "Yep. You'll love the dog."

"Now, I really need to see this animal."

Sawyer opened the door. "Go on outside. I'll bring the dog to you in a minute."

Jesse set Simone on a bench and hung the bag on a nearby wooden post with thin pegs. Huh. Who knew a vet clinic would have a post like that set up in a pet play yard. Then again, if Dr. Sorenson treated operatives frequently, perhaps they needed some time outdoors with dogs and cats.

Sawyer returned, holding a small puffball of a dog.

Simone's heart melted. "Oh, my goodness. Look at that dog."

Jesse took the dog from Sawyer and cradled it in the palms of his hands. "Is this a puppy?"

"Nope. The doc says he's a full grown teacup poodle. His name is Goose."

The dog barked.

Simone grinned. "Hi, Goose."

Goose wiggled in Jesse's hands as though he wanted to go to Simone. "Want to hold him a minute or let him play a while first?"

"I'd love to hold him." She held out her hands and cradled the tiny dog against her chest. "Oh, man. You're one cute boy."

"He's up for adoption at the local shelter," Sawyer said. "If you want him, Sorenson will take care of the paperwork so you can take him back to Tennessee with you."

Goose stood on his hind legs and licked every part of Simone's face that he could reach.

She chuckled. "Okay, buddy. Want to play for a while?"

Jesse took him from her and set him on the ground.

For several minutes, Goose explored the play area, pouncing on sticks and balls, finally bringing a small ball to Jesse.

They played fetch until Goose's energy waned and he launched himself into Jesse's lap. After three turns to find the exact spot he wanted, the little dog settled down with a sigh and closed his eyes.

Still standing close by, Sawyer snorted. "Looks like you have a dog, Jesse."

"That depends on Simone. If she wants him, we'll take him home."

"How can you resist that face?" Sawyer teased. "Come on, man, have a heart. Goose needs a home, and you need someone to come home to."

Jesse looked at Simone. "I already have someone to come home to. What do you say, Simone? Are we adding this little guy to our pack?"

"Of course we are. Sawyer's right. How can we resist this face?" She stroked Goose's head.

"Great!" Sawyer turned toward the vet clinic. "I'll let Doc Sorenson know."

Jesse handed the dog to Simone, unhooked her IV from the wooden stand, and scooped her and the dog into his arms.

Sawyer held the door for them. "I'll see you in a minute."

After Simone settled back against the pillows, Goose circled three times, then flopped down beside her with a sigh and promptly dropped off the sleep. "Thank you, Jesse."

"I'd do anything for you," he murmured. "Adopting a dog who needs a family of his own is nothing if he makes you happy."

After a brisk knock, Dr. Sorenson walked in followed by Sawyer. "Well, I hear you've decided to keep Goose. He's a good boy. I must warn you, though, that he prefers to be with his people all the time. He doesn't do well alone. Separation anxiety."

Simone glanced at Brent who stood in the doorway, leaning against the jamb.

"Not a problem," he said. "You work in an enclosed space at headquarters. I suppose we can use a mascot, although he's a little small for the job."

"Small but fierce."

Her boss snorted. "We'll see."

"Thank you, Brent."

He winked at her, then turned his attention to Sorenson. "How is she, Doc?"

The doctor looked up from checking her vitals. "Everything looks wonderful. If nothing changes overnight, she'll be able to go home in the morning. Preferably before my patients arrive," he said pointedly.

Brent laughed. "Got the hint, Doc. We'll be out of here before the sun's up."

"I'll instruct two of my men to be available to help and for guard duty on the way to the airport. Although Bayside isn't a hotbed of terrorist activity, I won't have one of my favorite people caught in the crossfire."

Jesse grinned. "Aww, Doc. I didn't know you cared about me so much."

Sorenson glared at him. "You can take care of yourself most of the time. I'm talking about Simone."

Brent laughed. "I always knew you had a soft spot for beautiful women."

"Do you want me to stitch your wounds next time without numbing the injury first?"

His boss sobered. "No, sir. I'm going back to guard duty." He beat a hasty retreat to the hallway.

Simone stared after him. Wow. She'd never seen Brent back down. Then again, she hadn't been on staff with Fortress for long. What she knew of him, though, showed he never backed down.

"Young lady, you should be resting." Sorenson folded his arms. "If you don't rest, you will stay here longer than one night."

Oh, boy. Now she knew why everybody obeyed the doctor. He ruled this clinic with an iron fist. "Yes, sir."

"Unless Goose bothers your rest, keep him with you. He'll keep you warm. Phelps?"

"Sir?"

"Same order. Rest or you'll be staying with me. Do you want that?"

"No, sir. I have plans with Simone, and we need to get Goose set up at her place."

"The next time I check on the two of you, I expect to find you resting. Chapman, I assume you're not on duty yet?"

"No, sir."

"Out."

He saluted the doctor and left the room.

After a few more terse instructions, the doctor left Simone and Jesse alone.

"Whew." Simone wrinkled her nose. "You weren't kidding about the doctor."

"You're lucky. He has a soft spot for injured women." Jesse bent and kissed her. "You heard Sorenson. Rest. I don't want to stay here longer than I have to."

She rested her hand against Goose's back and let herself drift off to sleep. Her last thought was of the hunt for the leak. Someone had been giving Trevor White Simone's location every time she moved.

Time to uncover the identity of the traitor.

Chapter Twenty-Two

Jesse tossed the ball for Goose for the millionth time and chuckled as the little poodle raced after the round sphere and pounced on it. "Good job, buddy. Bring it back to me."

Goose nabbed the soft ball in his mouth and pranced back to Jesse, acting like the conquering hero returned from the war. He dropped the ball at Jesse's feet and laid down, panting.

"You tired, Goose?" Jesse crouched and stroked the dog's back. "Me, too. Don't tell Simone though. It will be our little secret, okay?"

"Too late," Simone said from the doorway of her home. "Come inside. Lunch is ready."

"Come on, Goose. The lady of the house has spoken." He picked up the dog and ball and followed Simone into her bright kitchen. On the table, Simone had set two plates filled with spaghetti and meatballs.

"Smells great." Jesse bent and kissed Simone before setting Goose on the floor near his food and water dishes, and dropped the ball into the dog's basket of toys. Wouldn't be long before every toy was strewn in whatever room Simone spent time in. When she moved to another room, Goose moved all the toys. Funny and sweet to watch.

"You didn't have to do all this, sweetheart." Jesse wrapped his arms around her. "A sandwich would have been fine."

"I'm allowed to spoil you while you're home. Gives you an incentive to come home to me when you're deployed."

He squeezed gently. "I'll always want to come home to you. The doctor at headquarters gave me a clean bill of health this morning."

She smiled. "That's great. When will your team go back on deployment rotation?"

"Next week. Are you really okay with me leaving so soon after our return from Mexico?"

"It's your job. I love you, so I'll deal."

"Well, at least your security systems are installed. I'd feel better if we knew which rock White crawled under."

She shrugged. "He'll show up, eventually."

Yeah, he would. The problem was, he could show up while Jesse was deployed and that would leave Simone to handle him alone. The last confrontation between them had ended with her in the hospital. He wouldn't let that happen again. "If we haven't run him to ground by the time my team deploys, I'll ask Maddox to assign another medic."

"No."

"Simone...."

"Your team needs you, not a substitute. They depend on you to get them home in one piece. Go with them. I'll be fine."

"You weren't fine the last time White came after you."

"That was years ago."

Jesse still felt responsible for her safety. "White's dangerous."

"You've been giving me more pointers in self-defense for two weeks and so has Sawyer. Not only that, you gave me this little jewel." She held up her small pink Taser and laid it on the kitchen counter. "Trust me to take care of myself while you're gone."

"Under normal circumstances, I would. White is obsessed with you. That makes him doubly dangerous. I've seen what obsessive stalkers can do, Simone. I want nothing to happen to you."

She remained silent a moment. "You mentioned before that you might ask another operative to monitor me while you're gone if Trevor was still MIA. What if we compromise? What if I stayed with Poppy or Sage, then you and their husbands work out who stays with all of us?"

The ball of ice in his stomach melted a little. "I can work with that."

"Good. That's settled." Simone stepped out of his embrace. "Come on. You need to eat before your food gets cold."

When they finished lunch, Jesse helped Simone clean up their dishes and the pots she'd used to cook for him. Afterward, they settled on the couch with Goose tucked on Simone's lap and watched a movie together.

He glanced down at her at the halfway mark to ask if she wanted popcorn or a drink. She was sound asleep with her head propped against his shoulder.

He tugged the blanket off the back of her couch and draped it over her. Goose wiggled out and climbed back on Simone's lap, this time on top of the blanket.

By the time the movie finished, Simone stirred. As the credits rolled, she blinked and looked up at him, a sheepish look in her eyes. "I fell asleep, didn't I?"

"You needed the rest. Feel better?"

She nodded. "Sorry I conked out on you."

"Don't be. I'm glad to serve as your pillow any time."

Simone nudged him. "What about dinner?"

Pleased, he bent and kissed her. "I'm taking you out. I need to rack up the dates before I'm deployed."

"Where are we going?"

"It's a surprise. I think you'll like it."

"Anything you do for me is wonderful. When do we leave?"

"An hour."

Simone handed Goose to Jesse. "I need to get ready. I'll be back in a few minutes, and we'll feed Goose before we go."

"Sounds good." He smiled as she hurried down the hall to her bedroom. Couldn't wait to see her expression when he slid the engagement ring on her finger.

When she returned minutes later, Simone had dressed in black half boots, black jeans, and a blue sweater.

Jesse's heart skipped a beat. His wife-to-be looked stunning. "You look amazing," he said. "I'll be the envy of all the guys at the restaurant."

She smiled, her cheeks turning a pretty shade of pink. "Thanks." Simone took Goose from him and carried the poodle to the kitchen. "All right, buddy. Time for dinner."

Goose danced with excitement, yapping and getting underfoot. As soon as Simone set his filled dish on the floor, the dog gulped down his food in two minutes flat and licked the bowl clean of any scraps.

Jesse chuckled. "All right, Goose. Time to visit the grass." He attached the leash to his collar and walked to the back door. "We'll be back in a minute, Simone, then you and I can leave."

When they returned, Jesse put Goose in his crate. "We'll be back soon, buddy." He handed the poodle a dog treat and closed the crate door. He stood. "Ready for your surprise, Simone?"

She nodded. "I love surprises."

He hoped she loved this one. A lot of planning had gone into this evening, including many suggestions from his teammates.

Jesse escorted her to his SUV and lifted her to the passenger seat. After he circled the hood, he climbed behind the wheel and drove to Opryland Hotel in Nashville where they had reservations at one restaurant inside the atrium.

During dinner, Simone talked about her search for the traitor and how she'd come up with a dead end so far. "I don't understand it," she complained. "I should have been able to track down the traitor by now. This is embarrassing."

"You're still taking the pain meds?"

She nodded.

"They cloud your thinking. Another thing to consider. Perhaps the traitor might be closer to you than you realize."

Simone blinked. "A friend or colleague?"

"Why not? People who are closest to us are the ones who slip under our guard. We never expect our friends and family to turn against us."

Her expression grew troubled. "You're right. I haven't even considered the possibility. Stupid of me."

"You're human. You'll look again and find the leak."

"I hope so because I'll never be safe until I do. I don't want to run again."

Jesse straightened. "You're taking a stand right here. We'll deal with White together."

"I don't want anyone I love or care about to die because of me, especially you."

"All the more reason to stop this from getting out of hand now. Trust me, sweetheart."

"I do, more than anyone I've ever known."

"Then know that I have your best interests at heart. I will never let White have you or allow him to take you away from me." He set his napkin to the side of his empty plate. "Are you ready to tour the atrium?" When Simone nodded, Jesse came around the table to offer his hand.

As they walked the lush gardens and walkways winding throughout the atrium, Simone paused frequently to examine plants and flowers and came to a stop to admire the waterfall. "This is so beautiful," she murmured. "I could sit here and watch the waterfall for hours."

"Anytime you want to come back, tell me. I love this place, too." He wrapped his arms around Simone. Time to go forward with the plan. She loved him. She'd say yes. Wouldn't she? "I love you, Simone."

She lifted her face toward his and stood on her tiptoes to kiss him. "I love you, too, Jesse. I'm so blessed to have you in my life."

He took a deep breath. "I'm glad to hear you say that." Jesse released her and knelt in front of the woman he loved with every cell in his body. He pulled out the platinum solitaire ring that had been burning a hole in his pocket all day. "I promise to cherish you above all others. I'll protect you with my body and love you until I draw my last breath on this earth. Will you do me the honor of becoming my wife, Simone Kent?"

Tears slipped down Simone's cheeks but her smile said it all. "Absolutely yes."

Thank God. Jesse slid the ring on her finger and stood to share a blistering kiss with the woman of his dreams. Dimly, he was aware of applause nearby. When he finally broke the kiss and looked over his shoulder, his teammates and their spouses were on a nearby trail, beaming at them.

Stunned, he said, "What are you doing here?"

"We couldn't let you do this without our support," his team leader said. Brody clapped him on the shoulder. "Congratulations, my friend. You, too, Simone."

"Welcome to the family, Simone," Sage, his wife, said.

The rest of Texas Team shook his hand and hugged Simone as did their wives. Sawyer was the last in line to congratulate them. "Good job, Jesse. Happy for you, man. Welcome to the Texas Team, Simone. So, when's the big day?"

"In June," Jesse said. "You'll be the first to know the date."

Max, one of his other teammates, said, "Time to celebrate a new team member. Who's up for ice cream floats? I know a place near here that serves the best milkshakes in town." He named the nearby ice cream shop, and the group left the atrium to reassemble at the shop for dessert.

Laughter and teasing from his teammates and their spouses filled the next hour. Jesse enjoyed every minute. These men were the reason he loved his job. Friends who were more like family than his own biological family.

After a final round of congratulations and best wishes from their friends, the couples parted ways and Jesse drove Simone back to her home.

"That was so much fun. How did you get your teammates and their families to be at the atrium at the right time?"

He chuckled. "I didn't plan for them to be there."

"Don't get me wrong. I'm glad they came but why did they show up?"

"I was nervous about tonight, and they knew it. I might have asked for their advice about how to propose to you."

"You had to know I'd say yes. I love you, Jesse. Why would I turn down a marriage proposal from the man I adore?"

"You saw up close and personal how dangerous our missions can be while we were in Mexico. You might have changed your mind about spending your life with me during the past two weeks."

"Being with you makes me so happy I can hardly contain my joy."

"I'll do my best to make sure you stay that way."

"You don't have to do anything, love. All I need is you." She leaned over the center console and kissed him for long minutes. When she drew back, her eyes were sparkling. "I have nothing so fine to offer you as this gorgeous ring but I have the makings of a great cup of coffee. Care to join me for a while?"

"I'd love to." He didn't want to leave her anymore. Bad timing, though. Their wedding was at least six months out. Patience and discipline were the name of the game until his wedding ring was on her finger. She'd be worth the wait.

He exited the SUV and came around to help Simone from the vehicle. With his arm around her, Jesse walked to the door with his girl, unlocked it, and turned off the alarm.

Goose yapped in excitement in the kitchen.

Simone laughed. "Someone is happy we're home."

"He doesn't fool me. Goose just wants another trip outside and a treat for doing his business in the yard instead of the house."

"As long as the bribes work, I don't mind giving him treats. He has enough energy to burn them off. If you don't mind taking him out, I'll put on the coffee."

"Deal."

Jesse and Goose returned a few minutes later. The medic crouched and gave the dog a treat. "Good work, buddy."

When Goose dashed over to Simone, she laughed and picked him up. "Yes, I'm proud of you, too. Coffee's almost ready, love."

He kissed her. "I enjoy hearing you call me that."

"Good. You'll be hearing it for the next 70 years."

After drinking a mug of coffee with Simone, Jesse knew he needed to go home before he wasn't able to make himself leave.

He tugged Simone into his arms and kissed her for long minutes before stepping back. "I'll see you tomorrow, baby. Sleep well."

Before he reached the front door, something beeped. Jesse paused and glanced at Simone over his shoulder. "What's that?"

"My computer. I set it to run a check on my circle of friends while you were outside with Goose."

"What does the beep mean?"

"The computer found a match." She looked ill. "One of my friends is a traitor."

Chapter Twenty-Three

"Show me." Jesse wrapped his hand around Simone's and followed her to the kitchen where her laptop sat on the breakfast bar.

Simone climbed atop a bar stool and tapped a few keys to bring up the search results. She scanned the screen and sat back, her face white. "Oh, no."

Jesse rested his hands on her shoulders as he looked at the screen. "Who is Ember Atkins?"

"My only remaining friend in San Francisco." She covered her face with her hands. "Oh, Jesse. How could she do this? Why? I thought we were friends. I set up the scan just to satisfy you, never considering that Ember would be the one to betray me. I honestly thought it might be someone at the think tank in D.C."

"Can you tell from the information what she did?"

"She's been in frequent contact with Trevor."

He stilled. "How do you know?"

"Do you want deniability?"

"I don't care about that. Tell me."

"I hacked into her cell phone records." Simone flipped to another screen to show him many calls to one number. She highlighted each one. "That number belongs to Trevor."

"How does Ember know where you are, Simone?"

"She's a hacker like I am. In fact, I'm the one who taught her all my tricks." She huffed out a breath. "I never thought she'd use those tricks against me."

"Can you block her access to you?"

"I've learned several new techniques since I started working for Zane. You can bet I'll start using them in my personal life. The problem is the damage has already been done."

"What do you mean?"

She pointed to the screen. "The last phone conversation between Trevor and Ember was two days ago. Trevor knows I'm here."

A muscle ticked in Jesse's jaw. The jerk was probably already in Hartman. He'd be a fool to try to take Simone from the Fortress compound. A security force that wouldn't give any quarter would take White down in a heartbeat. They took the protection of their Fortress family seriously. If White posed a threat, he would be stopped or killed without a second thought.

"I'm not leaving you here alone," Jesse said. "You have a choice. You can stay with me at my place, you can stay in a hotel suite where I'll sleep on the couch, or I'll be sleeping here on your couch. Bottom line is I'm staying with you."

She glanced at Goose. "A hotel wouldn't allow him to stay with me. I won't leave him alone. I wouldn't put it past Trevor to hurt Goose to get back at me."

"That leaves staying here or at my place. Which do you choose?"

"Do you mind staying here? Goose isn't housebroken yet. I don't want him to mess up your floors."

"Don't care about that. I only want you safe. I can replace floors but I can't replace you."

"Do you want my help keeping watch overnight?"

He shook his head. "You're still recovering from two gunshot wounds."

"Jesse, you can't stay awake all night."

"Baby, I do it all the time when we're on a mission."

"I realize that, but I'd rather you had someone to split a watch shift with so you're not exhausted when you're deployed."

Simone had a point. "All right. I'll call Sawyer and see if he can stay with us."

She beamed at him. "Thank you, Jesse. I'll make more coffee and lay out snacks for both of you."

After she went to the kitchen, Jesse pulled out his phone and called his teammate.

"Miss me already?" Sawyer said in greeting.

"Ha. You wish. I need a favor."

"Anything. What do you need?"

"Someone to spell me on night watch."

Silence, then, "What's going on?"

Jesse summarized what Simone discovered.

Sawyer whistled. "Whew. A betrayal like that is rough. I'm heading to Simone's house now. See you in a few minutes."

"Thanks, man. I owe you one."

"Nope. Glad to do it." He ended the call.

Jesse slid the phone into his pocket and went to the kitchen. "Sawyer is on his way."

"Great. I'm glad he could help." Simone slid a cookie sheet into the oven with round slices of dough scattered across the surface.

"What's this?"

"Chocolate chip cookies for the hard-working men in the house." She showed the various snacks on the tabletop. "Cookies, coffee, and a variety of snacks on the table should keep you guys fueled and ready for trouble throughout the night."

Jesse chuckled. "Although you didn't have to go to all this trouble, we appreciate it anyway. We never turn down cookies."

"I have enough for both of you."

"We'll be fine, Simone." Coffee would have done the trick but he wouldn't reject her gift.

Jesse played with Goose until a knock sounded on the front door. He scooped up the poodle and went to let in his teammate.

Sawyer set his Go bag against the wall and held out his hands for Goose. "Hey there, little man. You're looking good." He chuckled as the dog licked his face and neck. "What smells so good in here?"

"Simone's baking cookies for us. She didn't want us to go hungry on watch."

"If you let that girl slip through your fingers, I'm calling first dibs on her. She's a keeper."

"That she is, which is why you aren't getting a chance with her."

His friend sighed and looked mournfully at Goose. "See what happens when you're late to the party, Goose? You miss out on all the special girls. Don't take after me, buddy. You'll be sorry."

Jesse and Sawyer walked to the kitchen and saw Simone take the last batch of cookies from the oven.

"Those smell amazing," Sawyer said. "Thanks for the cookies, Simone."

"You're welcome. I wanted to do something for you since you're helping Jesse and me overnight."

"I'm glad to help, cookies or no cookies." He rubbed Goose's head. "I'm going to teach Goose how to keep watch."

Simone laughed. "Good luck with that."

"You just watch me. You might be surprised."

"And I might not." She yawned. "Oops. Sorry."

"Are you ready to go to bed now?" Jesse asked.

"Depends. Are you taking the first watch or the second?"

"Second," Sawyer said. "I have the watch until 3:00 a.m. Jesse can take over at that point while I catch a nap. Brody is a stickler for being on time to PT. Jesse might have a couple more days to lounge around and be a bum, but I don't."

"Since you're taking the first watch, I'll try to sleep for a few hours and get up at 3:00."

Jesse smiled. Had to love a woman who would give up sleep to stand watch with him. "I'll walk you to your room."

After a long, sizzling goodnight kiss, Jesse walked across the hall to Simone's guest room and laid across the bed.

His internal alarm woke him a few minutes before three o'clock. He rolled out of bed, took a quick shower and changed his clothes before making his way to the kitchen.

Sawyer handed him a mug of coffee. "Everything's been quiet."

Jesse scratched Goose between the ears. "Did you teach Goose everything you know about night watch?"

"Not yet, but he has good instincts and good ears. He'll be a delightful companion for Simone when we're deployed."

Deployed. Jesse sipped his coffee, uneasiness settling in his gut. He didn't want to leave his teammates without his help on a mission. At the same time, he refused to leave Simone alone and vulnerable to Trevor White in his absence.

If he did as Simone has asked and went with his teammates, Jesse would have to find someone he trusted with his wife-to-be to watch over her and the other women.

Simone staggered into the kitchen, dressed for another day of recovery and, knowing her, computer work. "Morning."

"Good morning, sweetheart." Jesse brushed his lips over hers. "Coffee?"

"Please." She accepted the mug Sawyer poured for her with a nod of thanks. At the first sip, she sighed. "This brew is strong enough to melt metal. It's perfect, Sawyer."

He chuckled. "Glad to know you appreciate my genuine talent in life."

"So, Sawyer, is Goose ready for night watch?" Simone teased.

"Almost. Might need another night or two but this little guy has great instincts. He has a nose for trouble."

"Good to know. Thanks for watching him."

"No problem. He's a wonderful dog." Sawyer set Goose on the floor. "On that note, I'm going to take a nap. I'll see you in a couple of hours."

Simone stared after him, then turned to Jesse. "Shouldn't he sleep longer?"

"Not if he wants to spare himself an extra mile running at top speed. We weren't kidding about Brody. He won't put up with tardiness."

"How many miles do you run on average?"

"Between five and ten miles, depends on how quickly we're being deployed. Because we go back on rotation next week, the team will probably run five miles, six if you're late, more if you badmouth the leader or give him attitude about any of the evil exercises he dreams up."

"Sounds like fun," Simone said dryly. "I'm glad I'm not training for a mission with you."

Never again if Jesse had his way. "You can run with me if you want the exercise."

"Ha! If I'm running, something is chasing me."

He laughed. "Got it. No running for you. Is walking more your speed?"

"I love a good walk." She eyed him over her coffee mug. "Not, however, before the worms are up."

Goose sat at Simone's feet and stared up at her.

"Uh oh. Someone needs to go outside."

Goose barked once as though in agreement.

Jesse picked up his leash and clipped it to the dog's collar. "We'll be back in a minute." He disarmed the alarm, unlocked the door, and walked outside with Goose.

The teacup poodle hurried to the grass, did his business, then investigated all the grass blades in the yard. He tugged the leash until Jesse obliged him by walking closer to the back fence. A cool breeze blew the leaves on the trees and bushes, the branches swaying and causing shadows to dance on the fence.

Goose growled and barked.

Behind Jesse, a twig snapped.

He pivoted and saw Trevor White with a Glock pointed at him.

"You shouldn't have interfered," White said, and pulled the trigger.

Chapter Twenty-Four

Simone dropped two slices of bread into the toaster and paused, frowning. Why was Goose barking like crazy?

Then she heard a gunshot.

She dropped her coffee mug on the counter and ran. Simone threw open the back door and raced outside to find Jesse sprawled on the ground with Goose barking continuously nearby as though guarding him.

When she recognized Trevor White who was holding a gun pointed at Jesse, ice water flowed through Simone's veins. "Jesse!"

She ran to his side and would have fallen to her knees beside him except Trevor wrapped his arm around her throat and squeezed. "No!" she wheezed out.

"You're coming with me or your boyfriend dies right now. If he's not already dead." Trevor dragged her away from Jesse.

"Let me go." Simone clawed at Trevor's arm. She had to help Jesse.

"Simone!" Sawyer barreled from the house, weapon up and aimed at Trevor. "Let her go now, White."

"No way. She's mine. You have a choice. You can save your buddy's life or you can die along with your friend on the ground." Trevor's muscles tightened. He was going to shoot Sawyer. She couldn't let him shoot Jesse's friend.

"Don't, Trevor," she pleaded. "I'll go with you. Don't hurt Sawyer. Please."

Trevor laughed. "I love it when you beg. You'll be doing a lot more begging before I finish punishing you for turning me over to the cops."

"Anything you want. Just don't hurt him."

"Simone, no," Sawyer said, voice low. "Don't."

"I'll be fine." She tapped her watch band, hoping he got her meaning. "Save Jesse."

He looked torn. "You're asking too much, kid."

"Please. Save Jesse for me. Let's go, Trevor."

Trevor tightened his grip on Simone, using her body as a shield, and dragged her from the yard. "You follow us, and she dies."

Sawyer kept his weapon aimed at Trevor, looking for an opening. He didn't get one.

Simone stumbled as her ex-boyfriend forced her to his car parked down the street. She needed to escape and return to Jesse. How badly was he hurt?

Tears stung her eyes. He had to be all right. She'd never forgive herself if Jesse didn't make it.

Trevor yanked open the car's passenger-side door and shoved Simone inside. "Climb into the driver's seat."

"What?"

"Shut up and move over. You're driving." He motioned her to the driver's side with the barrel of the gun. "Hurry."

Heart sinking, she scrambled to the driver's seat, strapped on her seatbelt, and pushed the start button. "Where are we going?"

"Interstate 40 West. We're leaving this little town in our rearview mirror."

Simone's watch vibrated. Her screen remained dark, however. She breathed easier. Sawyer must have contacted Fortress. Thank goodness someone was tracking her. She did not know when Trevor would stop.

Somewhere along this journey, she'd escape. She must be ready. Jesse was everything to her, and she'd fight with every breath she had to go back to him. Simone wanted that life about which she'd only dreamed. The medic who held her heart was a key part of that dream. If he survived.

Pain ripped through Simone, almost paralyzing her in its intensity. No, she couldn't think that way. If she did, she wouldn't be able to help herself. Sawyer would take care of Jesse, and the man she loved would survive. She knew he would. He must. The alternative was unthinkable.

Trevor laughed suddenly.

"What's so funny?" she snapped. The Jerk thought he was so clever. What she wouldn't give to take him down a peg or two.

"Your boyfriend thought he was so tough. He died just like everyone else I've killed."

Stunned, her head whipped his direction. "What did you say?"

"You heard me. He died as easy as everyone else I killed."

"You killed other people?"

"What did you think, that I was an angel or something?"

Not in her wildest imagination did Simone believe Trevor would end someone's life. "Who?"

He named three people from their old neighborhood in San Francisco, long-time friends.

"Why? They were your friends."

"At one time, they were. They dissed me." He jabbed the barrel into her side. "Just like you did. You'll pay for that, Simone. No one treats me with disrespect and gets by with it. Even you."

"Why did you kidnap me? If you're angry with me, why would you force me to go with you?"

He snorted. "To punish you, of course. You deserve everything you get. Years I spent in prison because of you. I'm thinking about keeping you locked up for the same amount of days I was in prison."

That wouldn't happen if she could help it. "Oh, come on," she scoffed. "You spent two years in jail. Big deal. You've been living it up since your release while I spent my life on the run, always looking over my shoulder, watching for you."

He smirked. "And I kept finding you, didn't I? You thought you were so clever. You're as stupid as all the other women I've known."

"Really? If you're so smart, why did you have to use Ember to find me every time I moved?"

Trevor jabbed the gun into her side again. "Shut up, Simone, or I'll take you out right now instead of keeping you around."

She sucked in a breath as pain rocketed through her body. "Knock it off, Trevor. If I lose control of the car, both of us might die."

He backed off a little. "Your friends will pay the price if you trash my car. I'll go back and kill them all, one by one."

"You'll never get away with this. You know that, don't you?"

"Oh, I already have, baby," he crowed. "Your big, tough boyfriend is dead and his friend is powerless to do anything about it. Where I'm taking you, no one will ever find you."

That's what he thought. However, Trevor needed to believe she had lost hope. Otherwise, he'd be too vigilant. Simone wanted that chance to escape. "Where are we going, Trevor?"

"You'll see."

Great. She was driving without a destination. Simone glanced at the fuel gauge. Her hands tightened around the steering wheel. The Jerk had filled the gas tank before shooting Jesse and kidnapping her which meant the gas would hold out for about 500 miles. For the record, she was tired of being kidnapped. It sucked.

To keep from antagonizing Trevor more, Simone remained silent while she drove. If she was lucky, her ex would fall asleep. Stranger things had happened. After all, he was on an adrenaline high. She knew from experience after the high came a crash.

Instead of falling asleep, though, he stayed wide awake, popping a pill every once in a while. "What are you taking?" she asked when the sun had finally risen.

"Energy, babe. Pure, sweet energy." He laughed, using the barrel of the gun to brush her hair away from her face. "I can stay awake for hours with these little babies."

Her heart sank. Trevor was taking uppers while she was becoming more exhausted with each passing mile. Looked like the joke was on her. She was the one fighting an adrenaline dump while Trevor was still riding a high. At some point, though, he'd have to sleep. Even he couldn't stay awake indefinitely. When he fell asleep, all bets were off. She'd find a way back to Jesse either on her own or with the help of Fortress.

At noon, Trevor said, "Take this exit. We're going to fill up here and maybe grab a bite to eat. We'll take it to go, so no funny business."

She followed his instructions, drove to the nearest gas station connected to a truck stop, and parked beside a pump.

"Get out and fill the tank. I'll be right beside you so don't try anything. Anyone you ask for help, I'll kill. Got that?"

"Yeah, yeah. I got it." She climbed out of the car, groaning at her stiff muscles. Man, she hated driving that long without a break.

Simone glowered at Trevor who came around the back of the car to grasp her arm in a strong hold.

"Bad attitudes will cost you, baby," he murmured as he glanced around. "Don't tempt me to increase your punishment."

She held out her hand.

"What?"

"We have to pay for the gas." Simone raised her eyebrow. "You kidnapped me with no warning. I don't have a penny to my name. That means you pay for the gas or we walk."

He dug into his pocket and pulled out his wallet. Trevor grabbed a card and thrust it into her hand. "Use this."

She glanced at the name on the card and flinched when she recognized the name of one of his victims. "Seriously?"

"Just use it," he snapped, then rattled off the code.

"What if the account has been closed?"

"We'll go inside and pay cash. Hurry. I'm hungry."

Simone rolled her eyes and filled the tank. Why hadn't the victim's family closed the account? She shuddered to think how many charges Trevor had racked up on the account.

After she filled the tank, Trevor slung his arm around Simone's shoulders and held her tight against his side. "Remember what I told you. All the people we meet? Their lives are in your hands."

He went to a food counter and ordered two sub sandwiches to go along with drinks and chips. While the food workers prepared the sandwiches, Simone tried to pull away.

"Where do you think you're going?" Trevor hissed. "I told you no funny stuff."

"Bathroom. It's been hours since we started driving."

He scowled. "You'll have to wait until our food is ready."

At least he hadn't told her she'd have to find a bush on the side of the road. When their food was ready, Trevor thrust the bag of sandwiches at her and picked up the drink carrier in his free hand.

He hustled her toward the restrooms and pushed her toward the door marked women. "You have two minutes. After that, I'll come in and drag you out."

Simone hurried inside, used the facilities, and washed her hands all in under 90 seconds. She glanced around for anything she might use to escape or maybe a window to climb out. Nothing.

Twenty-five seconds to go.

She had just enough time to contact Fortress. Hopefully, someone could tell her Jesse's condition.

She pressed the emergency button.

A message appeared on the screen. Can you talk?

"For a few seconds," she whispered. "How is Jesse?"

"At the emergency room receiving treatment. No word on prognosis," Zane murmured.

"Tell Jesse I love him."

"You can tell him yourself."

Trevor banged on the door. "Simone, you've got fifteen seconds."

"Are you all right?" Zane asked.

"For now. I won't be for long."

"Help is coming."

"Tell them to hurry. Trevor is taking uppers. His behavior is becoming more aggressive and erratic." She gave him the car's description and the license plate number, the name on the credit card she'd used, and their present location. "I don't know where we're going."

"I'm leaving our communication open. Don't antagonize him, Simone. Play along."

More banging on the door. "Simone!"

"Coming," she called, grabbed their food bag, and unlocked the door.

As soon as she opened the door, Trevor crowded her back into the bathroom and slapped her. Simone's head whipped to the side as she cried out in pain. Man, that hurt.

"That's for keeping me waiting." He grabbed her arm in a painful grip and propelled her from the bathroom.

Her face burning, Simone stumbled along beside Trevor as they exited the building and walked to the car.

Once again, he opened the passenger side door, shoved her inside, and said, "Scoot over."

Without arguing, she did as he instructed and strapped on her seatbelt. Once he was inside the vehicle, she started the car and drove back onto the Interstate.

Trevor tore into the sandwich and wolfed it down in minutes along with the chips, then downed his soft drink.

Simone watched him from the corner of her eye and wondered if he would give her the other sub. No way would she beg him for food. She'd rather starve first. Trevor would enjoy her groveling and his ego boost at holding her in his power.

Just like she had expected, Trevor closed the bag of food and set it by his feet. The Jerk was probably going to hold the food for himself, making her go hungry to satisfy his own power trip.

The lack of food didn't bother her as much as the lack of sleep and water. The next time they stopped, she'd have to get water somehow.

"Aren't you going to ask me for food?"

"Nope."

He scowled. "Why not?"

"You bought food for yourself."

"Think you're pretty smart, don't you?"

She shrugged, flinching as her shoulder protested the movement. One more thing she needed. Pain meds.

"You'll eat when I say you can." Trevor trailed the barrel of the pistol from her cheek down her neck to her side. "And when you beg me on your knees. You'll only eat from my hand, baby, or you won't eat at all."

Oh, yeah. Definitely an ego trip. She didn't respond. Why bother? She'd never beg for Trevor to feed her.

She focused on driving, following the speed limit and praying her help from Fortress would find her soon. She needed to be by Jesse's side.

Mile after mile passed with Trevor alternating between taunting or threatening her and popping another pill to keep himself awake.

He couldn't sit still. One minute he was facing the window. The next he twisted in the seat to stare at Simone.

She much preferred for him to watch the scenery out the window as they passed. When Trevor watched her, he couldn't keep his hands to himself. He kept touching her leg, her arm, face, and finally sliding his hand under her shirt.

"Knock it off, Trevor," she snapped. "You're distracting me."

He grabbed her side and squeezed hard. "You don't tell me no. Ever," he yelled. "Do you understand me, Simone? I'm in charge now, not you. You're nothing."

Her watch vibrated twice against her wrist. A warning to cooperate and not tick off her crazy ex-boyfriend? A signal that help was close? She prayed the latter was true.

"Okay, okay. You're the boss. I'm just reminding you that if you distract me, I could run us off the road. Neither of us wants that." Especially her.

His fingers gripped her side harder. "Better not or you'll pay the price."

Despite her best efforts to contain them, tears trickled down her cheeks.

"That's better," he gloated. "I like it when you cry. You'll be doing a lot of that for the rest of your life, baby."

Not if she could help it. At the first opportunity, she was gone.

Two hours later, Trevor said, "Take this exit."

Mindful of Zane listening and watching their progress on his computer, she said, "Exit 52?"

"Yeah. When you get off, turn left."

"But there's nothing here."

He laughed. "That's the point. I'm taking you to the middle of nowhere. No one will be around to hear you scream."

#

Chapter Twenty-Five

Jesse glared at the doctor. "Patch me up. I have to leave." Hadn't this guy listened to a word Jesse said? His future wife was in the hands of her ex. He had to find her before White hurt her.

"Are you out of your mind?" The doctor folded his arms across his chest. "Someone shot you less than two hours ago. You'll be here at least the rest of the night and probably most of the day tomorrow, too."

"Can't, Doc Martin. Told you. My woman was kidnapped. The man who took Simone will hurt her if I don't stop him."

"Let the police handle it."

"Not happening. Finish the patch job now or I'll do it myself and check myself out against medical advice."

"You're not a doctor."

"I'm a medic."

"The police will want to talk to you. This is a gunshot wound. I had to report it."

"Fine. I'll talk to them after Simone is safe."

Martin stared at him a moment as though assessing whether Jesse meant what he said. He did. Nothing would stop him from going after Simone, not even a bullet wound in the side.

The doctor sighed. "All right. Don't say I didn't warn you when the cops track you down and read you the riot act."

"Won't be the first time."

"What about infection?"

"I'll take care of it. Finish the patch job. You have two minutes."

Muttering and cursing under his breath the whole time, Martin finished the stitching job and tossed his gloves in the trash. "I urge you to reconsider, Mr. Phelps. Checking yourself out of this hospital isn't wise."

"I'm aware, Doc. I'll seek further medical treatment after I find Simone."

Martin shook his head. "I hope she's worth endangering your life."

He slid from the exam table, masking the wince. "She is." Without a backward glance, he strode from the room without a shirt. He'd get one from his Go bag or from Sawyer's. Didn't matter to him. His only goal was to get to Simone as fast as possible.

Sawyer glanced up as Jesse walked out of the exam room. "Sweet-talked your way out of staying overnight?"

He snorted. "I'm leaving against medical advice."

"Figured that's what you'd do." He handed Jesse a shirt and walked toward the exit with him. "Zane's tracking Simone as we speak."

"Where are they headed?"

"West out of the state. Z doesn't know where White's taking her. Simone's ex didn't tell her their destination. He's making her drive."

His hands clenched. "Let's go."

"Just so you know, I'm driving."

"Don't care as long as we get moving."

"Your mike bag is in the back of the SUV. Did the doc give you anything?"

"Nope." Jesse's lips curved. "He wasn't happy when I refused medication."

"You need to be ready to handle White."

"I will be. I have what I need in the mike bag."

Sawyer shook his head. "I hope you know what you're doing, buddy. We could have handled this without you."

"She's mine to protect. I'm going with you. End of discussion."

"At the first sign of infection, extreme blood loss, or you lose consciousness, we're dumping you at the nearest emergency room and continuing with the rescue mission."

"Yeah, yeah. You won't have to dump me at a hospital. I'm fine." Mostly.

Sawyer snorted as he unlocked the vehicle. "I've heard that story before, my friend."

Jesse climbed into the passenger seat while Sawyer opened the cargo hatch to retrieve the mike bag. He handed the medical kit to Jesse. "Thanks."

"Yep." Sawyer circled the hood and slipped behind the steering wheel. As soon as he started the engine and drove from the lot, he activated the Bluetooth system.

"Got him?" Brody said instead of a greeting.

"He's in the passenger seat, digging through his mike bag for medication."

Silence, then, "The doctor gave you clearance to leave the hospital, Jesse?" his team leader asked.

"I walked out. Deal with it. And save the lectures. I already got a boatload of them from the ER doc and Sawyer. How far ahead of us are you?"

"Ninety minutes. Zane sent us Simone's GPS tracker signal."

"Have they stopped yet?"

"Nope. White must have filled the tank before he shot you and took your woman."

"Great." How far could he go on one tank of gas before they stopped?

"Yeah. Zane is listening to what's happening."

"Is Simone all right?"

"For the moment. He thinks White is popping pills to stay awake."

Not good. Pop enough uppers, and he would become irritable and jittery. He could hurt Simone by accident with a twitchy trigger finger or knife hand.

"Keep in touch," Brody ordered. "And don't be a fool, Jesse. If you need Sawyer to drop you at the nearest hospital, you better say so. Simone needs you alive."

"I hear you." Didn't mean he'd obey the order. His only priority was to save Simone.

"You are one stubborn man, Phelps."

"Like every member of Texas Team."

"We aren't the walking wounded, my friend. Don't push too far or I will bench you. Understood?"

"Yes, sir."

After Brody ended the call, Sawyer placed another call to Zane. "It's Sawyer. Send Simone's tracker signal to Jesse. We're about 90 minutes behind the rest of the team."

Zane whistled softly. "You should be in bed, Jesse."

"Would you stay in bed if your woman had been kidnapped?"

"Nope. I'd load up with every weapon I could carry, track her down, and kill every person involved in taking Claire from me and our son."

"Exactly."

"How can I help?"

"Keep me updated on their progress and if they stop for gas or food. Every stop gets help to Simone faster."

"Well, so far, you're out of luck. They haven't stopped for any reason."

"They have to pull over soon."

"If you think of anything I can do, let me know." Zane ended the call.

"You should rest," Sawyer said. "You'll need every bit of your strength to get through this."

He knew. Didn't make him happy. "How's our fuel level?"

"We need to fill up," his friend admitted.

"Good. When we do, I'll go inside the station and buy what we need to keep going."

Sawyer glanced at him. "You sure you're okay, Jesse?"

"I will be. I need fluids to help replace the blood I lost."

After reaching down to the side pocket of his door, Sawyer handed Jesse an unopened bottle of water. "Start with this."

"Perfect. Thanks." Jesse grabbed a packet of pain meds and another of antibiotics. He'd take a couple of each to hold him off until he freed Simone. Once she was safe, he would go to Fortress headquarters and have the doctor on staff look over him and Simone.

He keyed the GPS tracker signal into the SUV's navigation system, a handy addition to the retrofitted Fortress vehicles, and settled back to watch the flashing dot on the map.

As soon as he could, Sawyer exited the Interstate and filled the fuel tank. Jesse made a trip into the station to purchase supplies for the journey. When he returned, Sawyer dumped the supplies in the mike bag.

"Ready?"

Jesse nodded.

"Let's go, then. Simone and White are still on Interstate 40."

Where was White planning to hide out with Simone? Couldn't be anywhere densely populated. Too many chances for Simone to attract attention and get help.

He eyed the map. They were heading for wide open spaces. Where had White secured a place that was safe and out of the way?

Jesse called Zane.

"Yeah, Murphy."

"It's Jesse with Sawyer. Can you do research for me?"

"I'll try. If I can't, I'll put one of my best techs on it. What do you need?"

"You're watching the tracker on a map, right?"

"I am."

"White wouldn't take Simone where many people were around. Too easy for her to get help."

Silence, then, "You're right. Looks like they're heading toward less populated areas."

"White has to have a place ready. He can't just rent a place with Simone in tow. He has a plan, Z."

"I already looked for properties associated with his name or his family. Nothing. The family isn't rolling in money, Jesse."

"Maybe not, but White's tied to the drug trade. I didn't see signs he was a user, and he was in Mexico to talk business with the drug cartels."

"I still need a name." He paused. "Hold." Zane's voice filled the cabin, ten minutes later. "I might have a place to start. I'll let you know if I find anything."

"What happened, Z?"

"Simone and White stopped to put fuel in the tank and buy food."

Something in his voice clued Jesse in. "Something's wrong. What is it?"

"He's becoming more aggressive."

"What does that mean?" he demanded. "What did he do to Simone?"

"Slapped her and he's been groping her while she's driving. When she told him to knock it off, he hurt her. I don't know what he did, so don't ask. I can only tell you what I heard." Zane's anger, though, said enough.

"Are they still moving?"

"Yeah. One other thing."

"What?"

"He's not feeding her or giving her water."

Fury burned through Jesse, distracting him from pain and fatigue. "Why not?"

"He wants her to get on her knees and beg for it or he won't give her a thing and only if he feels like it."

"Brainwashing," Sawyer spat out. "The creep is trying to brainwash her."

"Won't work," Zane said. "She's a strong woman. She hasn't said a word since he told her about his condition for food and water."

Jesse frowned. "Her tactic will backfire as White becomes more irrational."

"Yep."

"All right. Thanks for telling me the truth, Z. Keep me updated on whatever you find on a location."

"You'll be the first person I call." Zane ended the call.

Sawyer glanced at him. "Finding the location is a long shot, Jesse."

"I know. If Zane comes up with something, though, we'll plan a rescue. Otherwise, we'll have to wing it."

"What else is new? We wing it all the time."

"Yeah, but this time, Simone is the victim. This isn't business as usual for me."

"For any of us. She's one of our own. We'll do this right and get her back, Jesse."

Yeah, they would. But how many injuries would White inflict on Simone before Jesse and his teammates arrived?

"Rest," Sawyer said. "The best way to help Simone is take care of yourself. For the moment, she's holding her own. That will have to be enough. We'll take care of White soon."

Although he hated to sleep when Simone was in trouble, Sawyer was right. He needed every minute he had to shore up his strength. He shifted in the seat until he found a semi-comfortable spot and dropped into a light sleep.

Sometime later, his phone signaled an incoming call. Jesse glanced at the screen and swiped his thumb across the glass. "It's Jesse. You're on speaker with Sawyer. What do you have for me, Z?"

"Simone and White got off the Interstate at exit 52. I think I know where they're headed."

#

Chapter Twenty-Six

Simone followed Trevor's directions and turned right onto a dirt road. Actually, the term road was a generous description for this rutted dirt track. If she owned a home out here, she'd insist on having this road paved or laying down a big load of crush-and-run rocks. This cow path would become a mud slide during heavy rains.

She grimaced as rocks pinged the undercarriage and tree limbs and bushes crowding the narrow track scraped the car as they drove along the rutted lane.

Trevor cursed. "Watch what you're doing. You're scraping the paint."

"I'm trying to stay in the middle but the tree limbs and bushes haven't been trimmed in a long time."

"Don't make excuses," he yelled. "Just do what I said."

No reasoning with him, Simone realized. He was too irritable to be rational which wasn't good for her health.

She glanced at her watch, wishing she could talk to Zane or, better yet, Jesse. Was he in surgery? She couldn't tell how badly he was hurt.

Simone slowed the car to a crawl to spare herself bouncing along the track and hopefully steer clear of worse damage to the car. Every time she hit a deep rut or hole, Trevor yelled and jabbed the gun into her side.

Finally, she saw a structure looming in the darkness at the end of the dirt track. Simone stared and wondered if the place had running water.

"Park in front. I'll come around. If you know what's good for you, you won't run." Trevor opened the door, looked around a minute, then circled the hood to open her door. "Out."

Barely waiting until she removed her seatbelt, Trevor manacled her wrist with his hand and yanked Simone from the car.

She stumbled after him, wishing he'd slow down so she could get her balance. When she fell, he cursed, kicked her leg, and dragged her back to her feet.

Trevor's hand shook as he shoved a key in the lock and opened the door. After yanking Simone inside, he turned on a light and locked the door. "Welcome to your new prison, Simone."

She glanced around. Rustic was an understatement. Man. She'd hate to live like this all the time. Worn out furniture, dirt everywhere, even on the windows, and a ragged carpet. Newspapers and magazines along with empty fast-food containers littered every flat surface.

On the other side of the large room was the kitchen with more dirt and grime everywhere. Takeout containers and trash covered the counters. The garbage can was overflowing and flies buzzed around the container.

Off to the left was a short hall which Simone assumed led to bedrooms and hopefully a bathroom.

Trevor tugged her toward the hallway.

"Where are we going?"

"I'm locking you up. I'm sick of looking at you."

"I need a stop at the bathroom first."

He glared at her. "Make it fast."

Halfway down the hall, Trevor shoved her toward a small room. "One minute, Simone. Every second longer means another beating. If you lock this door, I'll break it down. I'll be waiting."

"All right." She closed the door and used the facilities.

Her watch vibrated. A message slid across the screen. *Jesse's okay. Help to arrive soon.*

Oh, thank God. "Thanks," she whispered.

Another message. *Hold on. Be strong.*

Easier said than done. However, now that Simone knew the man she loved was still alive, she'd do whatever she must to survive Trevor.

Her ex twisted the knob and shoved the door open so hard it banged against the wall and bounced back to hit him in the side.

"Out," he shouted. "I told you what would happen if you took more than a minute."

She hadn't gone over her deadline.

Trevor gripped her by the upper arm and propelled her from the bathroom to a room across the hall. He shoved her inside and followed her. Fists clenched, he advanced on her.

The first blow caught her off balance and sent her to the floor.

Trevor was on her in a flash. His fists flew. Blows rained down her torso and face. When he finished, he rose and kicked her in the side.

Simone cried out as pain ripped through her. He just had to kick her in the same side where she'd been shot.

Warm liquid trickled to her back. Oh, man. Her wound had reopened. She prayed help would arrive sooner than later. If they didn't, she'd have to find something to staunch the blood flow until operatives found her. She would not let Trevor win this battle. She wanted that life she'd dreamed of with Jesse.

Trevor swaggered from the room, shut the door, and locked it.

With shallow breaths, Simone struggled to sit up. Pain consumed her and her vision narrowed.

No. She couldn't pass out. If she did, she feared what Trevor might do to her while she was unconscious.

Her watch vibrated. Simone glanced at the screen. *Safe to talk?*

"I'm alone for now," she whispered.

"You okay?" Zane murmured.

"The wound in my side reopened."

"Don't lie to me," he snapped. "I heard what he did to you. Body blows and face, right?"

She rolled her eyes, the only body part that didn't hurt. "You have a camera?"

"Don't need one. I've been on the receiving end of beatings. How is your breathing?"

"Hampered. Not sure if it's the bruising or fractured ribs."

Zane hissed. "If an operative doesn't kill White, Brent and I will. No one beats our people and gets by with it."

"Don't get in trouble on my account."

"Look around you. What do you see?"

She obeyed Zane's order. "Nothing. This room is totally empty."

"Are you on the bottom floor?"

"Only one floor."

"Windows?"

She looked. "One."

"Find out if it's locked."

Simone groaned as she climbed to her feet. Gritting her teeth, she walked hunched over to check. She pulled aside worn curtains to peer at the grimy window. So much filth had built up that she couldn't see outside. She did, however, see bars across the window. Trevor hadn't been kidding about calling this her jail cell. "He put bars outside the window."

"Are you small enough to fit between them?"

"When I was five, maybe. Definitely not now. I'm a sitting duck in here, Zane."

"Rest. Move as little as possible."

"I'll do my best. That will be up to Trevor."

"Be ready."

"For what?"

"To defend yourself until help arrives."

She closed her eyes and sank to the floor to lean against the wall. "How long?"

"At least an hour."

An eternity if Trevor came back to work her over again before the operatives arrived. With a sigh, she laid on the floor and prayed.

#

Chapter Twenty-Seven

Jesse's phone signaled an incoming call. He glanced at the screen. Zane. "It's Jesse. You're on speaker with Sawyer."

"I know where he took Simone. It's an old hunting cabin that belongs to his last victim."

He frowned. "Victim?"

"White killed three people before last night. The cabin belongs to the man whose card White is using to finance Simone's kidnapping."

"Why hasn't the family canceled the vic's cards?"

"No clue. I just sent you the address for the cabin and the schematic for it. The cabin is off the paved road a good way. Very rustic. White wanted to make sure Simone couldn't get help."

Something in Zane's voice warned him that something had happened. "Spill it, Z."

His friend sighed. "You won't like it."

"I still need to know. Talk to me."

"White beat Simone as soon as they arrived at the cabin. The gunshot wound in her side reopened."

"How bad is she bleeding?"

"Unknown. She's locked in a room with bars on the window. So, no way to escape. I told her to rest. There was nothing I could do to help her." Frustration was evident in Zane's voice. "You and your team better take care of White. If you don't, I will."

His eyebrows rose. "I hear you." He wouldn't want a Navy SEAL after him any day. If he eluded them this time, White's days were numbered. No one could hide from Zane Murphy for long. "Can you loop me into Simone's comm with her watch?"

"I can. Are you sure you want me to do that?"

The warning was clear. "I need to talk to her, Z."

"All right. Don't say I didn't warn you." Seconds later, Zane said, "She's alone for the moment. Go."

Jesse drew in a breath. "Simone. Baby, can you hear me?" He heard a soft gasp over the speaker.

"Jesse. Are you okay?"

"I'm better now that I've heard your voice. Tell me your injuries so I'll be prepared to provide treatment."

"Mostly soft tissue damage. My face is swelling. I'm having trouble catching my breath." She paused. "My side injury has reopened."

"How much are you bleeding?"

"Not as much as you were, but the bleeding hasn't stopped."

"Your blood type?"

"O positive. Why?"

Excellent. Three members of Texas Team had the same blood type, including Jesse. "In case you need an emergency transfusion." Unfortunately, he wouldn't be the one to donate. He wasn't in good enough shape himself. If there were no other options, he'd do it anyway.

"I love you."

"Love you, too, Simone." She was fading on him. "Rest now, baby. I'll stay with you."

"Okay." She fell silent.

Jesse watched the clock, willing Sawyer to drive faster. As it was, his friend was going over the speed limit. If he drove too much faster, they could get pulled over for speeding, and that would slow them down.

The connection remained quiet for 30 minutes. Simone gasped.

"What's wrong?" Jesse asked.

"He's coming."

"Cooperate. We're almost there." Not close enough to stop whatever was about to happen but he wanted to give Simone hope to hold on to.

"Get up," White demanded. "The cabin's a mess. Get out here and clean it up. Now."

Simone's shallow breaths turned to panting.

Soon, the sounds of her shuffling things and tossing them into a bag came over the speaker interspersed with soft moans she tried to smother.

Ten minutes later, Jesse heard flesh hitting flesh.

Simone cried out.

"You're taking too long," White snapped. "Get moving or you'll get a lot worse."

Jesse had seen and heard almost everything in his time as a cop and an operative but hearing Simone beaten and abused gutted him.

Sawyer reached over and squeezed his shoulder, then pressed down on the accelerator.

The minutes ticked by in at a snail's pace. He watched the clock and map while listening to everything going on in the cabin.

Fifteen miles from the target location, Sawyer disconnected his phone from the Bluetooth system and made a call. After a low-voiced conversation, he glanced at Jesse. "They're on site," he murmured. "Holding."

He acknowledged the information with a nod. If things became dicey inside that cabin, he'd send his teammates in to pull Simone out. As much as he wanted to rescue Simone personally, Jesse refused to allow White to hurt her again.

When he and Sawyer reached the ten-mile mark, White said, "That's good enough. Clean up the bathroom."

More sounds of shuffling, then a hiss of pain from Simone. "Hurting me won't get the job done faster, Trevor."

"You're moving too slow," he yelled.

"Do you have cleaning supplies?"

"There's a bar of soap and a washcloth in there. Everything better sparkle when you're finished, Simone, and I want to see you on your hands and knees." He laughed. "You'll be spending a lot of time there from now on. Better get used to it." More laughter. "After you finish the bathroom, we'll go to the bedroom. You won't be leaving there for a long time, baby. Remember all those times you told me no?" he crowed. "Those times are over. Now, it's all about what I want, and you can't stop me."

Jesse's face burned. Five more miles. *Hold on, Simone. Hold on for me. For us.*

Sawyer exited the Interstate and turned at the bottom of the ramp. The SUV leaped forward, chewing up the miles between them and Simone.

Watching the map, Jesse signaled Sawyer when it was time to turn off the road onto the dirt path. His friend barreled up the miserable excuse for a lane as rocks pinged against the underside of the SUV.

A quarter of a mile from the cabin, Sawyer parked the vehicle and hurried to the cargo area to grab their Go bags. They quickly geared up, slipped comm devices into their ears, and set off at a fast clip to join their teammates.

They found Brody and Logan watching the front of the structure. "Where's Max?" Jesse asked Brody.

"Monitoring the back. Z said he looped you into the comm link between him and Simone. Sit rep."

"White beat her before Z hooked me into the loop. Simone says she's okay but the wound in her side has reopened and is continuing to bleed."

"What do you say?"

"She's having trouble breathing. I'm afraid she has fractured ribs and internal bleeding. She's not in a good way, Brody. White takes every excuse he can find to hit her. We've got to get her out of there."

"White?"

He scowled. "I don't care if he survives or not. He's still high as a kite on uppers so he's irritable and irrational. He's threatening to rape her."

Brody's and Logan's expressions darkened. "Let's take this guy out before he does any more damage to Simone," Logan said. He left unsaid the real possibility that White might kill her if he kept punching and kicking her. Simone needed to go to a hospital as soon as possible.

"We scouted the perimeter of the cabin while we waited for you and Sawyer," Brody said. "There are bars on all the windows. We won't be able to get inside that way."

Logan shrugged. "Kick down the door."

Jesse narrowed his eyes. "And give White the chance to shoot Simone? Forget it."

"Subtlety is in order," Brody said. He pulled up the schematics on his phone. "Not a lot of options here. Do you know where they are in the cabin, Jesse?"

"Bathroom for now." His hands fisted. "White forced Simone to her hands and knees to clean the room. When she finishes with that, he's taking her to the bedroom where he said she'd be for a long time."

Logan checked his weapon. "She'll be out of his hands inside of five minutes, Jesse. Whether he'll be breathing is up to him."

Brody sent a text to Max. After getting a response a second later, he stood. "Sawyer, join Max and pick the lock on the back door when I give the signal. Jesse will go in with us. One minute."

"Copy." Sawyer slipped away into the trees.

Brody signaled Logan and Jesse to follow him. They made their way to the front door, on alert in case White noticed their approach to the cabin.

Jesse eased the mike bag from his shoulder and set it near the front door. Although he wanted his medical supplies close, he didn't want to be hampered by the extra weight.

At the ten-second mark, Brody looked at him. "Your only focus is Simone. The rest of us will handle White. Hear me?"

He gritted his teeth. Simone was his future wife. He should be the one to take on Simone's ex. However, she was his priority and always would be. Only he had the medical expertise to help her.

Besides that, he wasn't in shape to take on a long fight with a man hopped up on drugs. Jesse gave a curt nod.

After another second of pointed staring by his team leader, Brody sent a text and signaled Logan. The tumblers on the lock shifted seconds later.

Jesse twisted the knob and pushed the door open a crack. Inside, White ranted angrily at Simone, threatening to kick her again if she didn't get back to work.

Weapon in hand, he eased inside the old structure as Sawyer and Max slipped into the kitchen from the back.

Brody moved past Jesse to press his back against the wall and glance down the hall. He looked at his teammates and shook his head.

Great. No one in sight which meant White was in the bathroom with Simone. That room was small with almost no room to maneuver. Taking him down in the bathroom would leave Simone too close to the action. The likelihood of her being injured further was too high for Jesse. Much as he hated to wait, they must hold off until White left the bathroom.

They waited for five minutes. Every second felt like an eternity to Jesse. To be so close and yet still unable to reach Simone was torturous.

Finally, White cursed. "Get up and go to the bedroom right now. Move it, Simone."

She cut off a cry of pain and seconds later, Jesse heard her feet shuffling down the hall followed by heavier footsteps.

"Strip. I'm not waiting anymore."

Jesse tensed. They had to move. He looked at Brody who gave a slight nod. Taking the lead, Jesse walked silently down the short hall and stopped just shy of the door frame to the bedroom. Logan stepped up beside him, glanced into the room, and started a countdown.

On five, he slipped into the room. "On your knees, White." Jesse and Brody entered the room, weapons up and ready.

In a flash, White grabbed Simone by the hair, yanked her head back, and rested the blade of his knife against Simone's carotid artery. He smiled. "Get out. She's mine now. If I can't have her, no one will." He pressed the knife into Simone's skin just enough to draw blood. "Think I won't kill her? You're wrong."

Logan shook his head, an expression of pity on his face. "Haven't you heard you should never bring a knife to a gunfight?"

"I'll kill her!"

Simone's gaze locked with Jesse's. She mouthed, "I love you."

He smiled. "Simone, do you trust me?" he asked softly.

"Shut up," White snapped. "You don't talk to her. Hear me? She's mine. She only talks to me and only when I say she can talk."

"Yes," she said, still focused on Jesse.

Logan gave a slight nod.

Jesse prayed she remembered the few sessions of self-defense training. "Drop," Jesse ordered.

Simone immediately lifted her feet. Although White struggled to keep his hold on her, he couldn't hold her weight with one arm. She slid out of his grasp to the floor.

Seconds later, Brody and Logan had a screaming and cursing White face down on the floor with his hands behind his back.

"I'll kill you. I'll kill you all."

"Yeah?" Logan said. "Come see me after you get out of prison. We'll go a round or two."

"I hate you."

"My feelings are hurt," Brody said. "I guess I shouldn't expect any Christmas cards from you."

Jesse knelt beside Simone, fury sizzling in his veins at the sight of her swollen face and bloody shirt. He shoved aside the emotions and got to work. Jesse gently ran his hands over one arm and then the other.

"Hey," Simone said, voice hoarse.

Jesse glanced up at her beloved face.

Her lips curved slightly and grimaced when her split lip bled. "I knew you would come."

"Always. I love you, Simone."

Brody and Logan hauled White to his feet. Before they could hustle him out the door and put zip ties on his wrists, White broke free and sprinted toward Jesse and Simone.

In an instant, Jesse leaped to his feet, placing his body between Simone and White. He grabbed White in a bear hug and took him to the ground. After one solid punch to the jaw, White went limp. "Get him out of here," he snapped and stood, watching as his team leader and friend gripped the fallen man by the biceps and hauled him outside the cabin.

In a minute, White began shouting threats and curses at them.

Ignoring his own pain, Jesse once again knelt beside Simone and resumed his assessment of the woman he loved. No fractures in her arms. Excellent. He shifted his attention to her legs and didn't feel a broken bone. With pants covering her legs, Jesse couldn't see bruises he felt sure covered her skin.

He raised his gaze to her face. "I need to raise your shirt enough to see your wound."

She nodded.

Jesse pushed the bottom of Simone's shirt halfway up her ribs and examined her gunshot wound. She was right. Her wound had reopened.

Sawyer poked his head around the doorjamb. "Need a hand?"

"Get my mike bag."

"You got it." He left only to return seconds later with the medical kit. "What do you need?"

"Alcohol wipes and two pressure bandages. I can control the bleeding for now but Simone needs to go to the hospital to have her stitches replaced."

She moaned. "Hate hospitals."

"Don't we all?" Sawyer said cheerfully. "You did good, kid."

"I couldn't stop Trevor from beating me. How is that good?" she groused.

"You survived. Haven't you heard any landing you walk away from is a good one?"

Simone rolled her eyes. "If you say so. Being on the receiving end of Trevor's fists doesn't feel like a good thing to me."

While Sawyer kept Simone distracted Jesse cleaned blood from her stomach and side and applied a pressure bandage to the entrance wound. When he finished, he said, "I need to roll you to your side, sweetheart. It's going to hurt. I'm sorry."

"Can't hurt worse than I already do."

"Let us do all the work."

Together, he and Sawyer rolled Simone to her side.

She moaned. "Oh, man."

"I'll work fast." He cleaned the blood from her back, frowning when more blood immediately flowed from the exit wound. Another swipe with the alcohol wipe and he applied the pressure bandage.

He nodded at Sawyer, and they gently rolled Simone to her back. "Grab my mike bag."

"Jesse, you have your own gunshot wound to worry about. Let me carry her to the vehicle."

Simone's hand covered Jesse's. "It's okay," she whispered. "I don't want to hurt you."

"You won't." No one was going to carry her but him. He'd almost lost her. Jesse could handle a short trek. Probably. "Sawyer, get the SUV and bring it to the front of the cabin. I'll carry her to the vehicle when you arrive."

Sawyer grabbed the mike bag and took off at a dead run.

When Jesse heard Sawyer drive up to the cabin, he scooped Simone into his arms and carried her from the cabin to the idling SUV.

Sawyer hopped out and opened the back door for them. "Mike bag's in the floor behind the driver's seat."

"Thanks." Once Jesse placed Simone on the seat and followed her inside, Sawyer closed the door and climbed behind the wheel.

"Cops will be here soon. They won't be happy that you and Simone left the scene."

"Don't care. Nothing matters but Simone's health. Brody can tell them where I'll be. I'm not leaving Simone's side."

"I hear you. Just a warning that we'll soon have ticked off law enforcement officers swarming the emergency room."

"I'll handle them."

A snort. "If you're still conscious."

Jesse frowned. "What are you yammering on about?"

"Look down at your shirt, buddy."

He did and made a face. Great. Looks like he's be needing more stitches himself and probably a pint or two or blood. What a fine pair he and Simone made.

"Jesse." Simone's voice broke. "I can't lose you."

He cradled her against him, his arm wrapped around her shoulders. "You won't. A few stitches broke loose. I'll be fine. I'm more worried about you."

"Does this mean you get more time off before you're deployed again?"

"That's right. For the first time since Brent hired me, I'm going to take every day the doc says I need to be off work."

"Good. I want to go on a date when I won't scare little kids with my bruised face."

"Yeah? My choice or do you have something in mind?"

"I want to do something normal."

Sounded good to him. "Name it."

"Dinner and a movie." She sighed. "As soon as I can eat."

"Any time you're ready, I'd be honored to take you on a date. I'm looking forward to it."

"Do you care what kind of movie?"

Although he wasn't a fan of sappy romance movies, he'd watch a hundred of them as long as they made Simone happy. "Nope. Anything that you want."

"Including an art film?"

He froze. "You want to watch an art film? I don't think Hartman has one in the theater at the moment." Man, really? What ever happened to a good old action film?

Simone snorted. "Gotcha."

Jesse mock frowned at her. "Seriously, woman? That wasn't nice."

"Deal with it, tough guy."

Minutes later, Sawyer pulled up to the emergency room entrance and came around to open the door for Jesse and Simone. "You guys look like refugees from a war," he murmured. "We're going to cause quite a stir in there."

He wasn't wrong.

As soon as Jesse carried Simone into the emergency room, the nursing staff hustled them into an exam room. A doctor soon hurried in.

"What happened?"

In clear, concise terms, he explained Simone's injuries.

The physician, a man named Forrest, frowned. "You're a paramedic?"

He nodded.

"Why is she in this shape?" Suspicion filled his gaze as he looked from Jesse to Simone and back.

"My ex-boyfriend kidnapped me," Simone said. "Jesse and his friends rescued me."

"Are you sure that's the truth, Ms. Kent? We'll protect you."

"Yes, sir. It is the truth."

He gave a brisk nod, then looked at Jesse more closely. "What about you? How much blood on your shirt is hers?"

"Some of it."

"But not all?"

"No, sir. I was injured last night when Simone was abducted."

"He was shot, too," Simone whispered. "Please, help him."

Forrest patted her hand. "We'll help you both. Let me see if another exam room is open."

"No." Jesse held up his hand. "I know the protocol but Simone was traumatized and we're engaged. After what she's been through, I don't want her out of my sight."

"Understandable. All right. Let's start with you, young lady." Forrest assessed her injuries. "We'll replace your stitches after we've determined if you have internal injuries."

He looked at Jesse. "Let me check you quickly to be sure all you need is a few stitches, then we'll go from there."

Within two hours, Jesse and Simone had been assessed and treated.

When Jesse insisted they occupy the same room, Forrest frowned. "This is highly irregular."

"I'm not taking chances. Simone's kidnapper might work with a partner."

A slight nod. "I'll make the arrangements. The police are here and insist on talking to both of you immediately. I can refuse to allow it. However, I try not to antagonize the local law if I can help it."

Jesse sighed. Time to face the music.

#

Chapter Twenty-Eight

Simone stared at the pair of detectives and scowled. "Are you kidding me?"

"No, ma'am. We're not." Detective Scott held his pen over his pad. "It's a legitimate question."

"It's a ridiculous question. I told you Trevor White kidnapped me and in the process shot Jesse who was simply taking my dog outside to visit the grass."

"That's not what White says."

"Trevor is a liar. You can't trust a word he says. He'll spout anything to save his own hide."

"He claims your boyfriend attacked him and he shot Phelps in self-defense."

"He lied," she said flatly. "Once Trevor forced me to drive away from Hartman, Tennessee, we drove for hours until we stopped at that rundown cabin where you found him. He beat me and forced me to clean the cabin he'd turned into a pigsty with his own slob tendencies. After I finished cleaning, he took me to the bedroom and ordered me to strip. If Jesse and his friends hadn't arrived when they did, Trevor would have raped me."

The detectives exchanged glances before refocusing on Simone. "Tell us everything again from the beginning," Detective Coleman said.

She sighed and started from her beating from Trevor in California until the latest escapade. Simone had to be a little creative when she told them about the trouble in Mexico, telling the men that she and Jesse had gone to Sayulita for a vacation and Trevor followed them down there.

When she finished telling them a sanitized version of events this time, she was exhausted and feeling sick. "Look, I know you have a job to do but I need a break."

"Just a few more questions, Ms. Kent."

"No more questions," Jesse said from the doorway where he'd been standing. "She's had enough. You want to ask more questions? Do it tomorrow after we're both released from the hospital. If you push her too hard, she'll have a setback and then you'll be even longer getting answers. You have enough to work with for now."

"You're not a cop," Scott snapped.

"I used to be on the job, Detective. Now take a hike before I have security escort you out."

Both men scowled at him. After a stare down they lost, the detectives left the hospital room.

Jesse resumed his place in the chair by Simone's bed. "Should I have the nurse bring you anything?"

She shook her head. "I'm tired and nauseated."

"You've been through a lot, baby. Your body needs rest to heal."

"So does yours." Simone eased over to the edge of the bed and patted the space beside her. "Come on. I'll sleep better with you beside me."

"Are you sure? I don't want to hurt you."

"Jesse." Why was he being so stubborn? Jesse was swaying where he stood. "Lay down. You won't rest well in a chair."

"I need to keep watch," he insisted.

Stubborn, wonderful man. "You sleep light. You'll hear if anyone comes into the room. Besides, Sawyer is on duty in the hall. Come on." She patted the mattress again.

Finally, Jesse gave in, made his way to the empty side of the hospital bed, and stretched out beside her. "If you're uncomfortable tell me and I'll go back to the chair."

"Hush," she murmured, snuggled against his side and dropped into sleep.

Some time later, Simone woke to the knowledge that someone else was in the room with her and Jesse. She tensed.

"It's okay," Jesse murmured. "Zane's on watch."

Her eyes flew open, and she looked to the foot of the bed where her boss sat in his wheelchair with a computer in his lap.

Zane saluted and said, "Sleep. I've got your back."

Taking her boss and friend at his word, Simone dropped back into a dreamless sleep beside the man she loved, secure knowing that he was protected, too. No one would slip past Zane Murphy to hurt either of them.

The next time she woke, Jesse and the hospitalist were speaking in low tones with Zane listening to everything being said.

"Jesse?"

He returned to the bed and bent to kiss her gently. "How do you feel?" he murmured.

"Better than I did when we arrived."

His eyebrow rose.

She rolled her eyes. "I hurt all over. Satisfied?"

He chuckled. "With the truth, yes. I hate that you're in pain."

"Do you need me to prescribe pain medicine before you leave?" the doctor asked. "With the amount of bruising you sustained, it's justified."

Simone shook her head. "I'd rather take over-the-counter medicine. The bruises will heal in a few days."

"While that's true, your gunshot wound is another matter. We had to do some additional repair work as well as replace the original stitches. You'll hurt for more than a day or two."

She glanced at Jesse who gave her a slight nod. Excellent. He could take care of the pain meds if she needed them. Hopefully, she wouldn't. "No, thanks. I'll be fine."

The doctor frowned and shook his head. "I'll have a prescription for pain medicine included with your discharge papers in case you change your mind."

"Appreciate it, Doc," Jesse said.

"Take care, both of you. A nurse will be around shortly with your paperwork, then you'll be free to go." He left the room.

"The police want another interview with you," Zane said. "Sorry, but Brent wasn't able to persuade them to drop the second interview."

"We'll deal with it."

As soon as they were discharged, Sawyer drove them to the local police station where they went through another round of questioning. Four hours later, the interviews were complete and Sawyer drove them away from the police station in Liberty, Kentucky.

"Where's Trevor?" Simone asked.

"Jail waiting for the FBI to pick him up," Sawyer said.

"The feds?" Her eyes widened. "Kentucky isn't prosecuting him?"

"He crossed state lines. It's the fed's jurisdiction. You'll have more interviews but Brent convinced the agents to interview you in Hartman. You can relax, Simone. White will never bother you again."

Relieved, she sighed and settled back against the seat and snuggled close to Jesse. "What about Griffin Daley? Do we know what happened to him?"

"Dead," he said, voice flat. "The boss received word earlier this morning. Sophie Westlake and Bastien Boudreax are also out of your life for good. You'll have to testify against them, Simone."

"I figured that would be the case."

"So, you can rest easy. All your enemies are behind bars."

She grimaced. "Not quite. There's one more."

"Who?"

"Ember Atkins. She's been feeding Trevor information on my whereabouts since I left San Francisco."

"A good friend of yours?"

"She was. Ember is a computer hacker. I trained her myself."

He snorted. "Looks like you did an excellent job of it. What do you want to do?"

"I should confront her face to face."

"But you'd rather not." Jesse squeezed her hand. "Give yourself time to heal, then you can decide what to do. If you choose to go to California, I'll go with you. We'll face her together."

Although she felt as though she was being a wuss, Simone saw the wisdom in his words. She wasn't up to a confrontation. Not yet.

When the time came, she'd talk to the woman who used to be one of her best friends and find out why she'd betrayed Simone's trust.

Chapter Twenty-Nine

Jesse circled the hood of the rented SUV and opened Simone's door. The bright early morning sunshine promised a beautiful day ahead. Too bad their task was a difficult one for Simone.

He held out his hand and helped her from the vehicle. "Ready to do this?"

Simone looked pale but composed. "No."

Wrapping his arms around her, Jesse held Simone against him, grateful she was alive and healthy. He still woke in the middle of the night with nightmares about her abduction. He probably would for a long time.

When she went boneless against him, he lifted her face to his and captured her mouth. Long minutes later, he broke the heated connection and stared into her beautiful face. "If you want to leave, I'll drive us back to the airport. We'll go back home, watch movies, and eat junk food all afternoon."

She laughed. "Tempting but we're already here."

"No pressure to do this, sweetheart. You can handle it by a simple phone call instead of in person."

"You wouldn't be upset at this wasted trip?"

"Nope. I got to spend time with you. I don't consider that a waste."

"You're one in a million, Jesse."

"I'll remind you of that when we're in a heated disagreement in the future. So, what's your decision? Do we stay or go?"

Simone looked at the little house, straightened, and said, "Come on."

He threaded their fingers together and accompanied her to the door. This was her show. He was the backup if Simone needed it, her support. Jesse planned to stay in the background unless things became dicey. No one was allowed to hurt Simone, especially a friend who had already betrayed her trust.

After a deep breath, Simone pressed the doorbell. They waited.

A minute later, a woman with red hair opened the door, looking frazzled. Her eyes widened when she recognized Simone. "Simone! What are you doing here?" Her gaze shifted to Jesse, then back. "I didn't know you were in the area."

"I need to talk to you. May we come in?"

"Sure." She sounded hesitant, but she stepped back to allow them inside. "Take a seat in the living room. Do you want coffee or something? I just brewed a fresh pot." She smiled a little. "You know me and my coffee addiction."

"We need nothing, Ember. We won't be here that long." Simone sat on the sofa with Jesse. "This is Jesse, the love of my life."

Ember's mouth gaped. "Seriously? Wow. Congratulations, Simone. I'm happy for you."

"Thanks."

"Are you in San Francisco on business?"

"You could say that." Simone watched her friend a moment. "I came to see you."

"Me?"

The other woman looked nervous. She should be. Jesse wanted to yank Ember to her feet by her shirt collar and demand answers. His wife-to-be, however, was more patient than he was.

"I came to ask you one question."

Ember blinked. "Okay. Shoot."

"Why?"

She paled. "I don't understand."

"Yeah, Ember, you do. Why did you do it?"

"Simone...."

"I thought we were friends. How could you throw me into Trevor's path every time I moved to get away from him? You know what he did to me."

"I do," she whispered, misery in her eyes. "I'm sorry."

"That's not good enough."

"What do you want?" Ember demanded, shoving her long hair away from her face with a trembling hand. "Blood?"

"There's been enough blood spilled."

Her former friend seemed appalled. "I don't know what you're talking about. What blood?"

"Trevor attempted to kill Jesse before he kidnapped and beat me. He would have raped me if not for Jesse and his friends finding me in time to stop him."

Ember covered her mouth with one hand and closed her eyes. "I'm sorry, Simone. So very sorry."

"Why did you betray me?"

"You don't understand."

"Then help me understand because this isn't like you at all. What happened, Ember?"

She gave a bitter laugh then. "Trevor White happened."

"You dated him, too?"

"No." Ember shuddered. "Never. I hate him, especially after what he did to you before you left San Francisco."

"Then why did you feed him information?"

"He threatened my mother." Simone's friend cried. "Trevor said he would hurt her and make Mom suffer for a long time before he finally killed her if I didn't cooperate. I didn't want to do it, Simone. I swear. I never would have done something so hideous if I wasn't terrified for my mother. Please, you have to understand. Forgive me."

"Why didn't you tell Simone?" Jesse asked. He could understand feeding White information under duress. What he didn't get was why Ember didn't call or email Simone to let her know, to give her time to escape before Trevor landed on Simone's doorstep again.

"He said he had someone watching every move I made, that he'd know if I warned Simone he was coming."

"And you believed him."

"Yes, I did. You don't know him like Simone and I do, Jesse. He's vicious. If Trevor found out what I'd done, he would have killed me, tortured my mother, and found someone else to do his dirty work of tracking Simone."

"Did you profit from the work?"

Ember's face appeared almost translucent. She swallowed hard. "He paid me. I didn't want the money but he made me take it. I dumped it all into an account. I haven't touched a penny of that blood money, and I won't."

She wiped her wet face with her hands. "So, what now? How can I make this up to you?"

Simone shook her head. "You can't. It's done. You don't have to worry about Trevor anymore. He won't hurt you or your mother ever again."

Ember stared. "He's dead?" she asked faintly.

"In the hands of the FBI," Jesse said. "He won't get out of prison until he's old. You and your mother are safe."

She closed her eyes for a moment, relief flooding her face. "Thank God."

Simone stood. "We know you have to get ready for work. We'll leave you to it."

"Are you going to be in town for a while? We could have dinner together. Mom would love to see you again."

She reached for Jesse's hand as she shook her head. "We appreciate the invitation but we have a flight to catch."

"Will I see you again?"

"Perhaps. We're busy these days."

Ember opened the door. "Is it all right if I call you sometime?"

Simone smiled. "Of course. We'll talk." She hugged Ember who clung to her for a long minute. "Tell your mother I said hello."

"I will." Ember watched them walk to the SUV.

Jesse unlocked the vehicle and helped Simone inside before circling to climb behind the wheel. "Where to, Simone?"

She looked at him. "Home. I just want to go home and start my life with you."

He leaned over and kissed her. "June can't come fast enough for me," he murmured. "But I'm going to enjoy romancing you over the next few months."

Simone beamed at him. "Just so you know, I'm planning to romance you as well. Get prepared to be treated like a prince."

He laughed. Yeah, he was going to enjoy life with this woman. Simone Kent was full of surprises and she loved him. Jesse couldn't wait to see what life held in store for them. Perhaps someday, they'd share their love and home with children and more pets.

Life was good, and it would only get better from here. "Let's go home."

#

About the Author

Rebecca Deel is a preacher's kid with a black belt in karate. She teaches business classes at a private four-year college in Nashville, Tennessee. She plays the piano for her church, writes freelance articles, and runs interference for the family dogs. She's married to an amazing husband and is the proud mom of two grown sons. She delivers occasional devotions to the women's group at her church and conducts seminars in personal safety, money management, and writing. Her articles have been published in *ONE Magazine*, *Contact*, and *Co-Laborer*, and she was profiled in the June 2010 Williamson edition of *Nashville Christian Family* magazine. Rebecca completed her Doctor of Arts degree in Economics and wears her favorite Dallas Cowboys sweatshirt when life turns ugly.

Read more at rebeccadeelbooks.com.

www.ingramcontent.com/pod-product-compliance
Lightning Source LLC
Chambersburg PA
CBHW060518160726
47991CB00001B/80